FICTION   Brown, Sam, 1945-
B   The trail to Honk Ballard's bones / Sam
          Brown. -- New York : Walker, c1990.

          222 p.

          ISBN 0-8027-4101-0: $17.95

                        23705

                                   APR 9 0

          I. Title.

                                        89-24947

THE TRAIL TO HONK
BALLARD'S BONES

Also by Sam Brown
THE LONG SEASON

THE TRAIL TO HONK BALLARD'S BONES

Sam Brown

Walker and Company
New York

This book is dedicated to my beautiful wife Vicki, and to our daughter Michael Rey and our son Brian Earl.

All the characters and events portrayed in this work are fictitious.

First published in the United States of America in 1990 by Walker Publishing Company, Inc.

Published simultaneously in Canada by Thomas Allen & Son Canada, Limited, Markham, Ontario

Library of Congress Cataloging-in-Publication Data

Brown, Sam, 1945–
The trail to Honk Ballard's bones / Sam Brown.
ISBN 0-8027-4101-0
I. Title.
PS3552.R717T7   1990   813'.54—dc20   89-24947

Printed in the United States of America

2   4   6   8   10   9   7   5   3   1

PROLOGUE

I WAS up on a high mesa on the eastern plains of New Mexico. It was late in the fall of 1983, and Christmas wasn't far off. The biggest, and sometimes the only Christmas bonus a cowboy is apt to get, is of the long-haired, prime-furred variety he catches for himself. We were about two weeks finished with fall works on the outfit, and I was in earnest pursuit of a Christmas bonus of the type mentioned—bobcats and coyotes, namely bobcats because they'll bring five times what a coyote will.

Bobcats like lonesome country, and that five-thousand-foot, rocky, windswept mesa was sure enough that. I'd packed a dozen number three longspring traps, stakes and chains, and other trapping supplies to the top of the mesa on a horse. After I'd been there for a couple of hours, I found just what I'd been hoping to find—fresh bobcat droppings and tracks in a narrow, sandy wash that ran through a scattered thicket of cedars.

I hobbled my horse and followed the wash on foot. I wanted to get the whole lay of the 'cat run before planting any steel—see where it began and ended and where it looked like the 'cats might meet and frolic.

This was on the west side of the mesa, and every now and then I could see through the cedars and occasional pinons to the rimrock. Out beyond the rimrock were miles of crisp, clean New Mexico air, turning a light shade of blue against the other far-off mesas.

I followed the wash for a quarter-mile from where I'd hobbled my horse. The cedars grew thicker and thicker until I had a hard time getting through them, but then I suddenly came upon a small clearing, the north side of which was a curved rock ledge about five feet high and forming an irregular quarter circle. Next to the rock ledge was a flattened pile of dead brush and rocks about six feet across.

Standing by the brush and rock pile for a closer look, I saw that it was hollowed out underneath. A perfect bobcat den if I ever saw one. But as I got down on my knees and looked closer, and as my eyes grew more accustomed to the darkness underneath the debris, I saw what looked like the bottom of a large rusty—rusted through—metal can.

Thoughts of bobcat sign and traps were now replaced by curiosity, and I began pulling away rocks and dried cedar branches and logs until I could not only see better inside, but could reach the metal can with my fingers.

When I pulled on the can it was so eaten with rust that it came apart. It was then I saw the yellowed and brittle papers that the can had been faithfully protecting while the lonely years had silently slipped into forgotten decades.

There were many, many leaves of paper. What I had found I did not know. But I gathered the papers together and sat on the ground and read while the sun slowly arched across the sky.

The first two pages came apart like ashes when I touched them. What follows is word for word what was contained in the rest of those barely legible papers that for so long had lain unread.

CHAPTER 1

. . . BUT what man can say that he has never taken a wrong turn along the way, Autumn? Maybe some men, the lucky ones, have a chance to backtrack over a wrong trail and get off it before it is too late. But how many others are like me? How many go so far in the wrong direction before they know it that there can be no turning back? Or maybe some trails can only be traveled in one direction, and once a man breaks dust on them, he is bound to follow that trail to its end?

But here's the truth—while there is still time, before the others follow my trail and meet me at the end.

I was born on my folk's farm, just outside Caldwell, Kansas. The folks were honest, hard-working, God-fearing farmers and good people—the salt of the earth. They raised six sons and four daughters. I was the third from the youngest, but the seed from which I must have sprouted wasn't like the rest of them. The others were all content to stay on the farm like stalks of corn, but not me. I guess I was the weed of the family, and my seed was dropped on the place by a passing wind.

The first thing I can remember about the homestead was sitting on the ground in front of the sod house on a cool fall day watching the geese flying over, instead of letting the milk-pen calves in with the milk cow like I had been told. Pa gave me a whipping for it, too.

"Gonna Strap that 'goose-honk' outa your ears for once and all," he said. And that's how I got the name "Honk." Before that it was William.

Caldwell was a trail town, a cowtown, and in a few years the cowboys who drifted in and out with the trail herds garnered my attention like the geese had earlier. They were like the geese in a lot of ways, too, and both of them were as different from corn stalks as day and night.

By the time I was twelve I had the itch bad. But it wasn't an itch that could be cured with any plaster or poultice. The itch I had was for saddle leather and cowhorses, branding fires and trail dust.

Pa said, "You best get that notion outa your head right now, or you'll never amount to nothin'. A man's got to get him a piece of land and put down roots. And he's got to take a wife before the sins of the flesh take him. Then he's got to rear a family up in the ways of the Lord.

"Those men," he went on, sounding like the good Reverend Blackburn did on Sunday mornings, "look like they're having a good time, but it's only a disguise put on by the devil to lure more young men into his ranks. Those men are penniless most of the time, spending a month's wages in one night on watered-down liquor and disease-infested harlots!"

Those were my pa's words—but all I could hear was the honk of the geese and the solid thud of a cowpony's hoofs on some distant trail. Maybe, if I'd have listened close enough, I could have heard the sound a gut-shot man makes—or maybe even the lonely sound of a pen scratching words down on paper as a cold nightwind prowls through high mesa cedars.

It was only four miles from our farm to Caldwell, and many is the time I would sneak out of the house after everyone else was asleep and go there. I would watch those Texas cowboys going into and coming out of the saloons and parlors, aways wearing big hats and jingling spurs. The pianos would be playing up a storm, and I could hear women laughing and singing and cowboys yeehawing. I thought, If they're only pretending to be having a good time like Pa said, then they're sure giving their all to it!

One night I snuck up to a back window of Peggy's Prairie Parlor and, wide-eyed, was studying basic female anatomy and the finer points of cowboy charm when Pa grabbed me from behind.

He thrashed me good that night. The worse he ever gave me—and the last.

I snuck out of the house before daylight, slipped a pair of work bits into the mouth of one of our old work horses, and left on him bareback before daylight of an August morning in 1874. I was fourteen years old, and I never heard from the folks again.

There's no need to tell of my trials and tribulations from then until I was a man and my beard was set, except to say that a few months after I left home I had a job as a choreboy with a big cattleman in Texas. From then on my growing up was done among cowboys, and they've been known to show a boy a few shortcuts on the road to manhood. Maybe I took too many shortcuts and grew up too quick, but who would ever take the long trail to anywhere when he doesn't have to?

CHAPTER 2

IF you could have seen me over the next twenty or so years, Autumn, what you would have seen would probably have been a pretty average cowhand. I rode many trails, far too many for me to tell you about now, all across Texas, New Mexico, and Arizona. That covers a lot of country, but that wide area would be as close to an answer as to where my home was in those years as I could give. I'd spend a few months here or there before drifting on to someplace new, or returning to someplace I'd been. I grew to be a raw-boned, six-foot-tall man with sun-baked skin. I went up the trail five times, always returning to the home range when the herd was delivered. Whenever I wore out a good Padgitt Brothers saddle, I would go back to Waco and get another one.

I suffered the things most any cowboy does, ranging from broken bones to hung over mornings. I never had any money in those days, not for very long anyway. Most of the time I didn't have anything but a saddle, bedroll, a couple of changes of clothes, and maybe a horse or two. But that didn't bother me. Most cowboys have the habit of not looking over a day or two into the future, and when you do that, a couple of dollars in your pocket and a chuck wagon to call home seem to be about all the security a man could want.

I lived unrefined and wild, but the only crimes I committed were the honorable kind, like public drunkenness or disturbing some genteel soul's peace. If I had been a bronc, I sure might have had some pitch in me, but I would have been pitching only because I was feeling good and not because I was mean.

A lot of folks—the man from whose loins I sprang included in that lot—would have called me useless. Looking back, I would have to say that when I hit a town that description would have been pretty hard to deny. But I was only in town maybe one month out of a whole year. And what man has ever been born who was not a little bit useless when it comes to unfamiliar things?

By that I mean that while I will admit to being useless in town, I sure wasn't that way on a cow outfit or on a trail drive. There, the town people and farmers who called me useless would have been as useless as wings on a wagon. Out there, I was as much at home as the sagebrush and the coyotes, and I gave a man a day's work for a day's wages. Out there, my word and my work were respected, and I took pride in both.

I could handle a rope about as good as anyone, or take a raw bronc and make a hand on him. I could tell an open cow from a springer, a wet from a dry, one that had just lost her calf from one that hadn't calved yet. I knew when to give a herd some air and when to crowd it, when to let it bed down and when to keep it moving. I could read brands like a store clerk reads his order book. There wasn't much that could be done around a cowhorse or a cow that I couldn't do. I set out to make a cowboy, and I made one.

But my life took a dark and rocky turn when I rode into Tascosa that early June day in 1895. I can't say for sure why I ended up there. I guess every trail I'd traveled since I'd left home had its part in delivering me there. For each separate trail carried me a little farther in life and a little closer to Tascosa that spring.

I'd wintered off the caprock on the Matador Ranch about two hundred miles southeast of there, but come good spring, I decided I'd get on up in the high plains country of the Panhandle where it's not as hot. Just about any cattle country is hot in the summer, but you stay beneath that caprock and you can melt your taler. I didn't figure I had any extra taler on me, so I bought me a packhorse, loaded my bed and war bag, and drifted to Tascosa, the Cowboy Capital of the Panhandle.

By that time the XIT Ranch had taken over nearly all of the open range country the LS used to run cattle on, and I guess they had more men on the payroll than any other ranch in Texas, maybe in the world. But I didn't light in Tascosa necessarily intending to go to work for them, because they sure weren't the only outfit in that country. It was just by chance I guess that when I got there they were needing a couple of hands, and needing them right then because they should have already been going up the trail.

Monte Canaster was sitting in the lobby of the Exchange Hotel when I first saw him. I walked over to him, hung a thumb in my Levi's pocket, and said, "I hear you're lookin' for some help."

Monte Canaster was not a man who liked to indulge in pleasant conversation about the weather or the state of national affairs or about anything, as far as I could tell.

"We're goin' up the trail to Montana with a bunch of steers," he said. "You ever been up the trail before?"

I grinned and said, "A couple of times, I guess."

He said, "The pay's thirty-five a month, and I'll be in charge of the herd. We were supposed to leave today, but yesterday we had a man get hurt, and then last night one came to camp drunk and I had to fire him. We leave at daybreak, so you'll need to come to the wagon with your bedroll and war bag this afternoon."

Seemed like Canaster already had me halfway to Montana before I even told him whether I'd go or not. Some bosses are like that. They take a man for granted. Some of them think that every cowpuncher in the world is just dying for an opportunity to work for their outfit, and they figure that all they have to do to hire a man is just offer him a job. I always figured you'd better watch that kind.

"I don't recollect telling anybody I was goin'," I said as I worked my big plug of Daniel Webster tobacco from one cheek to the other. Then I looked down at Canaster and didn't say anything else. I wasn't some skinny Kansas farm kid wanting to be a cowboy now. I *was* a cowboy, and a darned good one, and if any outfit, even the high-and-mighty XIT of Texas, wanted to hire me, they could *ask*.

I could tell Canaster knew what I was doing, and I could tell it galled him, too. But in a couple of seconds he let out a breath of air in resignation and said, "Do you want the goddamn job or not?"

I figured that could be considered asking, so I grinned and said, "Yeah, I'll take 'er. Tell me how to get to the camp and I'll be there later."

He jotted my name down in his book, closed it, and stood up. He was about my height but alot heavier set than me. He had red hair and those big, light-colored freckles on his face like some red-haired men have.

"We're west of here about three miles," he said. "On the north side of the river, just past Cheyenne Creek. Better not show up drunk or carrying any liquor, or I'll have to fire you. Company policy."

He stepped around me then and left the hotel. I started to go catch him and tell him what he could do with his "company policy." I always figured you hired a man thinking he could do the job. If he couldn't do it, then you fired him. I never did hold with the way some of those new outfits had "company policies" that were drawn up by somebody who hadn't ever ridden anything ranker than a swivel chair.

But I let it ride. I needed the job, and besides that I knew that once you had been on the trail a few days and things got to be pretty routine, the boss would usually relax a little, some even smiled—although I didn't think old Canaster would ever be guilty of that.

I sold my packhorse to the man at the livery. Then I visited a couple of Tascosa's drinking establishments and got shuck of the packhorse money and headed for the XIT camp about sundown.

I got to camp just as they were starting to eat supper. Canaster looked up from his plate, sort of waved to me, and then motioned to the grub with his head.

I filled my plate and then went over to where him and another cowboy were sitting cross-legged on the ground. That other cowboy was two inches taller than me and about twenty pounds heavier. He had a heavy black mustache, a slim nose, straight teeth, and was a good-looking man.

Canaster said, "This is Burl Lewis. Burl, this is Honk Ballard." Then he stood up, wiped his mouth on his shirt sleeve, and said, "The horse wrangler will have the remuda here before long. Before we catch night horses I'll show you two fellers your strings. Some men who aren't going up the trail with us are going to pull guard for ever'body tonight, so we'll all have a good night's sleep. The night horses are just in case something happens."

Burl Lewis and I didn't say much as we sat there on the ground and ate our beef and beans, but we'd stick pretty close to each other for the next few months. He was the other hand Canaster had just hired, and it was only natural I guess that we sort of paired up.

Before daylight the next morning, we'd had our breakfast, rolled our beds, loaded them on the wagon, and I thought we were about ready to head up the trail. The wagon and the remuda were ready to go and all we needed to do was to start pushing those twenty-five hundred head of steers off the bed ground.

Me and Burl were sitting next to each other on our XIT horses, along with the other six punchers who'd be going up the trail, waiting for Canaster to give us the word.

Then we hit a snag.

"Aw hell!" Canaster said, looking at me, "I plumb forgot about yours and Burl's horses."

Then he went trotting over to where the remuda was, and he was shaking out a big loop in his rope as he went.

For an instant me and Burl looked at each other. Then I

said to Canaster's trotting-off back, "Whoa there, Mister Canaster. What do you mean? What about our horses?"

Canaster pulled up and turned his horse around, a big limp loop hanging in his right hand. "You can't take your personal horses along," he said. "It's company policy. I'll have one of the men that's stayin' here take 'em and turn 'em out in a trap, and you can get 'em when we get back."

I didn't like that idea very much. Didn't like it at all. It wasn't that the sorrel of mine in the remunda was the best horse in the world or anything. In some ways about the best that could be said for him was that he'd keep your feet out of the dirt and that riding him beat walking and carrying your saddle. (I called him Pat because every now and then he'd slap his right forefoot on the ground two or three times like he was patting for a dance and then blow up.) So it wasn't because of any great love for him that I didn't want to leave him behind. I just wasn't any too anxious to start up the trail without knowing I had a horse of my own in the remuda. Maybe that was a trait in me that had been developing over the years, or maybe it was just a natural cowboy suspicion of any outfit that set so much store in doing *everything* by some stupid company policy.

I wanted to know that if somewhere up the trail—anywhere up the trail—me and Canaster got crossways, and I wanted to roll my bed and say adios, my own horse would be there waiting for me. I figured that would be a pretty good policy of my own to adopt, and I adopted it right there.

I picthed my horse some slack and rested my hands on the saddle horn. I wallered the chew around in my mouth, leaned to the side and spit, and then said, "If that sorrel horse of mine stays in Texas, I'll be in the middle of him."

"Same here," Burl Lewis said.

"Hell, fellers," Canaster said. "I didn't make the damn policy."

I stepped off the company horse I was on and unbuckled

the flank cinch. When I started loosening the front cince, Canaster said, "What'n the hell are you doin'?"

"Givin' the XIT of Texas back their XIT of Texas trail horse," I told him. "This is about as short a time as I ever stayed with an outfit—and that's saying something for me."

Then Burl stepped off his horse and went to unsaddling, too.

"Oh, goddammit!" Canaster said, and I thought his freckles were going to pop. "You two fellers aren't above takin' advantage of a man, are you?"

I don't guess we were. When Burl had sided with me, it put Canaster in a considerable bind. He couldn't leave when he was two hands short, and I knew how he hated to put off leaving again. But I wasn't bluffing, and I guess he could tell I wasn't.

"Okay," he said, with about as much enthusiasm as a condemned man telling the same thing to the hangman. "We'll just leave your goddamn horses in the remuda, but you'll have to ride 'em when it comes their turn, just like they were company horses."

I reached under my horse's belly and grabbed the front cinch easy and careful so as not to booger him. I looked at Canaster and grinned and said, "Let's go to Montana."

CHAPTER 3

WE'D been on the trail for close to sixty days, had driven all the way to the banks of the Niobrara River, and were camped about two miles west of Lusk, Wyoming, when trouble came.

Sixty days on the trail can leave a man mighty and uncomfortably thirsty, but it's a kind of thirst that can't be quenched by any amount of water.

"Boys," Canaster said the evening we reached the Niobrara, "we'll be camped here all day tomorrow getting resupplied. I don't want no goin' to town tonight, but you can all go tomorrow, and I'll give everyone a half-month's pay. Here's how we'll do it—after two men stand guard for three hours they get to go to town for three hours. Then they come back to the wagon and get six hours to sleep and sober up before going out on guard again. Burl, you and Honk can be the first ones to go to town in the mornin' . . . and don't forget, men, there will be *no* whiskey brought back to the wagon. Company policy."

You might think Canaster's plan seemed fair enough, and I guess it was. And I guess it might look like me and Burl were lucky to get to go in first, and maybe we were. But that "fair plan" and that "good luck" had some flaws in them, and those flaws stood out to me and Burl like a lump-jawed steer would to a Chicago cattle buyer.

Oh, the flaws might not have looked so big when we first came back to camp about the middle of the morning, rocking in our saddles and talking like our mouths were full of oatmeal. There wasn't anything bothering us then except finding our bedrolls. But as our six hours of sobering and sleeping rolled along, and with it the coming of night and us

13

going out on guard again, those flaws in Canaster's plan got easier and easier to see.

But we hadn't talked about it any then, and I didn't know if Burl was seeing those flaws like I was or not. So after we'd been on guard for about an hour and the sun had gone down, I rode around to where he was and said, "Looks to me like we sorta got stuck with a hind tit on goin' to town."

I was just feeling him out, seeing how he felt about it, because if he wasn't seeing it like I was, I wasn't going to bellyache about it anymore.

"Yeah," Burl said, looking out across the herd that you could just barely see the backside of in the twilight. "I sorta been thinkin' the same thing."

That remark perked me up some, because when a man thinks the world has kicked him in the teeth, it helps to know there's someone else who thinks the same thing.

"By being first to go in," I said, "and having to go so early in the mornin', there was two joints still closed, remember?"

"Yeah," Burl said, "and I'll betcha all the gals weren't up yet in them ones that *were* open."

By then it appeared plenty plain that the flaw in Canaster's plan looked the same to Burl as it did to me, but just to be sure we were chewing off the same plug, I said, "What's worse, by bein' first it's been so long since we were there, it don't seem to me like we've been there hardly at all."

"Why, hell no, it don't," Burl agreed. "If we'd been the last ones to go, we'd either still be asleep or maybe just comin' back to the wagon."

When he said that, I knew we were on the same plug, right down to the last brown burley leaf.

It got quiet then for a while with neither of us saying anything. And it got darker, too. The stars came out and I said to Burl, straightening in the saddle and giving my horse some rein, "Guess I'd better ride around these sons-a-bitches."

"Yeah," Burl drawled, pulling his horse's head around. "I'll meetcha on the other side."

When we got to the other side of the herd just about all the stars had popped out, and it wasn't any lighter in the west than it was in the east. In fact, it was lighter in the *east* because that was the direction Lusk was in. And we were craving those lights like a pair of candle bugs in a broom closet.

"Looks like they're beddin' down pretty good," Burl said, talking a little softer now in the darkness.

"They shore are," I agreed, and without catching a breath I said, "You goin' first or am I?"

"Have you got any money left from this mornin'?" Burl asked.

"Why, godda—"I said louder than I aimed to. "Hell no, I don't, and I plumb forgot about it!"

"Well," Burl lamented, "I hate to be the one to bring it up, but I don't either."

After about a minute of listening to some coyotes yelp and some steers shuffling around, Burl said, "The outfit still owes us what—a month-and-a-half's back wages?"

"Well, yeah," I said, "they do. But so what? Do you want to go ask Canaster for it? You don't reckon he'd figger we was up to something, do you? I mean, two old boys standin' night guard two miles from a trail town asking for their money . . ."

"Okay, okay," Burl said. "Maybe we can't ask for the cash, but why can't we use it as clabber for a loan?"

Burl had lost me somewhere on that one, and I told him so in as vulgar a way as I knew how.

"Honk," Burl said calmly, like he hadn't heard me telling him what he could do with his loan clabber, "between the two of us we got three months wages comin', and I figger any-body would loan a feller a little spendin' money with that for a backup."

I got vulgar with Burl again. I told him sure, if we were a

couple of store clerks that had been living in Lusk for a couple of years they might, but who'd trust us?

He kind of threw his head back and said, "Honk, sometimes you ain't got a lick of sense. The place to go for this kind of loan is the outfit a feller is workin' for."

I was wishing he would just come out and say what was on his mind, because I sure as thunder couldn't figure it out.

"Let me put it to you this way, Honk—if you owned one of these trail-lean steers, wouldn't you be willing to put it up against three-months back pay?"

Well, I sure enough savvied what he meant by that, and I could see where his idea had a lot of merit.

I said, "Why anybody on God's green earth would be a fool not to want a deal like that, wouldn't they? It's such a surefire cinch that the outfit will want to do it, that there ain't no sense in even askin' them until we get to Montana. Then we'll just pay 'em back when we get paid. Is that what you had in mind, Burl?"

That is *exactly* what Burl had in mind.

"I'll slip around the herd till I find an old steer sort of off by himself, where I can ooze him away from the rest of them without makin' any commotion. Then I'll get him to town someway and sell him. After a while, I'll come back and watch the herd while you go to town, okay?"

Well, I guess it was, because Burl trotted off in the dark before I had a chance to vote one way or the other. Not long after that I heard his horse's hoofs clattering on some sandstone and him cussing. I was worried that the men around the wagon might hear all the racket he was making, but they were too busy telling each other all about the places of culture they'd visited while they were in Lusk to hear anything going on around the herd. Then I heard a steer beller and I knew that he'd had his last bit of grass—and it had come in the form of a thirty-foot catch rope with a Texas night horse anchored on the other end.

When Burl headed that steer toward Lusk we had been on

guard for a little over an hour, and most of the herd was bedded down. I had them all by myself after he left, but they didn't give me any trouble. It was a dark, dark night with no moon, just big and bright stars. It was also still, with now and then just a whisper of a breeze. Those things make for a quiet night on guard, especially around a herd of trail-wise and weary steers. All I had to do was just to move around enough so they would know someone was there.

Time passed and Burl never showed up back at the herd.

When the next guard came up from the wagon to relieve us, Burl was still gone.

"Ever'thing been quiet, Honk?" asked my relief, just to make a little conversation because he knew it had been.

"Go to hell," I said and rode off.

When I got to the wagon everybody was in their bedrolls asleep. I stuffed some wadded-up blankets in Burl's bedroll and laid my hat at the head of it. Then I got in my own bedroll, but not to sleep. In fifteen minutes, the man who had gone to relieve Burl came trotting up to the camp, stopped his horse, mumbled something, and then rode back to the herd. He had done just what I was waiting for him to do—he'd come to see if Burl was in bed, and then, thinking he was, rode off cussing because he had been looking for him for a quarter of an hour around the herd in the dark.

I laid in bed a few more minutes and then snuck out and headed for Lusk.

CHAPTER 4

LUSK wasn't a town that it took all night to search, and I hadn't been there more than twenty minutes when I spotted Burl's hatchet-butted blue roan tied to a railing in front of—what else—the Texas Hotel and Saloon.

I couldn't see Burl anywhere inside, so I leaned on the bar and described him to the bartender and asked if he'd been in there.

"Could he a been the one that come in leadin' that steer?"

I indicated that that was a distinct possibility.

The bartender leaned toward me, lowered his voice, and said, "You got one, too, feller?"

"No," I said, "I ain't got one too. Where's he at?"

The bartender tilted his head toward a door that lead to some back rooms and said, "Back yonder."

I couldn't think of but one thing Burl could be doing in the "back yonder" rooms, and it wasn't playing checkers. I guess maybe I should have waited for him to come out, but I didn't. I figured I'd waited on him enough for one night.

There were two things making me want to find Burl pretty quick, and I'm not sure which was the stronger of the two—although I have a pretty good hunch. One, I was uneasy about both of us being gone from camp at the same time. We were off guard duty all right, and had gotten by with one man pulling the guard for two. But both of us being gone at once meant that if something happened where all the hands and the cook were needed, then Canaster and the rest of the men would be put in a bind. Wanting to correct the flaw in Canaster's town-rotation system was one thing, but putting the other cowboys in a pinch was something else.

The second thing that had me riled was the sure knowledge that the price Burl got for the steer we "borrowed" probably had not been one that would have set the cattle market on its heels. He would have been in a hurry to sell and any cowtown butcher or saloon keeper would have known that, and his offer would have reflected that knowledge. I figured ten, maybe twelve dollars tops, and although that's a lot of money for a cowboy, I had faith in Burl's ability to go through every last cent of it before he remembered our agreement as to the allocation and distribution of the proceeds from the sale of said steer.

I opened the door to the back rooms and found a narrow hall with three doors on each side, and a door at the far end leading outside. A single, dingy-globed lantern provided just enough light that I didn't have to feel for the door handles on the doors.

The first two rooms were empty, and the third had a man and a woman in it. They didn't know me and I didn't know them, but just the same they didn't hesitate to invite me to leave at once. The fourth room was empty, and I never found out about the sixth because Burl was in the fifth.

A squatty, stringy-haired, redheaded woman was on the bed beside him. She had a black cheroot hanging out of her red mouth and a nearly empty bottle of whiskey laying across her belly. If it hadn't been for the whiskey bottle she would have been naked—she would have been as naked as Burl was. The only thing he was wearing was a glazed-over look, like he'd been dead for a week or so. There was another bottle on the floor and it was as empty. I would have shot Burl right then and there, but it would have been a waste because he was too drunk to suffer any.

The woman flashed me a yellow grin, turned on the charm, and said, "Cowboy, if you're bullin' and have my price, then just drag thisun out of the way and come on." Then she did some things that had nothing to do with modesty.

It's funny how some things can look one way when you

peek at them over the rim of rum-soaked and bloodshot eyes and then look so different when you see the same things through stone-sober eyes. If I had had the time—if I'd had the *money*, I guess I would have *found* the time—to stop at the bar for thirty minutes before coming "back yonder," then what I was seeing might have looked as inviting to me as a warm rock to a cold lizard. But stone-sober as I was, what I was seeing made me think that maybe all three of us could have been things that had crawled out from under a rock somewhere. All of a sudden, all I wanted to do was to smell the clean sage of the outdoors and see the bright stars over a herd of sleeping steers, things I had been aching to get away from not long ago.

Just to set the record straight, if *I* had been the one who brought that steer to town, chances are I would have been the one on the bed wearing my skin on the outside and looking as contented as axle grease in a wheel hub instead of Burl. And the next day I would have been remembering how sweet and delicate that little prairie flower with the red hair had been.

"I reckon I'll pass," I said to the flower.

"Aw, come on," she said, rubbing her legs together like a cricket. "Bein's how you came at just the right time, and I won't have to get dressed again, I'll do it for a dollar."

Some things are sure tempting, but I didn't think there was enough liquor in Lusk to make her one of them. I just wanted to get Burl's clothes back on him and get out of there.

When I got Burl back to the wagon, Canaster was up waiting for us. I never did figure out how he knew we were gone, and I don't guess it really matters. All that matters is that he was swelled up like a toad and dying to ream us out good—which would have been all right and is what he should have done. We had that coming and we knew it, or at least I did. Burl still didn't know anything yet.

But Canaster wasn't content to just give us a little private reaming and let it go, like most trail bosses would have.

"Where have you two bastards been?" he bellered like a mad bull. It was plain he was making a point to wake everybody up so they could hear. I guess he wanted to make examples out of us.

Burl was walking some by then, mostly on four legs though—his and mine—so I helped him over to his bedroll and let him down. Then I looked at Canaster and said, "Cattle rustlers. We been after 'em all night. If you fellers had've come and lent a hand, we might have got 'em."

A couple of the boys laughed, but not Canaster, and I think them laughing made him all the madder.

I could have guessed what his first two words would be—company policy.

"Company policy," he said, "is that there will be no unauthorized absences from a trail herd. Now just who in the hell do you two sons-a-bitches think you are?"

I could tell Canaster was pushing—not with his hands but with his mouth. We had a reprimand coming, but I wasn't going to take a cussing out, and I don't know of many cowboys who would have.

I bowed up and said, "Whoa there, Canaster, let's get one damn thing straight. We went to town when we shouldn't have, that's for sure. And I'll tell you something else we did, we took one of them steers with us to finance the trip, and we sure as hell oughtn't have done that either—but we did and it'll have to come out of our wages. Now, you can chew me out or you can fire me. Either way, I'll just grin and go on because it don't matter much to me one way or the other. But that don't go for cussin' me. You do that, Mr. Canaster, and I don't give a tinker's damn who you're trail boss for, you're gonna have to whip my butt, or else I'm gonna whip yours."

I'd like to say that from there I proceeded to give Monte Canaster the shellacking of his life. But the truth of the matter is we both fought until we gave out and then we just quit. We were both Christian about it, though, and gave about as much as we took. Each of us did a lot of grunting and groaning; we drew blood and donated some, and we were encouraged to no end by the other cowboys, all of whom were disappointed as hell that we couldn't fight until daylight.

The herd left early the next morning, and it left without Burl and me. When Canaster was roping horses out of the remuda, I just told him to catch my and Burl's personal horses. There wasn't anything said about us quitting or getting fired; it was just time for us to leave and everybody knew it. As far as I know, there was no hard feelings, although it was for sure that Canaster and I didn't say any more to each other than we had to.

"Here's how I figure your pay, Ballard," Canaster said to me as I was saddling up. "You have one and a half months coming at thirty-five per, that's fifty-two-fifty. Then outa that you owe the company a dollar for a new cinch and seventy-five cents for that new rope I saw you get out of the wagon. That brings it down to fifty dollars and six bits. Then there's your half of the steer, which is twelve dollars. That means the company owes you thirty-eight dollars and seventy-five cents. Agreed?"

I was agreed on everything but the price of the steer—of course, I didn't know until then that he'd seen me get the rope out of the wagon. But that steer . . . that animal wouldn't have brought twenty-four dollars if he'd been made out of gold instead of hide and horns. On the other hand, I could see where I didn't have much bargaining power, so I bit my bruised lip and kept my mouth shut.

Burl's pay came to forty dollars and fifty cents because the only thing Canaster took out of his pay was twelve dollars for half of the steer. Burl didn't agree or disagree because he was still asleep on his bedroll, and he was still that way when

I waved good-bye to the rest of the men when they were leaving with the herd.

"Where'n the hell's ever'body at?" Burl asked when he finally woke up about two hours after the herd had disappeared to the north. "And why ain't we with 'em?"

"Ever'body else is headed for Montana, 'cept me and you, and we quit."

"We did?" Burl said rubbing his head. "Why'd we do that? Holy cow, Honk, what happened to your face? That bay son-of-a-bitch fart you off again? "No, I didn't get bucked off. Yeah, we quit—I'm not sure why. Now, do you have anymore stupid questions before we leave?"

Burl looked at me and grinned. "Honk, you bastard. What'd you do, bring a girl back to camp?"

I looked at him. "You don't remember nothin', do you?"

He said, "I don't remember a damn thing, except for that beautiful little redhead I was with . . . Uh oh, I bet I overstayed in town a little, didn't I?"

"Maybe a little," I said.

"You come and get me?"

I told him that I had.

"You seen her then, didn't you . . . I mean, you saw the redhead? Wasn't she the kind . . ."

"I seen her, Burl," I assured him. "And she was damn sure the kind all right. One look at her and I could see why a man would forget about the time—or anything else."

I handed Burl an empty tomato can full of black XIT coffee and said, "Drink this and let's drift."

He took the cup and looked at the horses that I already had saddled. Then he noticed the third horse, a little cow-hocked bay.

"I went to town and bought him and an old packsaddle for twenty dollars," I informed him. "Figured we'd need 'em to carry our bedrolls and a little grub that I bought. I got the money Canaster left for you. He took out twelve dollars for your half of the steer. That left you with forty dollars and fifty cents. Then I took out another twelve for your share of the horse and packsaddle and grub."

Burl looked down at the money that I handed him and started counting it.

"Oh, yeah," I said, getting on my horse, "I took out another two and a half from your money and bought a bottle of Hermitage whiskey."

Burl just grinned and didn't say anything. He knew better.

In a minute he said, "How in the hell did Canaster find out about the steer anyway?"

"I told him," I said.

"Like I said, Honk, sometimes you ain't got a lick of sense."

I just grinned because I figured he was right—sometimes I didn't.

We trotted out, headed south. I don't guess either one of us had the least idea of where we were going. For that matter, I don't guess either one of us cared where we were going, at least I didn't, and I didn't think Burl did. There were a lot of things, though, that I didn't know about Burl Lewis.

Burl pulled up once not long after we left and said he was thinking about going back to see that pretty redhead one more time and asked what did I think of the idea. I told him I didn't think too much of it since we were already on our way and all. He said he guessed I was right, but wasn't she hard to get out of a feller's mind. I told him she sure was that all right, that I'd been trying all morning and hadn't been able to get her out of my mind yet.

CHAPTER 5

IT had been around the first week of August that the little blowup with Canaster occurred, and me and Burl were left on the south bank of the Niobrara River while the herd of steers we'd followed all the way from Texas forded it and went on north. For myself, I didn't feel better for having been employed by the famous XIT, nor worse for having left that employment. If I had any regrets at all in that regard, it would have been due to the fact that Burl was the one who had all the fun, while I was the one who pulled guard for both of us and the one who danced a prairie-land set with Monte Canaster to the tune of Burl's snoring. But the more I thought about *that* as we trotted along, the less cruel a trick of fate it seemed to be, and I realized—with a silent smile—that if I was going to roll around in Wyoming with either redhead—that ugly, overbearing Canaster or Burl's delicate flower—I'd pick the former every time.

As we trotted away from the Niobrara River, we didn't discuss where we were going. Since both of our home ranges were south of Wyoming, we just naturally drifted in that direction like a couple of fat coyotes automatically drift toward their home country as fall rolls down from the north.

Up to that point I'd known Burl about sixty days. We'd pulled most every guard together while going up the trail, and it would be fair to say that we got along all right. It would also be fair to say that we weren't thick as flies or that we were riding together because we were such great friends. More than anything, I think we were riding together for the simple reason that there wasn't any reason *not* to ride together and we were both headed south.

We made our way across the land in no particular hurry, stopping at most any ranch we came across and always getting fed and a lot of the time getting put up for the night. Sometimes the accommodations were nothing more than a barn, but after sixty days on the trail, anything with walls and a roof seemed first class and the height of sophistication.

We struck Rawhide Creek and followed it until we crossed the North Platte River and just kept bearing south. Sometimes we would shade up during the hottest part of the day, take a little nap, and let the horses graze. Then after it cooled off enough and we didn't think the sun would hurt our complexions any, we would stretch and saddle up again. As you can see, we seemed to be adjusting quite well to our unemployed status.

After a while we came upon a fair-sized creek called Horse Creek, and we followed it until it met Bear Creek. Right at that juncture was a pretty ranch nestled among some trees and surrounded by green, rolling hills. It was about as pretty a place as you are ever apt to see.

That was the Castle Ranch, owned by old Charlie Castle. We stayed in the bunkhouse that night, and the next morning before we were through with breakfast in the cookhouse an old halfbreed Indian gent came in and said that Mr. Castle would like to see us in his house before we pulled out.

All the ranch buildings there were built out of lodgepole pines, and the main house was as nice as any hotel I'd ever stayed in.

I guess Charlie Castle was a man in his early or middle sixties who had gray hair and blue eyes and looked like he could shoe a dozen head of horses all the way around without ever stopping. But while he looked so hard, he talked in a voice so soft you found yourself leaning toward him without realizing you were doing so.

"You two boys don't need to be ridin' the grub line," he said. While he was talking he wasn't looking at us but through a big window that opened toward the west and overlooked

Bear Creek. Then he turned toward us and said, "If you're lookin' for work, I can use you right here, at least for awhile."

That was sort of a surprise to me because the bunkhouse had seemed pretty well stocked with cowboys, and besides, this was the slack time of the summer—after spring branding and before fall gathering.

"Well," I said, "we were sorta driftin' back south where we came from."

"Suit yourselves," he said, turning his back on us again so we really had to strain to hear him, "but if you wanted to stay for a month or so, you could head on south then with probably seventy or eighty dollars apiece more than you got now."

I looked at Burl and he raised his eyebrows.

"Doin' what?" I asked, because I knew the kind of money Castle was talking about wasn't cowboy wages.

Charlie Castle turned around to face us again and said, "I see you boys are ridin' double-rigged saddles and carryin' short ropes."

I shrugged my shoulders and said, "We came up from Texas." I didn't offer that as an excuse for our rigs, but only an explanation. I didn't figure on debating him over whether a man ought to use a long rope and dally on a center-fire rig like the northern boys did or use a shorter rope and tie hard and fast to a double-rigged saddle like they did in Texas.

"Mister Castle," Burl said, "why don't you just come out and say what's on your mind."

Castle walked over a bookcase that was built into a wall and reached up and pulled down a map that was so big it covered up most of the books. It was a map of the southern part of Wyoming.

The old man put a crooked finger in the space between Horse and Bear Creeks and slid it along the map. "This used to be all Castle range," he said, "all of this country between the Bear and the Horse. It was Castle range and every son of a bitch in the country knew it . . . Now nesters and homesteaders have come in and started claiming it. Started *hell!* They have over half of it. But where were they when we were fightin' the Sioux and the Cheyenne for it? Tell me where the bastards were then!"

The old man was pretty stirred up, and we—me and Burl—didn't figure the kind of questions Castle was asking were the kind we were supposed to answer, so we just looked out the window or down at the floor and didn't say anything.

Castle wasn't through yet. He said, "Do you boys know where you'll be when the country is taken over by nesters and homesteaders? Do you think *they* will be hirin' men like you two—men who can ride and rope and know how to handle a thousand wild steers and move 'em up the trail? You can bet your ass they won't. Oh, they may hire you all right, but it'll be to fence up some good cattle range into quarter-section farms and turn the grass over with a goddamn plow!"

I couldn't help but laugh a little at what Castle had said. I opened my right hand up and looked at it and said, "This hand fits a pair of bridle reins and catch rope real good, Mister Castle —but it sure as hell ain't ever gonna fit no wire pliers or plow handle." I held the left hand up then said, "And the same goes for this 'un."

Now it was old Charlie Castle who laughed a little when he said, "But they'll *have* to learn to fit 'em, Honk, if the nesters take over the free range, 'cause there won't be any more big cow outfits for men like you and Burl to ride for. And do you think those farmers will let a cowboy ride the grub line like we do? Hell no! They'll be meetin' you at the first row of corn with a shotgun . . . 'cause they're not our kind, boys, they're just *not* our kind."

That big old room got awful quiet for a while after that, with me and Burl not doing much at all and Charlie Castle standing there looking at his map. In a minute he started in again, but his voice had turned back soft like it had been when we first came into the room. He looked back at his map and said, "A man that won't fight for what he's got ain't much of a man in my books."

I looked over at Burl and he just shrugged his shoulders. Then I looked at Castle and said, "I can sure agree with what you're sayin', Mister Castle, but if you're wantin' a couple of gun hands . . ."

"Oh, no, boys," Castle hurriedly said, "you've misunderstood me. Maybe I got too carried away. Look, I'd like to hire you two boys to rope and earmark some calves for me, that's all. When I was talkin' about your rigs and your ropes, I was thinking you were probably Texas hands, and it's a rare one of you boys that can't rope damn good. That's what I'm after—a couple of good rope hands, not gun hands. And you two being strangers around here would just make it better."

I relaxed a little, pushed my hat back, and said, "Why don't you go over that part about us makin' seventy or eighty dollars in a month again." Then I glanced over to the Castle liquor cabinet, making dead sure that Charlie Castle saw me.

Castle grinned, and so did the two cowboys in his front room with him.

There might have been some cheap cowboy stuff in the Castle liquor cabinet, but if there was, it never left the shelf that morning. We drank the good stuff, and we drank it like citizens. That is, the bourbon we drank came from a bottle bearing the label of Denver's Grand Palace Hotel, and we drank it mixed with a little water in the bottom of tall glasses.

That afternoon we packed a lot of provisions on our packhorse—provisions that came from the commissary beside Charlie Castle's cookhouse. Castle followed us back and forth, telling us to be sure and get everything we wanted.

When all the provisions were packed, he told us to follow him down to the supply barn, where he gave each of us a brand new rope and a couple of piggin' strings apiece. Then he told us to follow him back to his house.

While we sat on our horses in front of his big lodgepole

house, he went inside and came back out carrying two fifths of that good Grand Palace Bourbon.

"Better take this along," he said as he tossed each of us a bottle. "It's good to douse on canker sores or to use in case a horse gets sored-up."

"You mean to rub it on like a liniment?" I asked.

"Well now, you know, I never thought of that," the old rancher said, letting a smile creep across his craggy face. "The way I always used it though, was to lay up somewhere and drink it till the damned horse got well."

We laughed and started to leave when he called us back.

"Boys," he said, serious now, "I'd just as soon you didn't come by here too often. I know you've been around enough to savvy the score on a game like this. You know the deal, and you can be sure I'll stick to it. Whenever you've had enough, or whenever you get to wantin' to head on south, just bring the ears you've got to me and we'll settle up."

CHAPTER 6

THE working arrangement we had with Charlie Castle was simple enough, and though it could be seen in a light that would not cast back a very favorable reflection of anybody involved, as seen through my cowboy eyes there was nothing in it to be ashamed of. I'm not going to spend a lot of time defending what we were doing; I'll just tell how it was and let it drift on its own from there.

I felt Charlie Castle had a legitimate complaint about the homesteaders for the reasons he told us that morning in his house. And what he had said about the homesteaders not being "our kind" rang true in my ears. Castle, though, was our kind. He would help a cowboy out when he needed it, and if he—Charlie Castle—needed a little help himself, and was willing to pay for it, then the only thing for a man to do was to throw in and give him that help.

That the homesteaders were legal in what they were doing didn't mean a hill of beans to me because I'd seen legal before, just like I'd seen right before—and just like I'd seen the times when the two weren't anywhere near the same thing. Land laws and such were drawn up by a bunch of politicians back East, and what they knew about a cow outfit you could've put in a thimble.

Another reason I could see nothing wrong in what we were doing was because nearly everybody in a big cattle country had, at one time or another, had his rope on beef that did not exactly belong to him. I knew a lot of big operators who got their start by catching and branding mavericks. Back in a little earlier time, some outfits would send a chuck wagon out with a crew of cowboys whose sole

31

job was to roam around and brand mavericks. It was accepted on the range that if a cow critter had been "kicked off the tit" and wore no brand on its hide, then it was first come, first served. Even that XIT trail herd that me and Burl had come up from Texas with—do you think it was XIT beef we ate on the trail?

So after all of that, do you see how I didn't bat an eye when Charlie Castle put his deal to us?

I said I wasn't going to defend what we were doing, but it looks like I have been. I guess it's only natural for a man to want to throw as good a light as he can on himself. So, in spite of all the "non-defending" I've gone through, maybe it was Charlie Castle himself who said it best when he told me and Burl that we'd been around enough to "know the score" on what we were doing.

Well, I've led the bronc around enough—it's time to cheek him up and get astraddle of him. This was the deal:

It was still mostly open range in that country and a general roundup was held in the spring and the fall. The homesteaders and the nester ranchers set up housekeeping on a quarter section of land beside some good watering hole and let their cattle run loose and mingle with everyone else's.

That spring, Charlie Castle and his men—and probably some of the other big outfits did the same thing—made no special effort to bring nester cattle in on the drives. If one head—or twenty head, it didn't matter—wanted to run off, the cowboys would just push their hats back and say, "God, look at 'em run." Then they would pull their hats back down and ride on. It even went a little farther than that. Many times they not only made no special effort to gather nester cattle—they made special effort *not* to gather them. The number "missed" on any given day would not have been large, but with several men doing it every day for thirty or forty days, the numbers finally would get big enough to amount to something.

What Burl and I were supposed to do was to prowl around

the range and find some of those nester cattle that had been "missed." Most likely, the calves would still be sucking their mammies and would not be mavericks yet. Under those circumstances, putting Castle's brand on them would have been rustling in anybody's book. But we didn't brand a single head; didn't singe a single hair; didn't rustle a single hoof.

What we would do when we came across some of those calves was to shake a loop out in our ropes and build to them. We'd run astraddle of 'em and get our twines on 'em as quick as we could. Then we'd take out our knives and earmark them. The earmark we'd put on them would be the same earmark their mammies wore—even if it was a nester's earmark.

Any earmarked cattle on the range are taken for granted to also be branded because no one would go to the trouble of doing the one without doing the other at the same time. At least, that's what the nesters were supposed to think. After the spring roundup, they might ride around and brand a few calves here and there that had been "missed." But anything they saw wearing an earmark they wouldn't disturb, as they would figure there was a brand there—it was just too haired-over to read.

After those earmarked—but unbranded—calves had been kicked off the tit—and after me and Burl were out of the country—Castle's cowboys would catch them again. They would whittle on their ears again, only *they* would make the earmark resemble Castle's as much as it did any homestead-er's, and by the time they put Castle's Slash Two brand on the right hip, nobody in the world could prove that they had not come out of Castle cows to begin with.

This method of increasing your herd is known as "sleeper-ing," and Charlie Castle sure wasn't the one who invented it. It had been around a long time, maybe ever since the first two men wanted the same range. But you've got to have a lot of cow-savvy to know when it's being worked against you, and most farmers and nesters would just scratch their heads and wonder what in the thunder had happened to their calf crop.

The money, or rather the ears that we could exchange for money, was not piling up like I thought it would. Either there were not as many unbranded nester cattle on the range as I thought, or the nesters were making better hands at finding them and branding them than they were supposed to. But I was still making more money than I'd ever made just punching cows.

Castle said he would pay us six bits for each ear we turned in. The first day I roped and earmarked three calves; the next day two; the next, two again; the next, only one. And so on, until at the end of two weeks the two of us together had in a greasy leather pouch a total of thirty-nine ears—or parts of ears.

The way we worked it was to camp in a place out of sight and close to water, and then work out from there for two or three days, going in a different direction each day. Usually, we'd leave camp about the time the coming sun doused the first stars in the east. We would find cattle grazing down in the draws or out on the flats, and we would hopefully pick up a couple of full-eared calves. After that, we'd lay up somewhere until the cows started drifting in toward water. When they did that, we would try to hit all the watering holes close by and with any luck get another couple of ears.

We were careful to keep on the watch all the time, knowing this was the kind of roping a man had better do before an empty grandstand—or not do at all. I learned then that looking over your shoulder can get to be a habit mighty fast, and after a few days of it a man stays nervous all the time, wondering what some sound was, or what that movement was he saw out of the corner of his eye.

About the second time we moved camp, Burl said to me, "If I was you, I'd carry that old Colt on my hip instead of leavin' it at camp."

He carried a gun on his hip all the time, but all I ever

carried was an old .44–40 Winchester carbine in a handmade scabbard under my right stirrup leather. I just hadn't ever gotten into the habit of having a heavy Colt on me all the time, preferring to leave it rolled up in my bedroll.

I considered what Burl said for a minute, and then I said, "I always carry that rifle. Besides, I don't think . . ."

"Suit yourself," he said, "but if you ever get caught away from your horse when things go to gettin' hot, you'll be cravin' Colt steel worse than you were cravin' to get your hands on that redhead I had in Lusk."

Like I said, I'd just met Burl when I hired on to the XIT in Tascosa, and I didn't know anything about him, except that he seemed like another drifting cowboy. We got along all right then. But now that it was just me and him camping and riding alone all day, every day, things had changed.

Sometimes he would get quiet and not say anything at all to me. Sometimes I would catch him watching me out of the corner of his eye, and then when I'd look at him he would look off and laugh to himself. Sometimes he would just start laughing, not loud, but laughing just the same and never tell me why.

As you can tell, Burl Lewis wasn't the same good-time cowboy he had been coming up the trail, and I'd just about had my fill of him. And I just about had my fill of him bragging about that whore in Lusk. I said, "If I'd been unlucky enough to've had my hands on that redhead, they'd probably be so rotten by now I couldn't even hold a gun."

"What's that supposed to mean?" he said.

"It's supposed to mean that I've seen dry cows I'd rather be caught with than her," I said and got up and started walking away. Then I saw the sack we were keeping the ears in and I stopped and turned back to him and said, "I think we oughta keep our ears separate."

We'd started out pooling the ears into a common sack with the agreement that when we cashed them in we would split the money down the middle. The trouble with that arrangement was that I was really working at it and he wasn't.

Whenever we came upon a little bunch of cattle that had some full-eared calves in it, I would run old Pat plumb down roping three or four head. Burl might have roped one in that same time, and his horse wouldn't even have broken a sweat.

Now that I'd brought our work habits out in the open and suggested we keep the ears separate, I thought he might get mad. But he didn't act like it bothered him at all. He just said, "Whatever you think." Then he added, "You think this is really makin' money, don't you?"

I said, "It's not bad . . . if a man wants to work at it. I guess you've made a lot more at times, uh?"

Burl was squatted down and for a little bit he just looked at the ground. When he looked up again he was wearing a mocking grin and he said, "Oh . . . I guess I have."

CHAPTER 7

AFTER things turned bitter between me and Burl I decided, late one evening, that I would pack up and leave without him. But while I was making up my mind to do that, I got to thinking that maybe I should stay for a couple of more days and really work hard at earmarking calves, keep all of those ears for myself and then leave. That way I could go with forty or fifty dollars more in my pockets—counting the ears in the sack that we would split—than I had when I got there a little over two weeks earlier.

The next day I worked hard and rode hard and earmarked five more calves. Burl hung around the camp and didn't even bother to go with me, which suited me fine. That day though I had a scare. It happened when I was untying a fat heifer calf and looked up and saw two riders coming down a long slope about a half a mile away. They weren't coming in a hurry, but they were sure coming right toward me.

I let the calf up and she ran back to her bawling mammie while I got back in my saddle and coiled up my rope. Then I pulled my hat down and trotted out to meet the riders.

They were a man about forty-five and a boy who was probably his son. I could tell the man was a homesteader because he didn't sit a horse like a cowboy.

He said, "Good mornin'," when they stopped in front of me.

I said, "Howdy," and let my eyes drop so I could see if he had a gun on his hip. He did, and all of a sudden I wished my old Colt was around my waist instead of back at camp in my bedroll. I didn't want to admit Burl had been right, but I sure couldn't forget his warning, either.

"Catch a maverick?" the homesteader asked.

"Yeah," I said.

"Funny," he said, looking around, "I don't see your brandin' fire anywhere."

I knew then that I'd better start thinking before I started talking. I said, "Well, I *thought* she was a maverick, but when I got her roped I found a brand on her, so I just turned her loose."

"You couldn't see the earmark on her either?" the homesteader asked.

"No," I said, "she had an underslope earmark and the hair was too long on her ear to see it."

"That happens," the homesteader said. Then he nodded at me, and him and his boy rode off.

The next morning, before I left camp for what was *definitely* to be my last day of sleepering calves for Charlie Castle, I buckled my old Colt around my waist. Burl saw me do it, but just smiled and didn't say anything.

I earned four more ears that day and was riding back to camp late in the afternoon, feeling good about almost everything. I was on an old wagon road that nobody used anymore—nobody but cowboys sleepering calves for Charlie Castle, that is—when I saw Burl sitting on the ground in front of his horse underneath a big cottonwood tree.

When I stopped under the tree he stood up and I saw that he was holding a pair of binoculars in his hands. I never knew he had any until that moment.

"What are you doin'?" I asked.

He handed me the glasses without saying anything. When I got off my horse, he said, "Look at that brush-covered ridge over there."

The ridge he was talking about was about two miles away and was easy to see through the glasses. It was easy to see, but all I could see *was* a brushy ridge.

"I don't see anything," I said.

"Get 'em steady on something and look at the bottom of the brush . . . right above that clay bank."

I sat down on the ground and braced my elbows on my knees. It took a little while for me to see him, but when I did I saw him clear as day. He was sitting on a slope with the brush behind him to break his outline. In a little bit I could see that he had his own binoculars and they were pointed right down to where we were.

"Who do you reckon it is?" I asked.

"Could be a hunter," Burl said, "or somebody that's just curious . . . or it could be the law."

"Hell," I said, "there ain't no law against earmarkin' calves, is there?"

Burl just grinned and shrugged his shoulders.

I stood up, handed the glasses back to Burl, and announced the decision to him that I'd made two days ago: "I'm cashin' in my ears and pullin' out."

"Me too," Burl said.

"I mean *tonight*," I said.

"So do I," Burl said.

Our camp was down in a grove of cottonwood trees in a slight depression of land and was hard to see until you were right on it. When we came over the rise and were no more than fifty yards away, a man stepped out of the trees and waved at us.

I was wishing right then that I was a long way from Wyoming, but it didn't seem like there was much to do but ride on into camp. It didn't help my feelings any when I saw Burl drop a hand and ease the little leather loop off the hammer of his Colt.

When we rode up to within earshot of the man standing in front of our trees, he said, "Are you the boys that's been stayin' here?" He said it friendly enough, and he didn't look to be on the warpath at all. He was a man carrying a little age on him, maybe fifty-five years old, with a big gray mustache on a wide face. He was a little under six feet tall and medium built. He looked like a cowboy. He had some kind of gun on his hip, but it was holstered in a flap-top rig that completely covered it. A rifle hung from his right hand, but it hung casual-like and not like he was fixing to go to war with it.

"Yeah," Burl said, "this is our camp." We walked our horses on up to him and I could see that Burl kept his right hand tolerable close to the butt of his gun.

"Hope you fellers don't mind us makin' ourselves at home," the man said when we stopped our horses in front of him, "but there wasn't anybody around and the coffee pot was just beggin' to be used."

"That's all right," Burl said. "We'll just join you."

"Good," the man said. "Come on then."

After the man turned his back on us and started to walk into the trees Burl got off his horse and tied him to a low-growing cottonwood branch. I did the same thing and then went into the trees behind Burl.

In a few places we had to lean over to duck under a low branch and I noticed that even then Burl did not move his hand away from his gun or take his eyes off the man's back.

When we got to the camp there was another man there, sitting on the ground with a cup in his hand. He was about forty years old and had a gun on his own hip. He looked at me and Burl and nodded his head a little, but didn't say anything.

"There's two good cups left in the pot," the older man said. "Sure hope you boys don't mind us doin' this."

Burl grinned and shook his head and then took a cup from the older man, tossed the little coffee in it out and filled it up again from the black pot that he picked up from a flat rock beside the small fire.

The other man handed me the other cup and I did the same as Burl.

The older man eased down on his hunkers not far from the other stranger. He still had the rifle in his hand but still held it casual. Burl and I were standing up drinking coffee and the two strangers were squatting down watching us. Once in a while one of us would grin, but I don't know what in the hell we were grinning at. It got quiet too, too quiet, and I was wishing somebody would say something.

But nobody said anything, and I could feel a real uneasiness set in among our little circle of friends. It wasn't an uneasiness you could see, not at all. In fact, I don't think an artist could have painted anything that looked more peaceful. It was way late in the day and those Wyoming hills that surrounded our little grove of cottonwoods were throwing their shadows down into the bottoms of the draws. The broad, flat leaves of the trees were hanging still and the smoke from the little fire rose straight up through them. It had been hot and humid all day, but now it had started to cool off and you could smell that coolness as it mixed with the wood smoke. I could hear a few birds in the trees, and away off somewhere a coyote barked a few times and finished off with a long howl.

The younger man of the two strangers stood up then, turned his back to us, walked out about ten feet, spread his legs and started peeing.

I was watching both of them over the rim of my cup when the older man said in a soft, easy voice, still squatted down and holding his rifle, "I'm Johnson Powers and this other man is Ben DuPree—"

Then there was a blur to my right where Burl was, followed by a deafening roar and two inches of bright flame almost under my nose coming from Burl's gun.

Johnson Powers's face turned to mush and he flipped backwards as loose as a rag doll, somehow firing his rifle as he went over, I think simply out of instinct. But his bullet hit Burl and knocked him down.

All of that happened in less than one whole second, so fast that a man's brain didn't really have time to sort it all out.

DuPree whirled around with his eyes as big as silver

dollars. His hand dropped and started back up with a gun in it, and somehow I knew, although I sure didn't have time to think about it, that when that gun stopped rising and leveled off, it would be leveled at me.

I don't remember reaching down and drawing my old Colt, but I remember feeling the heavy thing in my hand and my thumb hurrying for its hammer.

The gun in my hand erupted and a tongue of blue flame leaped out. My thumb moved again and again the flames licked out toward DuPree. I saw him jerk violently, his face contort in pain, two patches of blood appear on his shirt front. My thumb moved a third time, but before it could rotate the big .45 cylinder, DuPree was down.

CHAPTER 8

FOR getting a man a long ways down a bad trail, I don't think anything can beat a smoking gun. I bet if the devil was to be allowed only one tool for gathering in men's souls, he'd far and away rather have a smoking gun than anything else, even hard liquor and soft thighs, the other two mainstays of his trade. The charm of a smoking gun is that it can accomplish its mission so god-awful fast. It couldn't have been more than two seconds from the time I saw that first blur of movement out of the corner of my eye and heard that first deafening roar, until I was standing there with the smoke curling up out of the end of the barrel of my old Colt.

Two seconds. Four shots. Three men down on the ground running out blood like a cow-country spring runs out water. One tick of a clock I was looking at Powers and DuPree over the rim of a cup of smoking coffee, and two ticks later I was looking at them over a smoking gun barrel.

My ears were ringing pretty bad, but other than that there was a strange silence for the next couple of seconds. I just stood there holding the old Colt that had traveled a hundred miles rolled up in my bedroll for every one it had traveled strapped around my waist. There was a layer of gray gunsmoke about shoulder high that was silently twisting and drifting higher, but the only sound was the ringing in my ears.

Then some birds somewhere in the trees started singing again, a couple of the horses snorted and rustled leaves, and a low roll of thunder came drifting in from somewhere a long ways off. Then I heard a "ooug . . . ooug . . . ooug" sort of sound, like an old dying cow makes each time she breathes. That was Ben DuPree. To my left came a faint gurgling noise and that was Burl.

That smell. I'll never forget it. It wasn't any one smell by itself that made my stomach turn over, but a combination of them. There was the smell of the damp leaves, the wood smoke, the coffee, the burnt gunpowder, and mixed in with all of them was the smell of blood and something that was even worse. It reminded me of the smell you get when you're butchering a beef.

Burl coughed and gurgled and I turned my head and looked down at him. His front was covered in blood and he was holding a shaking hand out toward me. DuPree had fallen against an old log and was sort of leaning against it cocked over to one side. His gun was still in his hand and his hand was laying in his lap. His legs stirred a little bit and I figured I'd better get that gun out of his hand just in case he felt like hefting it again. I wasn't so embarrassed at being the only one not leaking blood that I was willing to give DuPree another chance to remedy that oversight.

I eased over to him and leaned over and flicked his gun onto the ground with the barrel of my Colt. It was then that my gun bumped against something metal in his shirt pocket and I reached in to see what it was. The full extent of what I'd done—other than to save my life—didn't hit me until I drug it out and looked at it laying so innocentlike in the palm of my shaking hand—a United States Deputy Marshal's badge!

I dropped the thing like it was hot. Two steps had me standing over Johnson Powers's body. Burl's bullet had caught him just below his right eye, and a man's face hit that close with a .45 caliber bullet sure's not something to admire. His face was already blue and swelled something terrible, and a big old green blowfly was already wading around in the sticky stuff oozing out the hole.

Powers had come calling wearing a black vest, and I leaned over to pull it out of the way to look in his pocket . . . but I didn't have to bother. His badge was pinned inside his vest. It only had one word on it—SHERIFF!

I heard Burl cough again and looked over there and he had rolled over and was propped up on one elbow. There was blood trinkling out the lower corner of his mouth and he looked pale as a ghost—but I swear the son of a bitch was grinning!

"Y-y-you"—he coughed and spit out some thick blood— "you done good, Honk," he finally managed to say.

I crammed my gun down in its leather and before I knew it I had ahold of Burl's shirt front, shaking him and screaming, "Why in the goddamn hell'd you do that!"

I shook him so hard some blood as thick and sticky as wild plum jelly came out the hole in his chest. He didn't have the strength to fight me, and when I let go he fell back to the ground.

"They was John Laws, wasn't they?" Burl asked, stretched out on his back. His voice was weak but it was clear now, and I guess I'd done him a favor by shaking the thick blood loose that had collected in his throat.

I was getting more nervous all the time. I hadn't had time to be that way during the shooting, but I was sure making up for lost time now. I went to pacing and pulling my hand over down my face and off my chin. The thunder was rolling in more regular now. I could hear the blowflies buzzing around Johnson Powers's ripe head, and DuPree was still groaning like a dying cow. Just as well not gloss it—I wasn't just nervous, I was *scared*. I guess the most scared I've ever been.

"I got a glimpse of Powers's badge underneath his vest," Burl said. "That's how I knew."

I stood over him and said, "Well, what'n the hell do you think they'd a done to us for just earmarkin' a few goddamn calves? You dumb . . ."

Before I got much chance to cuss Burl like I intended, he rolled back up on an elbow and started laughing—spitting blood and laughing. Gunsmoke and the sight and the stink of death and suffering were all around us . . . and he was laughing!

When he was finally about choked down, Burl quit laughing and concentrated on just breathing for a few seconds. He was lungshot and operating with only one wind-maker. I knew he was bad hurt, maybe "unto death," but somehow I couldn't muster up much sympathy for him.

I went back over to where DuPree was. He'd stopped groaning and was just laying there, but he was still breathing.

"Where's he hit?" Burl asked.

"Hell, I don't know," I said without taking my eyes off him, "somewhere in the innards is all I know. Twice."

"You better bury 'em before we ride," he said.

I looked over at Burl then. "Hell," I said, "DuPree ain't dead, and besides, I didn't exactly do anything wrong."

"Didn't exactly . . ." he tried laughing again, but choked down even quicker this time so he gave that up. "Nothing but shoot a U.S. Deputy Marshal, you mean, in the gut—twice. You'll give a jury a goddamn good laugh if you tell 'em that, Ballard. Now there ain't but one thing to do—kill DuPree, bury the bodies, and let's get the hell outa here."

I could see where Burl was probably right in what he said about getting a judge and jury to believe my innocence. How would I *ever* do that? The terrible truth was that I couldn't not in a million years. I had blood on my hands, regardless of how it got there, and there was no getting it off. If DuPree died, as nine times out of ten, a gutshot man will, there wouldn't be but one thing waiting for me if I was caught—a scratchy hemp rope at the top of a short flight of stairs.

Seeing one truth in what Burl was saying made me begin to see another truth in his words. I didn't willingly see it, any more than I willingtly shot DuPree, but the fact is that I saw it—if Powers and DuPree were *both* tucked safely to bed under three or four feet of sod. . . . But I didn't want to think about that anymore. DuPree was still breathing and might for several more hours. I'd seen cows worse off than him live for a day or more, after you couldn't see how they could draw one more breath.

"Honk," Burl said, "use your head. You know DuPree's gonna die, so what good will it do to let him live just long enough to tell somebody who done it?"

I didn't answer him. I just went to where our horses were, got Pat and the cow-hocked bay packhorse, led 'em up to the camp and started getting ready to leave. Burl kept asking me where I thought I was going and telling me how I didn't have a lick of sense if I didn't go ahead and kill DuPree. I just kept packing, and in ten minutes I was ready to go. I stepped astraddle of Pat with the bay's lead rope in hand and looked down at Burl Lewis for what I hoped was the last time—but he wasn't there.

I didn't figure he had the strength to get up but somehow he had, and he was over kneeling in front of DuPree—with his six-shooter full-cocked and held about a foot and a half from DuPree's chest-fallen head!

"Burl!" I hollered as I whipped out my own gun.

"I'm just doin' what's gotta be done, Honk. What you ain't got the guts to do," he said.

I lifted my Colt so I could sight down it to Burl's back. Then I eared back the hammer and I did it slow enough so he could hear each click of the thing.

"If you can't shoot DuPree," he said, still looking over his gun barrel at the marshal's head, "why in the hell would I think you could shoot me?"

"If you pull that trigger, I guess we'll both find out whether I can or not," I said. "But goddamn you, Burl, I sure as hell got it in my head to do it." I meant just that, and I guess it sounded like I did too, because Burl didn't kill DuPree.

"You know what I'd do if I was you, Honk?" Burl said.

"Don't rightly give a damn," I answered, with my gun still pointed at him.

"I'd kill me and DuPree both."

I laughed a little and said, "Looks to me like you're both gonna die anyway."

"But you can't count on that," Burl said, turning around to face me now and not lowering his .45, but raising its muzzle just enough so it centered on my chest. "If you're gonna survive in this business, you've got to learn to take those kind of things in your own hands and not leave 'em to chance."

"Maybe you're thinking about killin' me and leavin' me here, uh, Burl? Better not to leave any witnesses at all. Could you be thinkin' along them lines?"

Burl stretched his blood-rimmed lips into a wicked kind of grin. "Could be—if I wasn't shot up. Like it is though, I need your help to get outa the country. I guess you're just tolerable lucky, Ballard."

"I used to think I was pretty lucky—until I met up with you," I said, with my old Colt still held out at arm's length and the broad front sight wavering somewhere between his belly button and throat latch. "Since then my luck's been goin' downhill like a cold-jawed horse pitchin' off a tall bluff. And being as that's the case, and I sure as hell wish it was you layin' over there where DuPree is with two bullets in the gut instead of just one in the lung, what makes you think I'd help you get to anywhere this side of hell?"

Burl lowered his gun and let the hammer down easy. "Two things," he said. "One, if you ride off without me, you don't know but what I'll kill DuPree. And two, money—lots of it. Enough money so you can lay low for a long time—even go to Mexico or South America and get some pretty senorita to lay low with you."

I lowered my Colt, but kept it handy because I'd just as soon as trusted a coon-tailed rattlesnake as Burl. "You've got the fiddle," I said, "keep sawin' on it."

"The money come from the Hillsboro, New Mexico bank eight months ago. Ten thousand dollars in cash. I got it hid on a homestead I've got near Liberty . . . I'll split it with you."

"Burl," I looked at him hard and said, "if you tell me you're a sorry, lung-shot son-of-a-bitch, I might believe you. Other'n that, though, I'd put more faith in a pack mule's fart than in anything you could say."

Burl started coughing and spitting up blood again until he sank back to the ground on his knees. I just sat astraddle of Pat and watched. Finally, he sat down, pointed toward his warbag laying on the ground beside his bedroll, and said, "Look in there."

I thought about it a little bit, then wrapped the bay's lead rope around my saddle horn a couple of times and got off. When I opened up his warbag, he said, "There's kind of a hidden flap in the bottom—look inside it."

I found the flap and pulled out a folded-up piece of paper. I unfolded it and read what it had printed on it, in big black letters across the top: NOTICE—BANK ROBBERY! Below that was written: On October 11, 1895, the Miners State Bank in Hillsboro, New Mexico Territory was held up by three armed bandits. From there it went on to give some description of the three and one of the descriptions could have fit Burl, just like it could have probably fit a thousand other men. It didn't tell how much money was taken or give any names.

"Now maybe you believe me, huh?" said Burl. "There was a teller killed in that robbery, and I wasn't about to let these John Laws take me in. You don't really think I'd be stupid enough to start a shooting like the one we had here, just because we'd been earmarkin' a few calves, do you?"

"Hell," I said, "I've seen horses fall over backards for no reason—and they weren't near as stupid as you. Sometimes horses *and* people just come unraveled for no reason . . . Now I'm fixin' to rattle my hocks all the way to Mexico. You can go with me as long as you can keep up. The minute you start slowin' me down though, I'll leave you like I would a crippled horse."

Burl grinned. "You'll have to put my gear on the packhorse and then help me get on—after that I won't be no trouble at all."

But Burl wasn't as tough as he thought he was, and he cried out in pain when I shoved him into the saddle. And even then he had to ride slumped over with one hand pressing a neckerchief against his bullet wound. I told him again before we left, "Goddamn you, Burl, I mean what I said —you can't keep up, and I leave you. It ain't like I owe you."

Burl acted like he hadn't heard a word I'd said. He twisted around in the saddle enough until he could see DuPree leaning unconscious against the log, and said, "I'll bet some day you'll regret . . ."

I touched a spur to Pat's belly and started south saying, "The thing I regret *right now* is ever crossin' trails with you."

Maybe not trying to get DuPree to a doctor was just the same as putting a bullet in his brain, but it sure as hell didn't *feel* the same. Anyway, I always thought a man had some responsibility to look after his own hide. I hadn't asked for Powers and DuPree to ride into our camp any more than I'd asked for Burl to start the shooting. And I didn't shoot anybody there because I wanted to see them jump and fall, but only to stay alive. That's the same reason I went south as fast as I could too. Maybe those are wrong reasons for doing what I did, but they're sure honest ones. There may be people who will say they wouldn't have done it, and maybe they wouldn't have. But they weren't standing in Honk Ballard's boots that late afternoon when the guns started going off, and death was only a few ounces of trigger pressure away. At a time like that, you have to play the hand dealt to you, and there's no time for figuring discards or strategy because the cards are dealt face up with the winner getting another breath of life and the loser getting Death.

I stopped at the top of the rise for a last look at the little grove of cottonwoods and all of a sudden I wasn't as scared as I was mad. The trouble was, I didn't know who to be mad at, other than Burl, and I knew *he* hadn't had anything to do with me deciding to leave the Matador when I had and go to Tascosa. I didn't know who or what to blame for that, so I just pulled my hat down, reined the sorrel around, and struck a trail south about the same time the sun dipped into the faraway hills in the west.

CHAPTER 9

I TOLD Burl I wasn't going to let him slow me down, but I did. If it had just been me heading south, I could have put the horses into a long trot, held it most of the night, and been below Cheyenne and into Colorado by the next sun. But instead of that, and owing to nothing but Burl's poor road condition, I'd had to hold the horses down to a little short jig of a trot, and even walked them now and then. That being the case, the next morning when daylight cracked—as I read in a yellow-backed novel one time—" the ragged dawn of a wide land," it was still a wide *Wyoming* land.

I'd angled to the east of Cheyenne and was just getting to what I think was Crow Creek when I decided we'd better pull up and let the horses blow and take on a belly full of grass. Grass-fed horses can't take near the abuse grain-fed ones can, and I figured a man on the run had better not be caught out on the plains on a used-up horse, where a hard run might be needed to get him over the next hill and maybe out of the notched rear sight of some citizen-posseman's Winchester, especially if it happened to be one of those new level-shooting 30–30s, or even worse, one of those 30–40s I'd been hearing about. Just thinking about how far one of those new calibers could likely reach out across an open prairie and knock a man out of the saddle sent a chill down my spine.

"Give me a pack of old-time, scalp-hungry heathens any day," I muttered, " 'stead of one Christianized citizen with a 30–30 and a clear three-hundred-yard shot at some poor, wayward cowboy's back."

We spent that day—my first full and official one as an

outlaw and a man on the run—holed up in a brush thicket that surrounded a little hole of muddy water. I just came on it by accident, but it was a good place. The water hole wasn't over ten feet long and not even that wide, and from the looks of it, it couldn't have been over knee-deep anywhere. The brush patch around it didn't have any more than an acre in it, and there were several other brush patches in that draw that were about the same size. That meant that there was nothing peculiar about our patch, nothing to draw undue attention to it. The muddy water seemed to suit the horses just fine, and I wasn't near as particular about the color of the water that passed through my own gullet either, as I might have been under different circumstances.

I pulled the saddles off the horses and hobbled them, and they dropped their heads and started baling grass. Mine and Burl's breakfast was a can of cold tomatoes. When that chore was finished I laid back, smoked cigarettes, dozed in short, fitful stretches, and fought off gnats, deer flies, and mosquitoes.

I didn't ask Burl if the accommodations suited him and he never volunteered to tell me. In fact, we didn't say hardly three words all day. I didn't want to talk and Burl didn't feel like it. He grunted when I asked him if he wanted part of the tomatoes, and said, "Okay," when I asked how he was holding up to the jarring his horse had given him all night long. He slept most of the time when he wasn't coughing or spitting out blood, and I noticed that his face was about as pale as a cowboy's legs. He'd stuffed some rags over the hole in his chest, and the blood on his shirt had turned from red to black and was drawing green blowflies something awful. I hated to even look at him.

When the sun went down, I had the horses ready to go. I helped Burl on his dun and I could tell he was weaker than he had been the last time I'd done that. We rode through that night like we had the night before, but we covered even fewer miles because Burl's horse was giving out on him. One time I looked back and they were about a hundred yards behind. I hollered, "Looks to me like you could spur the son-of-a-bitch enough to make 'im keep up!" but I don't think he heard me or was conscious enough to know what I said if he did. Finally, I stopped and tied Burl's dun to the pack-horse's tail, but he led about like a sack, of wet sand, so it didn't help us make any better time.

I don't know exactly when, but sometime during that night we crossed over into Colorado. It was the first time in all of my wanderings that whenever I saw a ranch I rode wide around it. Always before when I saw one, I'd ride straight for it. But now when I saw one I'd cock an ear toward it like a spooky bronc and sidle away from it.

When that second night started turning into day, I stopped us in some tamaracks that were growing along a little boggy creek. The horses grazed and I rested and ate cold from a can again. Burl just shook his head when I asked if he was hungry. He'd come farther than I thought he could, but I could tell he was sinking fast now. His eyes were sunk way back in his head and looked like open-pit mines, and I was beginning to smell the infection and rot in him. Every time I looked at him he seemed worse than he had the time before. A couple of times I hollered at him and he didn't even raise his head or open his eyes. Sometimes I saw him shiver and I knew he had a fever. Death had been hounding him since the moment Johnson Powers's bullet had parted the hairs on his chest, and I figured for sure He was going to catch up with us while we were day-camped along that boggy creek.

The truth is, had Burl been a cow or a horse or any kind of critter like that, I'd have put a bullet in his brain, figuring that would have been the best thing for him. But I couldn't do that to Burl, anymore than I could have done it to DuPree.

I could have rode off and left him, but somehow that didn't seem to be the right thing to do either, not that I cared any for him, because I didn't, and I knew that if the tables had been turned around, Burl would have left me. It was true that he had brought his sad state on himself, and I would have been a lot better off to 've been bitten by a diamondback rattlesnake than to 've ever met him. But he was now a helpless, harmless, pitiful figure of a dying man, and it didn't seem right that he should die alone. I wasn't going to hold his head in my lap and wipe his feverish brow, but I would at least wait there until Death trotted up our trail, took his last breath and drug his soul to hell.

The day rolled on and Burl got worse, but somehow he was still alive at high noon. As the sun started on its downward course, I started getting impatient. Awhile before sundown I saddled the horses—mine, the packhorse, and Burl's dun. I didn't saddle Burl's horse for him, but just to get the horse and saddle out of the area. I didn't want any sign of us left around there when it came time to bury Burl. But Burl *still* wasn't in a burying state—wasn't dead yet, I mean. Wasn't exactly alive, but wasn't dead either.

After saddling the horses, I settled back down again and fell asleep. It seemed like I'd just dozed off when something woke me up. I'd been asleep longer than I thought, because the sun was slipping out of sight in the west. I laid there not moving for a minute or so, wondering just what it was that I'd heard. Then I heard it again—the faint sound of voices!

I peeked through the tamaracks and looked up that little boggy creek. About a half mile north I saw them. The creek wasn't running but had holes of water scattered up and down it, and around one of those holes four horses had their heads dropped and were drinking while the men forked over them talked and laughed. I spooked and threw my ears forward and snorted like a bronc smelling a grizzly.

I didn't study long or weigh my options, looking at the black and white or the right and wrong of it. What I did was to scoop out a shallow grave with my hands in the loose sand among the tamaracks as fast as I could, roll Burl into it, and push the sand back up around him. He still wasn't all the way out of sight, so I pulled some brush up over him, about like a panther covering a deer carcass. Then I led the horses out of the tamaracks on the off side and down a little incline until I was out of sight of the men in the creek, mounted up, and run my spurs shank-deep into Pat's sorrel belly. By the time the four horses in the creek had sucked in enough water around their bits to fill their stomachs and the men on them had rolled their smokes, I was long gone, shed of Burl Lewis like I'd promised myself a few days ago I would be— but hardly in the manner I'd imagined. It was a pretty rough thing, what I did with Burl, not knowing for sure whether he was dead yet or not, I'll admit that. But then life itself is a pretty rough game, especially when you find yourself running from brush patch to brush patch and smelling for trouble like an old renegade maverick cow.

As soon as I could, I buried all of Burl's things—except for his twenty-six dollars—and turned his horse loose, thinking it better to not have any trace of him around me. Just like I didn't shed any tears or say any words over Burl's sandy, shallow grave, I didn't feel lonesome going on south without him. In fact, I felt better, a world better, being by myself again, just me and Pat and the bay packhorse. At least I could carry on a decent kind of cowboy conversation with them, and Burl wasn't there dying while I had to watch.

I came on down across the breadth of Colorado staying in the eastern plains. I crossed both forks of the Republican River and by then began to drift again instead of run. A couple of days later, as I was camped somewhere in the big Two Buttes Creek country in the southeastern part of the state, I started thinking about Burl's story about a bank robbery and there being ten thousand dollars hid on a homestead he claimed to have. After a while I decided, since it wouldn't take me much out of the way on my way to Mexico, I'd swing over by Liberty, New Mexico, to this alleged homestead.

I figured every man ought to have at least *one* truth in him, and, as I never heard one from Burl up to the minute I pulled the brush over him, I thought the trip to Liberty might be worth it on the rare chance that him telling about the money buried there was the one truth he had. I also figured that if the money was there, I had more right to it than anybody else—who else had been put in so great a jeopardy of life and limb because of it? The fact that the money would legally belong to someone else didn't bother me, anymore than legal ownership of an abandoned calf would bother a wolf. In fact, I guess about the only real difference between me and a loafer wolf—besides me walking around reared up on my hind legs and preferring my beef to have the hide and hair knocked off and warmed up before I ate it—was the fact that I felt a pressing need for some quick cash and a desire to see how America looked from the off bank of the Rio Grande River.

CHAPTER 10

I WAS off my horse, sitting among some cedars on top of a long ridge that ran down and to the southwest from a tall mesa. At the foot of the ridge below me was a homestead. I'd been up there for close to three hours, letting the horses graze while I smoked cigarettes, and watched the homestead like a hungry hawk watches a ground squirrel.

It didn't look like that part of the country had summered very good. As a matter of fact, it was hot and dry as seven kinds of hell. The grass was brown and curled and even the sagebrush was drooping and covered with a thin layer of dust.

I could see the homestead below me about a half mile to the east: the square, flat-roofed, adobe house; the wooden barn south of the house; the corrals set out east of the barn; the windmill just east of the house; and a small patch of green earth just north of the windmill that I took to be a garden. I'll tell you, it was a pretty drab picture, that little homestead set out on that big, sage-and-sand flat, and everything as dry as a deacon's whistle. Dust devils building up out of nothing and sometimes their tops rising higher than I was up on that ridge. They would build up out of nothing and disappear the same way. Dust to dust, I thought watching one start up, get big and tall and then get little again and finally disappear altogether. Dust to dust.

When the sun had slid down the western sky and was not far above that edge of the world, I thumbed a rock at a big green lizard panting in sagebrush shade and stood up. I unhobbled the horses, cinched up Pat, checked the cylinder on my old Colt, putting in the sixth cartridge, and making sure it was riding easy in the holster. I pulled out the Winchester, too, levered a shell into the chamber, and put one in the magazine to replace that one. I was a long ways now from the man I had been in Wyoming, when me and Burl first rode into Charlie Castle's ranch. Then, I didn't like the feel of a gun on my hip at all. Now, I wanted one within easy reach at all times. That was the new man I was, and I couldn't see any way of ever getting back to being an easygoing cowboy again.

After I reached the flat at the bottom of the slope of the ridge I was still three hundred yards to the homestead. There I stopped and studied again. I didn't have much in the way of a plan—just get in there some way, size up the situation, and get the money (if it was there) in the quickest and safest way, then shagtail it out again. But I didn't like the lay of the cards on the table before me. It was too quiet. From up on the ridge I'd seen somebody in the garden, and there had been, and still was, smoke coming out of the stovepipe on the house. But the only life I could see now was a black cur dog standing at the corner of the house barking and some chickens scratching in the dirt between the house and the barn. I got to thinking, Could be somebody's got me in their rifle sights right now.

Just then a tall auburn-haired woman stepped around the corner of the house, holding her long skirt with one hand and shading her eyes with the other. She stood beside a small cottonwood tree not much taller than she was and looked at me.

The dog stopped barking and sat down between the tall woman and the small cottonwood. I studied for a few more seconds, reached up, pulled my hat a little further down on my head, and rode slowly up to her.

(That was the first time I ever saw you, Autumn, and I guess I was struck by you even then. Of course, you weren't really you then, just a tall, auburn-haired woman standing at the corner of a little adobe shack of a house built on a dry, starved-out homestead in the middle of nowhere.)

I gave the woman a pretty quick, but cowboy-thorough, saddle inspection. She wasn't the draft-horse type, but more on the thoroughbred order—smooth of conformation; straight of bone; long of leg; glossy of hair; a little high-headed with bright intelligent eyes of a sparkling blue color, shallow mouth, good jaw outline, straight nose, and a small beauty mark on her right cheek.

All of that was fine, good to look at, and well worth the long wait on the ridge and the short ride down from it. What wasn't so good about it, though, was the fact that I had to be at the wrong homestead. I didn't need a second saddle-glance at the woman in front of me to know she wasn't one likely to be playing house with Burl Lewis. She was as far from being that squatty, yellow-toothed, redheaded, delicate prairie flower of a whore I'd found him with in Lusk as I was from being the man in the moon.

"Howdy, Ma'am," I said, lifting my hat a little and then pulling it back down. "I'm lookin' for the Lewis place."

I read something akin to concern in her sparkling blue eyes and, remembering the way I looked, I could understand where it was coming from. "Sorry about my appearance, ma'am, but I've been on the trail quite awhile," I said. I guess I was a little nervous. This lady was the one and only person I'd talked to since the shooting in Wyoming, not counting the few times me and Burl talked before he got too bad off, and on top of that, she was the first woman I'd seen outside of a saloon in over three months. Sometimes a man forgets how pretty a woman can be in a plain gingham dress and an unpainted face. When I realized I was staring more than was decent, I straightened in the saddle and said, "I'd be obliged if you could tell me if you know of a Lewis homestead around here. Could be just a place that's been abandoned. A man in Liberty said it was about six miles northeast of there and about a mile south of the Canadian River, but . . ."

"This is the Lewis place," she said, still holding a hand over her eyes. "I'm Mrs. Lewis . . . have you been with Burl?"

"Mrs. Lewis?" That was a surprise. No—it was a *hell of a surprise!*. "You're Burl Lewis's *wife?*"

"I am," she said. "You never did answer me—have you been with Burl?"

"Well," I hesitated, "Yes, ma'am, I have been. I went up the trail from Tascosa with him driving a herd of XIT steers."

"And why have you come here?"

I pulled at my hat again and squirmed in the saddle.

While I was wondering what I was going to say, I saw the dog pick up his ears and look back around the corner of the house where I couldn't see. My right hand dropped down toward the butt of the old Colt.

"Better tell whoever's back there to step out here where I can see 'em, ma'am," I said. "And you better tell 'em to be careful about it, too."

She hesitated and I picked up on it real quick. I brought the gun out of its holster and it was full-cocked by the time the muzzle came up.

She looked straight at me and said, "All right then . . . Come here, Casey." A barefoot boy in a pair of overalls came over to stand beside her, the top of his head not coming much past her waist. A tousle-headed boy with big eyes trying not to be afraid, looking me hard in the eye, and doubling up a mean-looking fist at his side.

"You better look out, mister," he said.

Feeling kind of foolish, I lowered the hammer on the Colt and let it slide back into its holster.

"It's okay," the woman said, putting a hand on Casey's shoulder but not taking her eyes off me. "He says he's a friend of Burl's."

That's when I saw the barn door over to my right start to open and my hand dropped toward the Colt again. And what stepped out of the barn but a one-armed, white-headed old codger about as dried up as a corn husk. "That's Otis Trump," the woman informed me.

Then on my left, out of the house, came a short, Indian girl just as homely and pregnant as one can get in no more years than it looked like she'd been alive to work on it. Fourteen, maybe fifteen years old, I figured. The auburn-haired woman in the gingham dress looked over at the smiling girl standing on the porch and said, "And that happy young thing is Mary Walking Horse."

I leaned over in the saddle and spat tobacco juice out past the end of my boot, and then wiped the dribble out of my whiskers with the back of a hand.

I thought about it all and decided, with much relief, that the whole thing was a dream and I'd wake up before long inside my bedroll, and it would be rolled out beside a chuck wagon somewhere, maybe still down on the Matador Ranch off the caprock in Texas.

Just then a squawking Rhode Island Red hen came up behind old Pat and caught me and him both napping. Pat dropped an ear, jumped sideways, and kicked, not being a barnyard kind of horse, and then swallered his head and really came apart. The fool had been ridden nearly into the ground and I wondered how he kept going every time I threw the saddle on him, but there he was—kissing his butt in that barnyard like a grain-fed bronc.

Caught napping like I was, I blew my right stirrup and dropped the left rein the first jump. I knew I was fixing to get my head stuck in the dirt and I couldn't believe it. I remember thinking, If it's a dream like I think it is, I'll wake up just before I hit the ground. But the ground was coming up awful fast and I knew I'd better be waking up pronto.

But I didn't wake up, and the way I splattered in that barnyard, I had to figure it wasn't a dream and everything that had happened to me so far was for absolute real, right down to having a wore-out, sore-backed horse part company with me in front of a bunch of nesters on account of a grasshopper-eating chicken running up under him.

I sat up in the dirt, looked at the sorrel, and said the only thing appropriate for the occasion: "Son of a bitch!"

Little Casey said, "You shouldn't talk like that, mister. The Lord don't like it."

I pushed my hat brim up so I could see him and said, "Well, just so you'll know, son, I ain't too sold on ever'thing He does neither!"

The grandstand at that particular one-horse pitchin' might have been sparse on numbers, but they all seemed to be enjoying themselves. The one-armed old coot, the springing squaw, the boy evangelist—they were all grinning till hell wouldn't have it. And the thoroughbred woman with the shining auburn mane? She grinned right along with the rest of them and said, "Casey, see if the hens have laid any more eggs. Since the Good Lord has seen fit to *land* this gentleman in our midst, the least we can do is to share our table with him."

CHAPTER 11

I PICKED my inglorious self up off the ground, cussing under my breath and dusting the barnyard litter off my clothes. All the spectators to my performance had disappeared except for the woman—Burl's woman. She was standing a few feet away, no longer smiling. The sun had slipped behind the ridge in the west, leaving everything except the windmill wheel and tail in shadow. A coyote yelped a few times from somewhere in the sage not far south of the homestead, and another one up in the hills to the north answered that one with a long wail.

"I'm Autumn Lewis," she said, "and you are . . ."

"Uh, Smith, ma'am," I said. "Will Smith." I figured one name was as good as another—as long as it wasn't Honk Ballard.

"Well, Mr. Smith, supper will be on shortly. There is a washbasin and soap and towel at the windmill."

"Mrs. Lewis, about Burl, I—"

"It'll keep till supper, Mr. Smith. I'll call you," she said and walked away.

While I was washing up at the water trough, I took a good look around the place, or, as us in the desperado business say, "I studied the layout." What I saw didn't impress me much—and I never was hard to impress when it came to homesteads.

The place was run-down and ill-kept. There were two blades missing out of the windmill wheel overhead, and the thing sounded like it hadn't been greased in a month of Sundays. Seeing the distance between the top-most water mark on the trough and the level of the water in it, I could tell the windmill wasn't pumping nearly as much as it had at one time. The barn was missing some boards and others were curling up on the ends. The pole corrals were falling down. The adobe on the house was weathering away and the porch was sagging. And those were just the starters! To tell the truth, the place was in worse shape—except for the flowers planted on each side of the porch and the pretty little cottonwood on the corner—than most line camps I'd stayed in, and that's going some to say that.

I looked over at the garden, about thirty rows wide and forty feet long, and saw the wooden bucket that was used to dip water out of the trough and pour in the rows. The garden was dry then, judging from what little I knew about gardens, with the six rows of corn so dry it looked like they'd been frosted on. The watermelons looked like they might be making pretty good, but most of the ones I could see had been eaten into by coyotes. There wasn't one weed though among the garden plants, and I knew the hoe leaning against the house had seen plenty of hard labor.

Just east of the garden I saw two wooden crosses side-by-side marking two graves. The wind whipped the crosses and stirred up the sand around the graves.

The boy Casey came out of the house, walked over to the water trough, and said, "Mister, you can come eat now."

I said, "Boy, is Burl your daddy?"

He looked at me like I was crazy and said, "Naw, my mamma and daddy are over there," pointing to the two graves. When I looked back at him, he was already halfway to the house with the dog hanging onto one frayed cuff of his overalls.

I took off my chaps and laid them on the porch. Then I took off my hat, ducked my head, and walked through the door. In contrast to the run-down appearance of things on the outside of the house, the inside was clean and neat, although it took a little while for my eyes to adjust to the dim light to see that. Nothing was fancy or looked like it had cost a lot of money. In fact, about everything but the stove in the middle of the room looked like it had been handmade, but it was all clean and neat. The curtains on the windows on either side of the slab door were made from soft cotton sackcloth just like those hanging in front of the wooden crates nailed together and used for shelves. The house had only one room, but the left-hand third of it was partitioned off from the rest by blankets hanging from a rope. The floor was hard-packed earth, but swept clean and sprinkled. The smell of the sprinkled dirt made you think it was cooler inside than it really was. There were two rugs on the floor, too, that had been made by sewing pieces of cloth rags together.

Everybody was sitting at the table with an upside-down plate and a tin cup of water before them. Their hands were in their laps and all eyes were on me as I stood just inside the doorway.

"Mr. Smith," Autumn Lewis said, pointing to a place at the opposite end of the table from where she sat, "you may sit there. Would you like to take off your gun?"

"No, ma'am," I said as I strode over to the table, swung my leg over the stool like it was a horse, and sat down.

I turned my plate over and starting reaching for food when I realized that everybody was still just sitting there with their hands folded, watching me. It had been a long time, but I remembered a certain ritual more civilized people engaged in at mealtime, so I backed off gathering all the grub to my end of the table and sat there waiting for the ritual to be over and the eating to commence, those fried hen eggs sure beckoning to a cowboy who hadn't seen one in weeks.

When everyone bowed their heads, I did likewise. I'm not sure, but that might have been the first prayer—other than at a burying—I'd heard since I'd left home all those many long years ago. And I *know* it was the first time I'd *ever* heard a woman praying. Not that I ever gave it much thought, but I don't guess I was even aware that a woman *could* pray.

"Our most wonderful Saviour and Redeemer," she began in a clear, soft voice, accompanied by the banging in the wind of a loose board on the barn and by the faint noise of wind-blown sand striking a loose window pane, "Who in His most infinite wisdom knows and supplies our every need . . ." I cocked my head and raised an eyebrow and looked at the pregnant Indian girl who no doubt needed a buck husband; the old man who no doubt needed that arm he was missing; the boy in tattered overalls and bare feet who anybody could see needed a mother and daddy above the earth instead of returning to dust within it. It was easy for me to see that if those three thought their every need was being supplied by the Lord—or anybody else—then they needed to reinventory.

And the woman doing the praying? Looking at her there with her head bowed in prayer, I decided that what she needed most of all was about thirty minutes alone with a handsome, bowlegged drifter of the plains. I had one such hombre in particular mind, of course—me. I thought it with an inside chuckle though, like a rough-hewed man will, and with no malicious intent. Maybe a man ought to be able to keep a tight rein on the thoughts that run through his head, but I never could—and with my eyes on that silky hair falling down over those gingham-clad shoulders and resting on gingham-gathered breasts, my thoughts were running as wild and free as a whole herd of desert mustangs.

". . . and we thank Thee most of all Father for the guest at our table tonight, trusting that he was led here by Thy divine guidance. Amen.

"I'm sorry, Mr. Smith, we haven't had any meat in two weeks." This from the one who just a second ago was giving thanks to the Lord for supplying their every need?

"What about the chickens?" I asked, already stuffing the

second egg into my mouth and holding my head over my plate to catch any spillage that might occur.

"You can eat a chicken only once, Mister Smith: you can eat her egg everyday."

Then something struck me as funny. These people are living like they are on the poor farm, when they might very well be sitting on ten thousand dollars in cash! It didn't make any sense, and then I thought—looking at Autumn Lewis again—that her and Burl Lewis in the same bed makes even less sense!

"Well, Mr. Smith, why don't you tell us what word you have from Burl. Is he coming back soon?"

At that instant, like the world had stopped turning and everything in it suddenly froze, the other three people around the table stopped chewing, or held their forks in midair, or left their water cups touching their lips.

"Well . . ." I said. "I don't expect he'll be comin' back anytime soon at all." At that, the chewing, the fork lifting, and the drinking started up again.

"And just when *do* you expect he might be coming back?" This stopped the chewing, fork lifting, and drinking again.

I hesitated a little bit, considered the proper way to tell a lady that her husband won't be coming back ever again, and then said, "It ain't likely that he'll ever be back."

Chewing, fork lifting, and drinking commence again.

"Mr. Smith," Autumn Lewis said, "why don't you just tell me what it is you have to say."

"Well . . . Burl had a horse fall on him while we were goin' up the trail. We had a little run one night and Burl was ridin' fast trying to check the leaders, when his horse stepped in a gopher hole and went down."

"Mr. Smith," the lady again, "is Burl hurt or dead?"

"Dead is what he is, ma'am. Happened quick and he didn't suffer none. We buried him there on the prairie where it happened. I had to leave his saddle and bedroll, but I brought all of his money for you—twenty-six dollars."

I don't know what I expected. Tears maybe, because I always figured a woman would cry when she'd just been told that a hard-running cow pony had the knell for her beloved husband and he'd never again cross her threshold.

But this wife shed no tears. Instead, she looked up and said, "Thank you for coming all the way to tell me that, Mr. Smith . . . You're welcome to unroll your bedroll in the barn tonight if you wish."

CHAPTER 12

AFTER supper I unsaddled the horses and put my gear in the barn. I spent half an hour tying up poles in the corral before I slipped the bits out of the horses' mouths and watched them smell the ground and then lay down and roll. It was the first time in weeks that they had been turned plumb loose like that without any bridle or hobbles on and, even though they were in a corral, they were sure enjoying themselves. They needed a chance to rest up for a day or two, just like I did. They were also getting pretty long-toed and their shoes needed to be reset. I told myself that the next day I would look around in the barn and see if I could find a pair of hoof nippers, a rasp, a hammer, and some horseshoe nails. I grinned as I watched the horses stand up and shake the dust off their backs, thinking what a good excuse that would be to prowl around the barn.

When I left the horses and walked into the barn it was as black as the ace of spades inside, except for a dim yellow light coming out of the doorway leading to a small corner room. I migrated to the light like a candle bug, and looking inside the room I saw Otis Trump sitting on a cot. "Thought I might find some oats in here for my horses," I said.

The old gent looked me up and down and then said, "If that skinny sorrel can fart you off now, just think what he might do after a big bait of oats. Was I you, I'd think again about feedin' him anything. Come to think on it," he said with a nearly toothless grin, "was I you, I might just leave the horses be and carry the saddle myself."

"Listen, Pop," I said, "if I ever need your advice, you'll be the first one to know it. Right now though I'm a little give out and plumb out of sorts, so if you'll just tell me where the oat bin is, I'd appreciate the hell out of it."

"Well, excuse me for ever bein' born," he said. "Just 'cause you got the round ass and rolled off and embarrassed yourself ain't hardly *my* fault, you know."

"I guess *you* can really spur the hair off a pitchin' horse, huh?" I said. I wasn't in any mood to argue, but neither was I in any mood to be mouth-abused by some toothless old goat.

"Ain't likely," he admitted, still grinning, "but one just crow-hoppin' like that sorrel was, I reckon I could."

"Listen, Pop, just tell me where the goddamn oat bin is, and I'll get outa your way before you get so wild you spur somethin' right over the top of me."

He grinned again and rubbed at the white stubble on his face with his single hand. "Oat bin, uh? It's along about the middle of the east wall."

I figured now we were getting somewhere. "Got any morrals to feed the oats in?"

"Hangin' this side of the oat bin," he said.

"Now that wasn't so hard, was it?" I asked.

"No," he said, grinning nearly toothless again, "that was plumb easy."

"Would there be any way you'd let a feller use that candle for a few minutes?" I asked.

"No," he said. "It'd be dark in here without it."

I pointed a thumb back over my shoulder and said, "And it's goin' be dark out there without it too."

"But I ain't out there," he said. "I'm in here—where the candle is."

I could have taken the candle anyway and there wasn't anything he could have done about it, other than maybe gum me to death, but I figured it wasn't worth the hassle, so I stepped out of the little room and started feeling my way down the east wall. I tripped over a wagon tongue and knocked some hide off my shin, and then I knocked some harness off the wall and it fell on my head.

Finally I felt the morrals and the lid to the oat bin. I opened the wooden lid back on its hinges and lowered the two morrals—but they didn't stop lowering until they were sitting on the floor inside the oat bin. The oat bin was empty!

After I tripped over the wagon tongue again and knocked off some more hide, I stepped inside the old man's room and said, "The goddamn oat bin's empty!"

"Well, of course it is," he said. "I could have told you that, if you'd a asked. Ain't had no oats for nigh on two months. That's the reason you didn't see no horse here neither. We keep him staked out in the grass. All you asked was where the oat bin and the morrals was, and I told you."

While I was thinking how bad that old man needed a choking, I looked over into a corner of the room and saw a long-necked bottle laying on a wadded-up blanket. I walked over and picked the bottle up. There was nothing written on it by label or mold, but it was half full of something that *looked* like whiskey. I pulled out the cork and smelled the stuff, and it *smelled* something like whiskey. I put my tongue on the cork and it *tasted* something like whiskey—not anything like Charlie Castle's Grand Palace sipping whiskey though. This stuff was stout as wild mare's milk.

"That's *Desierto de Pena*," the old man said. "At least that's what the old Mexican who left it here called it, and he said it was *mucho veneno*."

"Poison, huh?" I said. "Well, hell, that oughta mean it's pretty good cowboy stuff then." So I tilted the bottle up and took me a big old cow swaller of that *Desierto de Pena*.

It felt like a branding iron had been run down my gullet.

My eyes watered and my face heated up and turned red as a sandy-creek plum.

I wiped my mouth with the back of a hand and said, "Boy, that's good stuff. Wonder what *Desierto de Pena* means anyway?"

"Means Desert of Trouble," the old man informed me as I stepped into the dark hallway of the barn with my right hand gripping the bottle.

I rolled my bedroll out on the barn floor and sat down on it. I figured on having two, maybe three more drinks out of the bottle and then sticking the cork back in it—but things didn't work out that way. I'd been on the wagon by necessity ever since me and Burl had finished off the two bottles Charlie Castle gave us the day we hired out to him to earmark a few calves. But that night in the dark barn, I got knocked off the wagon by that *Desierto de Pena* and run over lengthways by its wheels!

I remember sitting on my bedroll, having a drink now and then and feeling sorry for myself like only a man nursing a bottle of rotgut whiskey can. I was also trying to figure, if I was Burl and had ten thousands dollars in bank money to hide, just where I might hide it.

On top of those things, I was trying to figure out what kind of a crazy place Burl's homestead was! "Maybe a warm-up for some kinda goddamn road circus," I mumbled as I took another drink.

Then there was Autumn Lewis's sky-blue eyes—not to mention the rest of her—and her being a *praying* woman, too! And married Burl Lewis? There was just *no* figuring that one, not even with the help of the *Desierto de Pena*.

The next thing I knew I was standing in a crowd of people and we were milling around like a bunch of cattle that had just been thrown onto a roundup ground. There were several figures on horses around the crowd and they started shouting and waving ropes and long whips. The crowd—mostly men but a few women—started moving, and I heard a lot of crying and begging. I got scared and broke free from the crowd and took off running. One of the figures on a horse— I don't remember what they looked like, but I remember they had short horns like a Jersey cow—ran up behind me and roped me around the neck. I tried to slip it off but I couldn't get enough slack in it before I was jerked to the ground and drug all the way back to the crowd of men, across rocks and cactus with my tongue lolled out. When the rope was taken off, I was kicked in the butt and the Jersey-horned figure said, "Another bunch-quitter for hell."

I remember seeing some terrible critters that night, some serpents and monsters. And then the next thing I knew I was laying belly-up in the dirt between the barn and the house—and I still had a deathgrip on the neck of the bottle that had brought me down. It was still about a third full, too, but I wasn't tempted to partake of any more of it right then. Chickens were scratching in the dirt all around me, and the sun was so bright I had to shut my eyes for a while. I tried to sit up but didn't get the job done until the third try, and then the dog came over and licked me in the mouth. I looked around and saw Autumn Lewis and the boy working in the garden and the pregnant Indian swishing some clothes around in a steaming pot with a long stick.

In the shade of the barn not twenty feet away was the old one-armed man. He was sitting on the ground, chewing tobacco and spitting the juice into a little hole he'd wallered out in the ground with a rusty nail. When he saw me looking at him, he grinned like a possum but didn't say anything.

I tried to get up, but the world started getting out from under me like a spinning bronc, so I sat back down. My head felt like it was about as big as a number two washtub with about five gallons of sour blood in it. I looked up at the sun, or at least as close to it as I could.

" 'Bout midway between high noon and plumb dark," the old man said. "Guess that Mexican knew what he was talking about, huh? Boy, you flopped around and screamed out here like one of them chickens do when she's had her neck wrung. You'd been quiet for a couple of hours though, and I was waitin' to see if one of them hens would lay a settin' of eggs on yore belly. Wouldn't that have been somethin' to talk about."

"I'd rather talk about how I nailed an old man to the side of the barn and let him dry out like an old cow hide," I said.

The old man just grinned and scratched his arm with his stubby white whiskers.

I finally made it to my feet and walked over to the water trough by the windmill and washed my face. Autumn Lewis and Casey stopped their work and watched me. The boy came over to me and said, "Mister, you were about the drunkest man I ever seen."

My head felt like somebody was driving a rail spike into it from each side, and my knees were wobbly as a fresh-foaled colt's. "Run along, son," I said to the boy without raising my head, "I ain't in no mood to be pestered."

I felt my stomach coming up and started for the barn, but didn't get any more than halfway there before I had to stop and lean over. That *Desierto de Pena* came up even ranker than it went down, and it didn't come up alone either, but brought everything with it that was in me. I sank to my knees and got sick again. I heaved so hard I don't know how my innards kept from tearing loose and coming out.

I laid down on the ground for a while because I just felt too bad and weak to do anything else. In a few minutes the chickens started pecking and scratching all around me, and I saw that the other people on the homestead had already gone back to what they had been doing before I came to— Autumn Lewis and Casey were working in the garden, the pregnant Indian was washing clothes, and the old one-armed man sat in the shade of the barn and grinned. Everything was going on just like I wasn't laying out there in front of the barn in my own mess.

In a few minutes I crawled into the barn and fell onto my bedroll. I wasn't even thinking about it then, but I'd made quite an impression in the short time I'd been there—in less than twenty-four hours I'd been bucked off by a sore-backed, chicken-scared horse, had been bad-whiskey drunk and sick, and had finally crawled into the barn on my hands and knees.

I got sick inside the barn several times after that and by sundown wasn't sure whether I was dead or alive. The only clue I had to either was my smell, and I'd never smelled anything like me that didn't either need to be buried or drug off.

I laid real quiet there in the darkening barn for a long time, not doing anything but breathing, blinking my eyes occasionally, and listening to the night sounds come in as the day went out. There was the deep-throated "wheeww-click-click" of a chaparral and the short whistle of blue quail; far-off in the distance a cow bawled for her calf; somewhere a dove made a lonesome sound like the desert wind blowing across the neck of an empty bottle; and of course the coyotes howled their usual lonely anthem.

Then floating in on the evening breeze, softer and purer and sweeter than any night sound has ever been, was a woman's voice singing: "We gather together to count the Lord's blessings . . ."

CHAPTER 13

SOMETIME during the dark of the night, after my stomach had stopped wretching and I lay asleep in a feverish sweat on top of my bedroll, I heard a high-pitched terrible scream. My first thought, coming from a brain still woozy from bad whiskey and weak from fever, was that the *Desierto de Pena* had a hold of me again. Then I considered the fact that I might have died and gone to hell, for it was dark as a pit inside the barn, and I was warned often enough by my pa and the Reverend Blackburn when I was a kid in Kansas about the terrible tortures that occurred in an Eternal Pit of some kind.

The more I listened though and the more my head cleared, the more convinced I was that the screams were of *this* world and coming from somewhere outside the barn. I filled my fist with Colt revolver and found my way to the door. I looked outside and saw the soft light of a candle coming through the window of the adobe house.

Then the scream came again—directly from the house.

I rushed across the space between the barn and the house, and just as I reached the door it was jerked open and Autumn Lewis and I collided.

I stepped back, looked at her in her long, blue flannel gown, and said, "What in the hell's happenin' in there?"

"Mary's having her baby!" she shouted. She shoved Casey past me and told him to go to the barn and sleep with Otis. Then she turned back inside and hollered at me, "Bring in some firewood from the corner of the house and put it in the stove and then get a bucket of water!"

When I carried the wood inside I saw Mary Walking Horse

laying on a narrow bed in the corner. She had kicked off the blanket that had been covering her and her gown was pulled up around her neck. She was laying with her knees up and her legs spread apart. I saw how terrible big her belly was, and then I saw all the blood soaking into the bed covers. I put the wood into the stove as quick as I could and then got out of there. I wasn't in any hurry to go back inside with the bucket of water either. I'd seen plenty of cows having calves and had pulled as many of the slimy things as any other cowboy I guess, but I'd never seen a woman giving birth and couldn't see how I'd be bettered any by watching it happen now. I was going to set the bucket by the door and leave it there, but Autumn Lewis said, "Bring it right on in, Mr. Smith, and start it to heating."

When I went back inside she was wiping the Indian girl's face with a towel.

The girl screamed again and cried out, "Oooh, God!"

I poured the water in two pans that were sitting on the stove and then got out of there quick.

In about thirty minutes Autumn Lewis came out of the house and sat down beside me on the porch. She was still in her long blue sleeping gown.

"It's been pretty quiet in there for a while," I said. "Is everything okay now?"

She didn't say anything, and when I looked at her she was shaking her head. "What's wrong with her?" I said. "I mean other than havin' a baby."

"What's *wrong* with her, Mr. Smith," she said, like I ought to have known without being told, "is that she is a child instead of a woman. I'm afraid she's not big enough."

"Well," I said, "she was big enough to get pregnant, I guess. So—"

"She was raped by a priest on the Bosque Redondo Reservation. When her father tried to kill the priest, he was put in jail. Mary was afraid the priest would kill her, so she ran away. I found her just this side of Liberty about three months ago, nearly dead from lack of water and scared as a wounded rabbit."

"Oh," I said. "So you just took her in, huh?"

Blue eyes looked at me, and though I could barely see them in the dim light coming through the door, they made me feel guilty.

"Yes," she said, "so I just took her in."

"And the old man?" I asked.

"Just an old man with no one to care for him anymore. He was sweeping out a saloon in Liberty for his room and board until the owner decided he wasn't earning his keep and threw him out. I invited him to come out here and live with us and help out around the place."

Then Mary Walking Horse screamed from inside the house again and Autumn rushed in to see about her.

During the next hour or so there were more screams and groans and words of encouragement coming from inside the house. I sat on the low porch and waited with my head in my hands, dozing off every now and then. I'm not sure what I was waiting for.

There was silence then from the house for a few minutes, and then—a baby crying!

I pulled myself up, went back to the barn, and fell on my bedroll asleep. It seemed like I had just closed my eyes when something forced them open again and I could see that it was just beginning to get light outside. I closed my eyes again, thinking how tired and weak I was, and how good it would be to sleep some more.

Then I heard something. A sort of strange and quiet sound. I listened to it for several minutes with my eyes closed, thinking it was maybe the wind blowing something back and forth, or one of my horses rubbing against something. Then it suddenly dawned on me what the noise sounded like— digging!

I got up and peeked out the barn door and saw Autumn

Lewis in the gray light of a brand new day, over by the windmill and the garden. And she *was* digging!

The first thing I thought was, The bank money! You don't reckon she's diggin' up the bank money, do you? Then I thought, Why not? Looks likes she's diggin' out there by the graves, which would be a good place to hide something. *And* she probably figures that as tired and weak as I am, I'll sleep till noon.

Seeing that her back was to me I slipped out of the barn and came up on the other side of the windmill. Her back was still turned to me and she was swinging a pick now so I walked around the windmill and stopped no more than six feet from her.

I said in a low voice, and expecting her to wheel around and be scared and surprised that I'd caught her digging, "Lose something, Mrs. Lewis?"

Far from doing what I'd expected she would, she said without even stopping digging, "Yes. I lost Mary Walking Horse last night in childbirth."

Then a baby's weak cry broke through the stillness of dawn and she dropped the shovel and rushed to the house.

I looked down at the hole she had been digging in the hard New Mexico ground that it was to be Mary Walking Horse's grave.

I leaned over, took the pick in hand, and started swinging it.

I watched from the doorway of the barn. I had found all the horseshoeing tools that I needed to reset my horses' shoes and was almost through with Pat, but now I stood in the doorway of the barn with a horseshoe in one hand and a pair of hoof nippers in the other watching them bury Mary Walking Horse and listening to her baby crying from inside the house. I'd dug the grave and helped lower the girl's body into the ground but then had returned to the barn to get on with resetting my horse's shoes while the rest of them did the official burying of the girl.

No, I hadn't found any money while I was looking for the horseshoeing tools, and I'd decided I was a fool for hanging around there any longer looking for something that might not even exist. I remembered what I'd said to Burl back up there in Wyoming—that I was going to rattle my hocks all the way to Mexico—and I could see how that was probably the smartest statement I'd ever come up with, especially in a pressure situation. And now I could see how stupid it was for me to have stopped that hock-rattlin' three hundred miles short of where I said I was going to. I could see that plain enough from the doorway of the barn, just like I could see them bowing their heads and praying over Mary Walking Horse.

I was ready to go by midmorning. I led the horses out of the barn; Pat was saddled and the little bay was loaded with my bedroll and the scant stock of supplies I had. I pulled on my leggin's and buckled them behind me and stepped in my saddle. I was feeling some better by then, the bad effects of that rotgut Mexican whiskey being about worn off. We had to be a sorry-looking bunch though—my two horses and me. I was needing a change of clothes along with a bath and shave when I rode in, and I was only in greater need of them now. The horses had time to rest up a bit, but the only thing they'd had to eat was a few dried weeds in the lot and the boards on the corrals and they looked like a couple of gutted snow birds.

I rode over to the windmill and let the horses take on a big fill of water. I looked at the place again and I could tell that—like me—it looked even worse than it had when I'd ridden in about a day and a half ago. The garden needed attention—and watering—badly. The plants that had been holding their heads high were now wilted and their leaves were beginning to curl. Same with the flowers beside the porch. The windmill still creaked and groaned for attention, and the water trough had sprung a new leak.

The place looked deserted now. There was no smoke coming out of the adobe's stovepipe, and nothing moved other than what was moved by the wind. I couldn't even see the dog or any of the chickens. Like I said, the place looked deserted that morning I was fixing to ride on south. It looked like it could have been deserted for some time, too, except for the fresh grave beside the two old ones. And it was quiet enough to be deserted. There were noises, but they were wind noises and not people noises.

When the horses finally lifted their noses out of the water, I reined them around and started on my way, passing between the barn and the house. The baby started crying from inside the house, and the horses raised their heads a little and pointed their ears in that direction.

Then the door opened and Autumn Lewis stepped out onto the sagging porch. She didn't say anything or do anything other than just look at me as I rode past in a walk. I'd thought some before that I might stop and tell her I was leaving, but then I figured I ought to just get on out of there before something else happened. Anyway, she'd be able to tell that I was gone. And I thought, I ought to thank her for feeding me, but then I remembered that I had just made the one meal and had thrown it up and then had been too sick on the *Desierto de Pena* to eat again. To tell the truth, I hadn't done anything I was very proud of while I was there, and I was just ready to leave it all on the trail behind me. But there Autumn Lewis was, standing tall on the porch and looking pretty, so I angled a little closer to the house and pulled to a stop in front of it.

"I see you're leaving, Mr. Smith," she said. "I want to thank you for all you've done."

I nodded my head and pulled at my hat brim. "Yes, ma'am," I said. "I gotta be goin' on. I left Burl's twenty-six dollars in the barn where Otis would be sure and see it. I didn't want to bother you none. Thank you for feeding me, and I'm sorry, ma'am, that I didn't conduct myself any better than I did. So long, ma'am . . . and I'm sorry about Burl. He was a mighty fine man and he sure spoke highly of you—and often too."

I started off again and the baby started to cry from inside the house again. "Mr. Smith," Autumn Lewis said and I pulled Pat up again, "wouldn't you like to see the baby. I mean, you did help to get her into this world."

I pulled my lean and whiskered face into something of a smile and said, "To tell the truth, Mrs. Lewis, I was doin' ever'thing I could *not* to help with that chore any."

"Please wait a minute, Mr. Smith," she said and then turned and went into the house.

In just a few seconds she stepped out again holding the baby wrapped in a blanket. She stepped off the porch and turned the bundle so I could see the baby's face. Pat boogered and snorted but then stood still with his neck arched and his nostrils flared, I guess not much different than I was because neither of us were used to fresh-born people.

"Looks like a pretty nice one," I said.

"It's a little girl," Autumn Lewis said, smiling like only a woman admiring a baby can.

"Got a lot more hair than I figured," I said, "and them eyes shore are big and dark. She's sure skinny though—of course most new calves are the same way. That changes soon enough though; after a few days of pullin' on a ti . . . I mean, after a few days of suckin' an ol' calf will be fat as a butter ball. Guess people babies are the same way."

All of a sudden the baby jerked her arms and started crying and my horses jumped over beside the barn. I eased them a little closer and said, "She sure cries a lot, seems to me like."

"She's hungry, Mr. Smith," Autumn Lewis said. "She sucked once before Mary died. Since then all she's had is a little water.

That was something of a puzzle to me. I wrinkled my eyebrows and said, "Why don't you feed her?"

"Babies need *milk*, Mr. Smith," she said. "They *have* to have milk."

What I was thinking must have been obvious in my face to Mrs. Lewis. She said, "Mr. Smith, you know a lot about cows, so I'm sure you know a dry cow can't nurse a calf."

I felt my face heat up and turn red. "And you don't have a milk cow, do you?"

"We have one somewhere out there," she made a small sweep with her hand to the south. "The man I bought her from in Liberty said she should come fresh in less than a month, but two months later she wasn't even making a bag yet, and we didn't have anything to feed her, so I turned her loose, thinking that when she finally calved we would get her back some way . . . But the Lord will provide," she said, smiling again, but somehow I didn't think she was as sure as she was pretending to be. "He always does. Anyway, it's not your problem, Mr. Smith. You've done enough for us as it is. Good-bye and good luck." Then she took the crying baby and went into the house.

CHAPTER 14

THE first thing I did after leaving the homestead was to ride to the top of the ridge to the west. There I pulled up and looked all around, feeling really good to be away from the place and on the move again, and thinking that in a few days I would be across the border into Mexico and could stop worrying about being a hunted man. A hawk circled and screamed high over head. Pat spotted something on the other side of the ridge and pointed his ears in that direction. Finally I saw what it was—a badger ambling along and stopping at every hole or bush to sniff and dig a little. Things seemed right with the world again about everywhere I looked—but then, even from way up on that ridge, I heard Mary Walking Horse's baby crying. I looked back down at the homestead for a few seconds, then slowly shook my head, and headed south.

When I rode off that ridge and pointed Pat's nose in the direction of Mexico there was no doubt in my mind but that in a few days I would be there. I don't remember even considering any other possibility. I had ridden along in a jig of a trot for three or four miles when I heard the honk of geese and looked up and saw a flight of them winging their way south ahead of the coming winter, the first I'd seen for the season. That was about as early as I'd ever seen them too, and I figured a bad winter might be coming. It was then that I also felt a cool breeze at my back, and, turning in the saddle, saw a dark cloud bank hovering close to the northern horizon.

When I turned back around there was a high-horned, red-and-white, spotted Longhorn cow just coming into my view over a sage-covered hill. She had a baby calf at her side not much more than two weeks old. The cow had her head down grazing and hadn't spotted me yet. I stopped the horses and sat still in the saddle and watched for a few minutes. I looked overhead and after a few seconds spotted the geese again on their way south.

I looked back down at the cow and all of a sudden felt some cowboy orneriness come upon me. I hadn't felt like building to something and roping it just to hear it beller in a long time, but I felt like it then. I got off and hobbled the packhorse and then pulled the cinches tighter on old Pat. As soon as I was back in the saddle, I reached down and slipped my ropestring off the saddle horn and started building a loop in my rope as Pat started off the hill.

About then the cow spotted us, threw her tail up, and took off, bawling for her calf but not waiting around to explain the particulars to him of what their hurry was. Pat wasn't a race horse but he savvied the catch rope pretty good and on top of that we'd gotten ourselves a pretty good jump on the cow. I dropped the horn loop over my saddle horn and pulled it snug and by the time I'd swung the loop over my head two or three times I was already close enough to mail it to her.

The weather being hot and dry like it was, my rope was limber as a dishrag, but my loop went after those horns like it had eyes, bumping the base of the right one and then curling out and around the left one. I drug the slack out of the loop with a smooth motion of the wrist while the old cow snorted and went to slinging her head.

I couldn't help but grin—maybe the first real grin I'd enjoyed since a day or two before that awful affair with the lawmen in our sleeper camp in Wyoming. Seeing my loop draw up around the horns of a wild cow like that out on the range was something that always did put a smile on my face. My smile got even bigger when she pawed over her head a time or two and bellered like an old thing will sometimes when you rope her.

I'd never "laid it behind" much grown stock on Pat and wasn't too sure how he would handle himself when I did, but I was feeling so wild and free right then, enjoying life for the first time in a long time, that I think I'd have laid it behind a bull elephant if that was what was tangled up in the other end of my rope.

With a wild "yee-haw," I flipped the slack in the rope over the cow's right hip and turned Pat off to the left, digging my spurs even deeper into his belly and really driving him to the end of the rope.

A horse tripping something as big as a cow has to be down close to the ground when the slack runs out. Old Pat wasn't. The fool jumped a bear grass and had all four feet off the ground when him and the cow hit opposite ends of the rope.

Pat was jerked out from underneath me and all of a sudden I was on the ground again. You might think that I'd really be cussing my string of bad luck. Well, although I can't remember the exact phrasing, I'm certain I did voice some disapproval of the happenstance that left me horizontal to the ground *again,* at a time when I wasn't the least bit sleepy. But when I found out I could still navigate with my forked end on the ground and the blunt end up in the air and the biggest piece of hide I'd lost was a patch about the size of a dollar in front of my left ear, I just picked up my hat and put it on with a grin. You see, getting bucked off and horses' jerked out from him are things that a cowboy might not ever look forward to, but they are sure things that he knows are going to happen and he learns to take them without kicking something and breaking his toe in disgust. Also, I didn't have a grandstand full of snickering spectators watching me this time like there had been when I got bucked off in front of the barn. This time there was just the packhorse hobbled and watching from a hilltop, me and Pat, and that Longhorn cow. But I guess the biggest reason for me not feeling bad and for the grin on my ugly face to stay there is that old Pat and that cow were tangled up in the rope like a kitten in a ball of yarn.

Pat had gotten astraddle of the rope and when it came up between his hind legs he went to kicking and spinning. The cow, not too content with the run of things herself, wiped her nose on the ground and jumped in amongst the flying hoofs to play skip rope with old Pat, slinging slobber and hooking at everything within horn-reach. I was kind of wishing my Padgitt Brothers kack wasn't in the middle of the fray, but it was such a nice wreck to watch I just pulled up a piece of New Mexico sand and sat down and watched them go at it. The bay nickered at old Pat from up on the hill and I was thinking the only thing that could have been better was if I'd had that squawking Rhode Island Red chicken to throw in the boil along with everything else.

Pat and that old cow went at it hard for five minutes. They filled the air with snorts, squeals, bellers, hair, blood, and dust. I knew Pat would get a better education in cow-ology and range etiquette in those few minutes than I could pound into his thick head in a year; and then when they'd wore themselves out, or got in such a mess neither of them could move, and I went over and untangled them, that dumb sorrel would think I was the most wonderful critter he'd ever seen.

I waited another five minutes, feeling like nothing other than a cowboy watching a good range wreck from a safe distance. When the action between Pat and the cow started to simmer down a little, I walked up to the hill where the bay was hobbled to get a piggin' string off the pack. I would need it to tie the cow down with, knowing her disposition would be such that she would love to snort in my hip pocket while I was trying to untangle her and old Pat. I had two piggin' strings tied on my saddle but figured getting one off the pack would be safer than trying to get at them.

When I was getting that piggin' string, I noticed the corked end of that half-full bottle of *Desierto de Pena* sticking out of the middle of my bedroll. I don't even know why I brought the poison stuff along, but I guess when I was rolling my bed and the bottle was laying right there beside it, it seemed more foolish at the time to leave it than it did to take it along. Maybe my thinking—supposing that I *was* thinking—was that a single drink here and there down the trail wouldn't make me sick. Or maybe I was just afraid that word would get out that Honk Ballard not only got bucked off because of a Rhode Island Red chicken, but that he left a half-full bottle of whiskey behind on top of that. Whatever the reason, I'd brought the rotten stuff along, and when I was getting a piggin' string to tie that cow down with that Pat was entertaining, I saw it.

I pulled the bottle out of my bedroll and uncorked it. I held it to my nose and when I got the first strong whiff of it, I nearly got sick again. That's when I poured the stuff out on the ground, grinning as I did so, thinking about what some of my noble compatriots would say if they had've rode up over the hill right then and seen me.

Just before I threw the empty bottle down, I looked at it in my hand—and then I looked down at the cow.

I can't explain why I did what I did next, anymore than I can explain why, at just about that exact moment, a pair of human wolves were riding up to the same starved-out homestead that not long before I'd ridden away from, sure that I'd never see it again. There's no way I can explain why an old cowboy in a little trouble with the law and rattling his hocks to Mexico will find himself, through a curious chain of events, with an empty bottle in his hand, a full-bagged cow tangled up nearly at his feet, and a hungry baby's cry lingering in his ear. All I know is that, the more I look back on it, I see that living life is sometimes like being on a runaway horse—you may be forked up there in the middle of him in your own saddle, but really you're just going along for the ride, watching the rocks and holes fly by without having any control over where you're going, or how long it takes you to get there.

But whatever the "why" of it, there I was in a sage-covered depression of land, squirting milk into an empty whiskey bottle while a mad cow bellered and thrashed and beat her head against the ground. Then a few minutes after that I was sitting on Pat again, holding a bottle of warm milk and watching the cow who had donated it trot off high-headed and stringing slobber across the sage.

There is no way I had planned milking that cow, it just happened—but since it had, I would trot the milk back to the Lewis homestead. This little milk run, I told myself silently, won't take much more than an hour and *then* I'll rattle my hocks to Mexico.

So blows the wind.

CHAPTER 15

I RODE through the scratching chickens and pulled to a stop in front of the house, expecting the door to open and Autumn Lewis to step out onto the porch. But the door didn't open, no one came outside.

"Hello," I hollered. But still the door didn't move. I cocked my ear a little towards the house, but all I heard was the morning cluck of scrounging chickens in the barnyard and the faraway roll of late-summer thunder.

"Hello . . ." I said again. "Mrs. Lewis . . . ?"

Then the door opened—but no Autumn Lewis was standing in it. Instead, the doorway was filled with a stocky man under a floppy brown hat with a big wad of tobacco in his cheek and an ugly smile on his lips!

I didn't know what else the big man was—but I knew he was trouble! You don't have to see a rattlesnake coiled on the porch to know he's trouble, him just being there and doing nothing but sunning is trouble enough.

I dropped the bottle of milk and reached for the Colt on my hip. I had it almost clear of leather when a shot rang out from behind me. The bay boogered and jerked the lead rope out of my other hand, and Pat reared up and spun around twice.

"That 'un was just over your goddamn head," a hard voice behind me said. "The next un will spatter your brains all over the front of that adobe, if you even take a breath without waitin' to be told."

"Boy!" the man in the doorway said. "Who this man be? Might he be that Will Smith you was tellin' about?"

Casey appeared in the doorway in front of the man. He swallowed hard and said, "That's him."

"The one who came here to tell the Missus Lewis that she was a widder lady?"

"Yes sir," Casey said.

"Casey," I said, "where's Mrs. Lewis?"

"Shut up!" the man in the doorway said, shoving Casey away and out of sight. Then he smiled again and said, "We'll take good care of Burl's missus, don't you worry none about that." The man behind me chuckled and said, "Why don't I kill him right now, Pole? He ain't goin' to do nothin' but cause trouble."

"Scalp, besides the smell you also got the brains of a boar hog," the big man in the doorway of the adobe said. "You don't kill men who're goin' to help you, you ought to know that. It ain't in the leastways polite.

"Now, mister, you ease that thunder iron outa its holster and drop it straight to the ground, and then you take off your hat and hold it in your right hand, and then you step offa that horse. Better be careful not to drop your lid though, 'cause if you do, old Scalp back there will pop your head like it 'as a overripe melon. Now do it!"

I did just like I was told, and when I was standing on the ground he said, "Now then, pick up that bottle you dropped while ago an' bring it here."

When I handed it to him I realized what a big man he was. He was a good head taller than me and the only thing I owned that was a big as his shirt was my bedroll tarp. A heavy black beard covered his face from just under his eyes to where the long chest hairs were poking out around his collar. It didn't look like he had more than a scattering of teeth in his mouth, and his nose had been broken some time and had healed up off center.

He took the bottle and looked at it while the second man came up to stand just off the porch behind me and said, "What'n the hell is it? Some kinda white licker?" I turned around to look at the man who asked that. He was carrying a rifle and was a lot smaller than the other man, more my own size. He was bareheaded and I could see how he came by the name Scalp—he was as slickheaded as a purple plum, hardly had any whiskers even, or eyebrows. His eyes were big and they bugged out like a frog's, and they had dark circles under them like somebody had been circling the wagons there all night.

"Looks like milk to me," the big man said.

"Oh, surely it ain't . . ." Scalp said.

The big man pulled out the cork and smelled it. "Smells like milk," he announced.

Scalp stuck me in the back with the muzzle of the rifle and said, "What *is* that stuff?"

"Milk," I said.

"Milk?" Scalp said, like it was the first time it had been mentioned.

"Yeah," I said. "It's a new drink—cows make it outa grass."

"Pole," Scalp screamed, "the son-of-a-bitch come acallin' on Burl's old lady with a bottle of goddamned milk!"

"I never heard of chasin' a skirt that way," Pole allowed.

"The world's gettin' in a hell of a fix, ain't it, Pole?" Scalp said. "Why I can remember back when a feller'd want a little whiskey to bring out his charm when he went to see a gal."

Pole grinned at me, big and ugly. "I guess one man's whiskey is another man's milk, don't you, Scalp?" he said.

"I reckon so," said Scalp, puckering his lips. "What does that mean, Pole?"

"Means that maybe this here smart-mouthed pilgrim gets his charm-starter elsewhere than you and me do. Go untie Burl's skirt and bring her here and we'll see."

"Whatcha gonna do?" Scalp asked with joy in his heart, handing the rifle to Pole.

"Just get the skirt."

In a little bit, Scalp stepped out the door leading Autumn Lewis by a short piece of rope tied around her neck like she was a dog or a horse. But she looked unhurt—scared and defiant and some strands of hair coming down from the tight bun on her head and falling to her shoulders, but unhurt. We—Autumn Lewis and me—looked at each other for a second or two and then the one called Pole handed me the bottle of milk and said, "Drink it."

"It's for the baby," I said.

"Drink it!" Pole said, sterner voiced. Scalp was standing to the side of Autumn, holding the rope and grinning like a kid at a sideshow.

I held the bottle out toward Autumn and said, "Give it to the baby."

Pole swung the butt of his rifle and hit me hard in the side with the steel butt plate. It felt like a mule had kicked me. I sank to my knees, trying to get air into my lungs.

"Please, Mr. Smith," Mrs. Lewis said in a quivering voice, "just do what he says."

I brought the bottle up slow to my lips and held it there, but I couldn't make my hand tilt it high enough so the milk would run into my mouth. It wasn't so much the fact that any sort of old cow-track water was a delicacy to me compared to milk, as it was the knowledge that not once since that day so many years ago when I left home riding one of Pa's workhorses bareback to make a place for myself in the world had I knuckled under to man or beast. I didn't win every tussle with either of them, that's for certain, but they always knew they'd been *in* a tussle, and I walked away with my head high, skinned up a little maybe, but held high on any account.

"Come on, cowboy, drink up!" Pole said, "and then show us how it turns on your charm. Ha. Ha."

I lowered the bottle, my mind made up past what I thought was a point of no return to not knuckle under to those two citizens who were having as much fun with me as a puppy with a toad.

Scalp said, "He ain't gonna do it, Pole. The-son-of-a-bitch-ain't-a-gonna-do-it."

I heard Pole say, "The hell he ain't!" and then the steel butt plate hit me under the right eye and the wood floor of the porch hit me behind the head.

Autumn screamed and knelt down beside me, but Scalp jerked her back with the rope around her neck.

I got my feet back under me, feeling the blood run over my cheek and off my chin. I looked down to where it was dripping on the porch. By then I was like a bronc that was hot and mad and sulled up, and anything you try to get him to do you're just bumping your head against a wall.

I looked at Pole and grinned.

"The son of a bitch!" Scalp said, nearly screaming. "The son-of-a-bitchin' no good bastard still ain't gonna do it, Pole!"

I saw Pole's big ugly face get red, and I knew he was mad enough to bite himself. That made me not hardly notice how much my ribs ached and my cheek throbbed. Then I saw the red leave Pole's big ugly face, and I didn't like that.

"Scalp," he said, now slow and cunning and keeping his eyes on me, "you know what you was tellin' me about what you'd like to do to the woman before we left?"

I looked at Autumn Lewis and then at Scalp. Scalp looked at Pole and then Autumn Lewis.

"Yeah," Scalp said, "I shore 'nough do," like just the mere thought of it brought him wicked satisfaction.

Pole leaned way over and spit tobacco juice off the porch, wiped his mouth with the back of a hand, and said, "Then why don't you take her on out to the barn."

On one hand I figured it might be a bluff, but on the other hand I figured those two were capable of carrying out in hellishly exact detail anything the devil could dream up for one man to do to another—or for a man to do to a woman.

"Seems like I got a sudden cravin' for *leche*," I said, reaching for the bottle.

I drank all of the milk, being allowed to stop and get my

air and gag twice before I was looking up through empty glass.

"Now let's see if that stuff turned on your charm like whiskey used to turn on a real man's charm—back before the world got in such a terrible fix," Pole said.

"Whatcha mean? Whatcha gonna do now, Pole?" said Scalp.

"Well," said the big one, "since this here cowboy came acallin' on the lady with some milk to give him the backbone to get romantical . . ."

"And since he's already drank the milk, huh, it's time for the romantical part? Is that what you mean, Pole?" Scalp was grinning till I thought he might bite his bugged eyeballs.

"Yeah," Pole said, "that's what I mean. Let's see you kiss this widder lady, cowboy. You bein' the good friend to Burl that you were, just act like we wasn't even here and your doin' it for your old long-lost saddle pard."

I looked at Mrs. Lewis again, but neither of us moved. Then she dropped her eyes. I can't deny that what Pole was telling me to do, I'd thought about. Thought about more than just kissing, I've already told that. But I've also already told how that was just a man's mind wandering off on its own, with him really not meaning anything indecent toward the lady at all.

But this was something else entirely. It wasn't even close to anywhere my mind had ever strayed, because everything I ever thought about doing with *any* woman she had to be as willing as me. I shook my head, more to myself than to Pole, thinking there was no way I could do what he said.

"Hey, Pole!" exclaimed Scalp. "Maybe I oughta do the lady a favor and hold her nose for her!" Looking back on it, that *would* have been a favor because I hadn't had a bath or shave in a long time and the clothes I was wearing had been worn for days and days and had been slept in and sick on.

"Do it, cowboy, or I'll have to let Scalp do it for you."

"I'm sorry, ma'am," I said, "but I guess . . ."

"It's okay," she said. "I understand." She was trying to be brave but when I leaned over to kiss her I saw her lips quivering and heard her trying to muffle a sob in her throat.

Just before our lips touched, I saw out of the corner of my right eye how Pole was watching us so hard, how big his eyes were, and how he had let his finger slip out of the trigger guard of the rifle he was holding. I thought it might be a chance. Not a good one, but at the moment chances seemed to be in short supply, and I couldn't see where culling this one would be a healthy idea.

I jerked my head back at just the last instant and brought a right cross between my face and Mrs. Lewis's. I tried to drive Pole's off-center nose back between his ears with my fist. I'd been in plenty of fights and brawls before, and I knew when I got a good lick in on a man. I got that kind of a lick in on Pole. His nose flattened under my knuckles like a half-ripe grape and blood splattered over his face. That felt as good to me as dragging the slack out of my loop had earlier that morning when I roped that cow.

But the feeling didn't last very long, because when Pole sunk to his knees, and I was about to kick him under the chin, Scalp flipped Mrs. Lewis's lead rope around my neck, and I found out how an old cow feels when she gets roped around the neck and chokes till she can't do anything but loll her tongue out and fall over in a stiff-legged strain.

CHAPTER 16

SCALP choked me with that rope until I passed out. I came to laying on the hard floor of the feed room out in the barn. There was no window and the only light was what filtered in through cracks in the two outside walls. It was enough though, so I could see where I was and who was with me. Casey and old Otis Trump were both sitting on Otis's cot looking at me.

"That baldheaded 'un drug you in here with a rope around your throat like you were a dead dog," Otis said. "I'll swear, mister, if you ain't passed out, you're gettin' throwed or drug. You spend so much time lengthways on the ground, I'm beginnin' to wonder if you ain't part rotten log or serpent."

I sat up and felt my rope-burned neck, making a vow I knew I'd never keep to not rope anything ever again. "And judging from your ugly, snaggle-toothed grin," I said, "you've enjoyed every minute of it, too. How long've I been in here?" I was feeling my aching head now.

" 'Bout half an hour," Otis said, still grinning. "You got them bumps on your noggin' 'cause them fellers used it to kindle up a two-by-scantlin' out there before they drug you on in here. I think you kept callin' 'em bad names and makin' 'em lots of rash promises. I guess you wasn't satisfied with just gettin' a good chokin'."

"Yeah," I says, "I always was one that wanted more outa life."

I looked at Casey, sitting on the cot beside Otis. He was scared and it looked like he'd been crying. I said, "Casey . . ." and he started up a quiet cry again. I said, "It's all right, boy." But, in spite of what I said, I knew there wasn't a solitary thing right about it. And I was as scared as he was, too.

"Did you see 'em do anything to Mrs. Lewis?" I asked.

Casey sniffled a couple of times and swung his feet back and forth. "Just the one with the beard—he tried to bite her on the neck and squeeze her back here." He touched a hand to his bottom.

I was nearly afraid to ask, "And then what happened?"

"Then Autumn slapped him and he laughed and said if she didn't like that, then maybe she ought to tell him where the money was."

That didn't come as any surprise to me, but only confirmed what I'd been suspicioning. Those two had come to the homestead for the same reason I had—Burl's money—and it didn't take a criminal genius to see that most likely they were the other two involved in the robbery where the money came from.

"And *then* what happened?" I said. "Come on, boy, don't make me have to drag it out of you!"

"S-s-she said she didn't know what he was talking about, so he had the other man tie her up and put her on the bed and he said to Autumn that if they couldn't find the money Burl was supposed to have for 'em, then Burl's woman would have to settle up with them. He said that was only fair and she ought to be able to see that."

It was pretty clear to me by then that Burl had lied to his two partners about where the money was, just like he'd lied to me. I believed the money existed now, but knew that Burl had surely hidden it somewhere else, and, with him dead, that somewhere else would probably never be known. The only satisfaction I got out of thinking that, was that Burl had died without ever having gotten to spend the money himself.

"Was that all?" I asked.

"Y-y-yes sir," he said, "except that the one without any hair asked what about the other people, and the big one said they'd have to figure on that later. He said they'd have to find out where that"—Casey looked up at me like he didn't know whether he should say it or not—"where that stupid cowboy fit in on the deal, but he said he figured what the cowboy was after was more apt to be found under a calico skirt than it was in a money bag. Then they both laughed and brought me out here and locked me up."

It thundered outside—a long, deep rumble. Then there was a clap of thunder that shook the barn. Pretty soon we could hear it raining.

"Rain," Otis said. "We need it."

We sat there listening to the thunder and the rain for quite a while after that. Once I got up and tried to break down the door, but my shoulder gave a lot more than the door did. In my mind I kept seeing those filthy hands of Pole's on Autumn Lewis and his vulgar lips on her throat. Somehow, I kept thinking that everything that was happening was my fault, but I really knew it wasn't. It was all Burl's fault. It was his fault—what I was afraid was happening in the house right then and what would happen to the rest of us once Scalp and Pole were ready to ride out. It was all Burl's fault and I nearly wished he was alive to see it instead of rotting underneath a brush pile in Colorado.

"Mr. Smith," Casey said after about an hour.

"Yeah," I answered without looking at him.

"What're you gonna do?"

"This oughta be good," Otis said.

"Mister Smith?" Casey said.

"Just hush, boy!" I snapped. "Can't you see that I'm in pretty much the same predicament as you and that grinnin' old wart beside you. I can't hardly walk through doors or walls, you know."

"That means," Otis said, leaning closer to the boy beside him, "that if he could just get at them two fellers, they'd think a cyclone had been unleashed. They'd think a whole regiment of horse soldiers was upon 'em. They'd think—

Woops, looks like we got company. Mister, it ain't none of my business, but unless you're so mean that you bite the heads off diamondbacks, then you might oughta git off your butt."

His last comment was the first thing Otis had ever said that I took seriously. I had been sitting on the floor and leaning against the north wall, but before God even had time to get the news I was *standing* against the south wall.

Otis hadn't been lying. Just a couple of feet from where I'd been sitting, the broad, mean head of a snake was sticking through a crack where the wall and the floor didn't quite meet. I couldn't tell the brand of our caller though, whether he was a bullsnake or a rattlesnake, but to me *all* snakes were rattlesnakes.

Otis picked up an old boot to bounce off Mr. Snake's head to let him know the premises were occupied and how unsociable the occupants were—an understandable reaction, and one which, had I been given the opportunity, I would have cast a yea vote on.

But then, before Otis's one-armed launch of curled-toed boot could be gotten underway, I heard myself saying, "Wait!"

"Wait hell!" Otis said. "He may be one of your double-first cousins bringing news from home, but there ain't room in here for me and him both."

I grabbed the boot just before it left Otis's hand. "You just sit there and be still," I said.

"You ain't got a lick of sense, Smith. Not one goddamn bit, you know that?"

My hands were already sweating, just thinking about what I was thinking about.

The snake poked his head in the crack, flicked his dark, forked tongue out a time or two for whatever reason snakes do that, and then dropped his head onto the floor and came on in. But it took him a while to get all of himself in, partly because he was slithering slowly, but mainly because there was so much of him to get slithered in.

He kept coming in, slow and mean-looking, like he was the meanest thing on earth, until at last his body started to taper and I saw the first black ring around his tail. There were a couple of more black rings and then about three inches of rattlers.

He was a *big* snake. A big old diamondback or coontail as some people call them. He was three and a half feet long and as big around as a cedar post. He froze against the wall for a few seconds and then started angling across the dim room.

Otis started to get up, but I clamped a hand on his shoulder and shoved him back down on the cot. He started to say something and I dug my fingers into his bony shoulder and shut him up.

It took three or four minutes for the snake to crawl across the room. When I thought he was far enough away from his entrance hole, or any hole on an outside wall big enough to crawl through, I whispered, "Now."

Casey and Otis both looked up at me. Otis whispered, "Now *what*?"

I released my grip on his shoulder and whispered, "Now we're gonna catch him."

"We're gonna play hell!" Otis whispered.

"We've gotta have a weapon of *some kind* to use against Pole 'n Scalp," I said.

"And you think that snake's . . ."

"He's the nearest thing to a weapon I see," I said.

"Just outa idle curiousness," Otis said, "are you planning on using him for a club, or are you figurin' on chocking 'em to death with him?"

"We'll take this blanket you and Casey are sittin' on and throw it over him."

"And then what?"

"How the hell should *I* know?" I said. "Just ease up off the blanket and we'll stretch it out between us, throw it over the snake, and see what happens next. Listen, Pop, I don't have any answers. Maybe at one time I thought I did, but now I know I don't have an answer for anything. I'm just tryin' to figure out something here. There ain't no tellin' what's happening to Mrs. Lewis right now, or what's gonna happen to us a little later . . . So, are you gonna try to help me, or are you just gonna sit there and grin like a possum eatin' persimmons?"

CHAPTER 17

WE didn't have any trouble getting the blanket spread out over the snake. The first thing we did was to make him coil up. That was easy enough but kind of unnerving, because when he started rattling in that little closed room, it was just about the scariest thing I'd ever heard. But then we spread the blanket out and dropped it over him without much trouble. He took offense to that though, like I was afraid he might. He could crawl as fast with that blanket spread over him as without it, and in nothing flat he was out from under it.

"Keep 'im away from the walls," I said, "or he'll get away!"

Saying that is one thing, but doing it is something else. A three-and-a-half-foot diamondback rattlesnake that's on the peck pretty well chooses where he wants to go by himself. I was the one standing between him and the hole in the north wall where he'd come in, and, in spite of all the instructions I'd been doling out, I was the one who couldn't make himself stand his ground and head him off. I wanted to, but I couldn't. I stood my ground about as long as I would have if that ten-pound snake headed for me had've been a fifteen-hundred-pound bull wiping his nose on the ground and stringing slobber out of his mouth.

I let him have his hole with so little interference from me that I'm embarrassed to tell about it, but I jumped back toward it before he'd got plumb through it, and put a boot on the last eight angry inches of him. You talk about a rattlesnake singing and a cowboy wondering what in the hell he was doing! He doubled back and I saw the tip of his forked tongue coming back inside.

"Don't move your foot!" Otis yelled and shoved the wadded-up blanket down over the snake's tail and my foot. The blanket kept the snake from coming back *inside*, and my boot kept him from getting all the way *outside*.

"I'll be damned," I said. "That was pretty quick thinkin' for an old wore-out fart like you. We got him now."

"From where I am," Otis said, looking up and grinning big as ever, "I cain't hardly tell just who's got who."

"What're we gonna do?" I said.

"Well, let's see . . . Now, *you* were the one who said you wanted to catch him. Ain't that the way of it?" Otis asked.

Suddenly, there was a knock on the door and Scalp's inquiring voice, "Hey, what's goin' on in nare? What's all the racket been for? Cain't a man get no honest sleep around you people? Cowboy, are you up to somethin' agin?"

"Yeah," I said, "we're catchin' big ol' rattlers in here." Then I whispered to Otis, "Keep that blanket pressed down so he can't double back. Whatever you do, *don't* let him come in headfirst."

Then, with nervous hands and sweaty lips, I leaned over and grabbed the snake just behind my boot and started dragging him slowly—and with a chill down my backbone every time he moved—back inside.

"What'n the hell you bein' so quiet about now?" Scalp said.

"That's the way you gotta be to catch big rattlers," I said. "So will you please go away and leave us alone."

"What's *that* noise?" Scalp asked.

"That's a goddamn rattlesnake!" I said. "They rattle that loud sometimes when you catch 'em bare-handed."

"You all must think I'm a dumb bastard, if you think that I'd believe you're catchin' rattlesnakes with your bare hands in there," Scalp said, nearly laughing.

I was dragging the snake out now with my right hand and keeping my left one pressed against his back, so I could grab him behind the head when it came along. Hunting for a snake's neck to grab ahold of is not that much fun, knowing what can happen if you miss it.

'Now why would anyone ever think *you* were a dumb bastard, Scalp? Why, just now I was just sittin' here askin' Otis which back-East finishin' school did he reckon you got your diploma from."

I was worried, not only about what I was going to do with the snake when I got him—like I'd have to get him if I got him at all—but I was even more worried because evidently Scalp had been asleep out in the barn for a while. That meant that Pole was alone with Autumn. Thinking about both of those snakes—the one I had my hands on and the one who had his hands on Autumn Lewis—and what they were both capable of made my blood run cold.

Finally I felt the snake's body start to taper in my left hand and I knew his head—and his fangs—were just inches away. I pulled him out slower than ever now—I knew I had to, even though I could hear Scalp unlocking the door and pulling away whatever it was that had been pulled against it.

"I'm comin' in," Scalp announced. "I want all of you against the north wall when this door opens. We'll see how smart you are then, cowboy."

"Aw, I wish you wouldn't, Scalp," I said, " 'Cause if you do I'll probably wind up throwin' this big old diamondback on you."

The door started swinging open. When I stood up and turned around, there was Otis and Casey standing in front of me, between me and Scalp, so Scalp couldn't see what I had.

There is no way anyone could have planned the things that happened next. It's like riding a bucking horse you've never been on before. You don't try to anticipate what he'll do, you just try to keep a leg on each side of him, your mind in the middle, and be ready for whatever comes. You hope he'll buck straight and honest, but you know that he could fall over backwards and crush you to death.

"Now let's just see what'n the hell you all are up to in here," Scalp said, standing in the doorway and scowling.

"Who?" I said, trying to hold the squirming snake so Scalp couldn't see him and he couldn't bite either me or Otis or Casey. "You mean *us*?"

What's you got there?" Scalp said, stepping forward and pulling the hammer of his Colt to full cock.

"I ain't got nothing' here that you'd be interested in," I told Scalp. "Just a big old mad rattlesnake."

"There ain't nobody gonna tell me what I'm interested in or what I'm not interested in," Scalp said. "You're standin' there holding a live rattlesnake, huh? Well, let's just see it."

"Scalp," I said, trying to draw him closer, "I'm tellin' you, I don't think you want to." Then I gave Scalp something that surprised him—a mad rattlesnake in his face!

That big old coontail landed right around Scalp's neck like a live snakeskin necklace.

Scalp yelled and shot, his bullet going into the floor between us. He spun around twice like he was doing some kind of Indian dance, grabbing at the snake with one hand and hitting at it with the gun that was in the other. He was saying something, but his words were coming out so fast I couldn't understand them. He shot again, this time in the air. He spun around another time or two and stomped his feet like he was standing in red ants.

Scalp ran out the door. I'd never heard a man scream like he did or see one go as crazy. It wasn't pretty and I almost felt sorry for him, but I did what I had to do.

I was thinking that he would drop the gun and I was going to be ready to grab it when he did, so when he ran out the door I was right behind him. He shot again and I ducked because I didn't have any idea where the gun was pointed.

He shot again, that bullet going through the barn wall just above my head. He was spinning again and had managed to get the snake from around his neck, but a pair of long fangs held the snake's head to the spot below his right ear like a giant leech.

That's when I saw the broken-handled pitchfork laying beside a small pile of old hay. I grabbed it. Then out of the corner of my eye, I saw the outside door start to open.

I knew I didn't have much time, but I didn't know what I didn't have much time for, except to get to that door. I ran, somehow knowing that the difference between getting there before it opened and not was the difference between life and death.

The door jerked open and there was Pole, his gun ready for business, a giant silhouette of meanness against a flood of rain-soaked daylight.

I was two steps away, maybe too late, but still running hard.

I guess it took a second or two for Pole's eyes to adjust to the darkness inside the barn.

"Scalp!" Pole yelled. "What'n the hell—"

I never let up. I ran into Pole like a charging bull, the pitchfork held chest-high. I felt the steel prongs sink into his big chest and then felt one of them hit something hard, scrape it, and then sink deeper.

Pole's gun went off. There was a blinding, burning flash in my face. I began to fall, slow, like I was in molasses, into a silent, black world where creatures of the light are not allowed.

CHAPTER 18

I HEARD someone calling for a man named Smith and felt someone pulling on my arm. It was dark. I turned my head both ways to look for light, but there was no light. Someone called for Smith again and someone pulled my arm.

I was in a bed. I tried to get up, but someone held me down. "You son-of-a-bitches!" I yelled. "Let me up! Let me go! I got to go! Saddle the horses! Rattle my hocks! Goddamn you, Burl!"

"Dr. Russell! Come here quick!" someone yelled. "He's talking out of his head again, and trying to get up!"

I had to get my arms free, get up, and get away. Run. Run. Run.

"Where am I! Let me up! Got to leave! Light a lantern! Throw my saddle on old Pat!"

"Mr. Smith! Stop it! Lie still! This is Dr. Russell! Your eyes are bandaged, and you're in my office in Liberty! You're okay, but you can't get up! Do you hear me . . . Mr. Smith, do you hear me? I'll tie you to the bed if I have to. Is that what you want?"

I let my body go limp. Whoever was holding me was too strong for me to pull away from.

"That's better . . . Now, can you hear me?"

"I . . . Yes, but . . ."

"Well, thank God! Finally. Mr. Smith, you've been injured. Do you remember?"

I was confused. My mind was like a puzzle in a box. I had a feeling all the pieces were there, but I couldn't get them to fit together. I remembered what happened in Wyoming and

109

that I was running away from it, but I couldn't remember much else.

"Mr. Smith, do you remember me—Autumn Lewis, Burl's wife? You came to tell me that he had been killed."

A few of the pieces were coming together. I suddenly remembered the homestead and why I'd gone there. And I did remember Autumn Lewis and how she didn't seem like she could have been married to Burl. I remembered eating in her house and watching her. Then I remembered that *I* was Will Smith!

"I remember," I said. "The adobe house . . . and the big barn."

"And do you remember leaving and then coming back with a whiskey bottle full of milk for the baby you helped deliver?"

"Yeah," I said, "the baby's mother died. I roped a cow and . . . that's about all I remember. Did Pat fall with me?"

"No, I'm afraid not," the man's voice again. "There were two men at Mrs. Lewis's when you came back. Remember? God knows what they were up to—although we've all got a pretty good idea. But thanks to you, they got about what they had coming to them."

"I can't remember anything after roping that cow," I said. "I don't even remember goin' back to the homestead. I just roped that cow for the fun of it . . ."

"Well, whether you remember or not," the man said, "you're quite a hero around here. God! I hate to think what would've happened out there if you hadn't gone back."

"You said the men got what they had comin'. What was that?" I asked.

"You killed 'em, Mr. Smith . . . Both of 'em."

"Good God!" I said.

"Well, it was pretty bad all right, but there's no one in Liberty doubts but what it would have been worse if you hadn't. It will probably all come back to you after a while."

It was a shock to me at the time. There I was running from

one killing, and now I'd just heard that I'd killed twice more? In a day or so most of what happened came back to me, although it always seemed more like a dream than a reality.

"Why can't I see?" I raised a hand to my eyes and felt the bandages covering them.

"Your eyes suffered powder burns when a gun went off in your face. The bullet creased your skull, too. You've been unconscious for two days and I was beginning to worry that you'd never come out of it. I've seen men with head wounds lay unconscious for months before they finally died. Seems like anything past two days and it's time to get worried—and you were about to close out your second day."

Two days! I thought. It seemed like a couple of hours ago that I was roping that cow. I should have been getting close to Mexico right then!

"How long before we can take the bandages off and I can ride?" I asked.

"Well, now there, Mr. Smith, let's just slow down a minute and take this a step at a time. Actually, we're about to take step number two right now. The first step was taken when you decided to join the living a few minutes ago. The next step will be to removed your bandages and see about your eyes." Then he started loosening them.

"What are you? A sawbones?" I asked.

"Dr. Whitney Russell at your service."

"What about my eyes, Doc? You ain't sayin' . . ."

"I'm sayin' let's take the bandages off and see what you can see and go from there."

"But what if I *can't* see? What if—"

"Please, Mr. Smith," Autumn Lewis said, "don't worry . . . Just have faith."

"Well, Ill tell you what, ma'am," I said, "just give me my eyesight and my horses, and I won't *need* any faith."

"Now, Mrs. Lewis," the doctor said, "if you'll pull the shades over the windows and the door to keep out some of the sunlight, we're just about ready.

"I'll have to warn you, Mr. Smith, that at the best you won't be able to see a whole lot, but just being able to see *anything* right now will be encouraging. Okay, open them up and let's see."

In spite of the doc's warning, I wasn't ready for what I could see—or couldn't see. "Nothin' but a couple of patches of fuzzy light, Doc!"

"Well, thank God!" the doctor said. "That's just about the most we could hope for right now."

Well, it wasn't anywhere near the most I was hoping for. Being able to see about as much as a man could on a new-moon night with a thin layer of clouds in the sky wasn't much cause for me to rejoice.

"Doc," I said, "didn't you hear me? I'm damn near blind!"

"But you're not!" Dr. Russell said, "Now calm down and let me finish my examination, will you?"

He held a hand gently over my left eye. "Now what do you see?"

"The same thing—two patches of light not bright enough to find your mouth by."

He held a hand over my right eye. "What about now? Are the lights any brighter or dimmer?"

"Gone, Doc," I said. "The fuzzy lights are gone now, and I can't see no more than if I was inside a cow's belly."

"M-m-m-m . . . Well, that's about what I expected. Now, Mr. Smith, I'm going to put some medicine in your eyes and then rebandage them."

Maybe he had expected that, but it seemed to me that he was no longer rejoicing in my two fuzzy patches of light as much as he had been a few minutes ago.

"Doc," I said, my voice low and meek, my heart pretty well tore-out, and my self-pity in full blossom picturing me pushing a blind man's cane around for the next thirty or forty years and begging for money in some sour-smelling saloon, "just give it to me straight out. About the only good I'll get out of my eyes from now on will be to keep my forehead off my chin, ain't that so?"

Dr. Russell hesitated a few seconds, then he cleared his throat and said as he pulled each eyelid up and dropped some stinging medicine in my eyes, "All right, I'll tell you my professional opinion on the matter—you're not going to be blind, *but* you're not going to ever see as good as you did before, either. I think this right eye has a good chance of returning to normal. It's still badly blistered. But once it heals—and it will only heal if you take care of it and do as I tell you—once it heals, unless scar tissue forms over the pupil, it should be about ninety percent as good as it was before."

"How long will it take to get that ninety percent, Doc?" I asked. "And what about the left one?"

"You should be able to notice almost daily improvement, but just exactly how long is hard to say. I'd say a couple of weeks, though, if I had to make a prediction."

I didn't say anything. I was too stunned, I guess. Dr. Russell could very well have just read my death sentence. Words just don't roll off a man's tongue at a time like that.

"Now, about this one," the doctor went on, putting a bandage over my left eye, "we have a problem here—on top of the powder burns, I mean. There was a thin sliver of metal that was probably shaved off the bullet as it went from the cylinder into the barrel. I had to dig that sliver out of the pupil. It had penetrated fairly deeply, I'm afraid."

"It'll never be as good as the other eye, will it, Doc?" I asked. "How much can I expect out of it?"

He didn't answer right off, but instead started bandaging the right eye. "How much?" I asked again.

"I'd say the chances of it *ever* getting any better than it is right now are . . . slim and none."

The doctor didn't say any more. I guess he couldn't think of anything else bad enough to top what he had already said.

"Mr. Smith," Autumn Lewis said, "I want you to know how grateful I am, and how terribly sorry I am . . ."

CHAPTER 19

I WAS asleep as much as I was awake for the next two days, which Dr. Russell said was normal for my type of head wound. My disposition couldn't have been much worse or my heart any lower. I was aware however, although I saw no reason for rejoicing over the matter, that the two dim, fuzzy patches of light I could see through my right eye were gradually getting bigger and less dim and fuzzy.

"How's the cowboy doin'?" I heard someone say. I opened my eyes and saw the dark silhouette of a man in the open doorway, the most distinct image I'd seen since Pole's gun exploded in my face—an event which, by then, I could remember as well as I wanted to. The man himself wasn't clear, just his dark outline against the daylight behind him.

"I'd say he was doing about like he ought to be, Sheriff," Dr. Russell said. "Why don't you ask him yourself, looks like he's awake again."

"Yeah, I see he is," the man said. Then he took a step inside the room, pushed his hat back, and said, "Fella, I'm Sheriff Joe Betters. You say your name is Smith?"

"Yeah, that's right—Will Smith." I hesitated and then asked, "Why?"

"Oh," he said, slow and deliberate, "I was just tryin' to get all of this straight for the reports I gotta fill out. You know anything about them two fellers you killed?"

"No," I said.

"Where'd you learn to handle yourself like that?"

"I . . . I don't know. I barely remember what happened."

"Shoot," the sheriff said, "now ain't you something. You kill two bad hombres—and do it practically bare-handed

114

too—and then you're bashful as a schoolboy about it. Yes, sir, you'd fit right in one of them yeller-backed novels they're writin' back East.

"Those two were treated about as rough as any men I've ever seen—and I was in Lincoln County when The Kid and Henry Brown and that bunch were there. The big one, the one called Pole, had that pitchfork run clear through his heart, between a couple of ribs and out his back. And that other one, the baldheaded one—glory be! I never seen one man kill another with a rattlesnake before. Took him more than a day and a half to die. Finally smothered to death because his head swelled so big he couldn't breath. Ain't that right, Doc?"

Dr. Russell grunted.

"Did you know them before?" Sheriff Betters asked.

"Uh, no," I said. "Never seen 'em before in my life."

"Just wonderin'. I mean, it seems kind of funny, the things they were supposed to have said about finding some money out there. And then you being there too, and being an old friend of Burl's—it just seems kind of funny. You know anything about any money hid out there?"

"No," I said. "I don't know anything about any money."

"Well, I'd better get back to the office and finish those reports. You say your name is Smith, huh? Will Smith? And you just came to tell Mrs. Lewis that Burl got killed goin' up north with a trail herd?"

"That's right," I said.

"And you were there when Burl Lewis was killed, and you don't have any idea what those two men were doing at the Lewis homestead?"

"That's what I said, Sheriff."

"Okay . . . Smith," the sheriff said, pulled his hat down and started out. When he got to the door and silhouetted himself in it again, he stopped and turned inside and said, "Say, Doc, how long till he'll be able to ride?"

"Guess he could ride right now, but how long it'll be till he can *see* where he's riding I can't say for sure. A week or two would be my guess, though."

"When'll you be letting him out of here?"

"Why?" I asked. I didn't like them talking about me like I wasn't there, and I sure didn't like the interest Sheriff Joe Betters was showing in me. Of course, I had a natural tendency to be suspicious of anybody wearing a badge, whether I thought he was showing undue interest in me or not.

"How long, Doc?" Betters asked again.

"Why, he can leave anytime he wants to, Joe," the doctor said. "This isn't a jail, you know. I can't hold a man against his will. He's not sick and I've done about all I can for him. He just needs some more time to recuperate—get his strength back and let that right eye continue to improve. I was going to suggest he get a room at the hotel tomorrow or the next day anyway."

"Is that what you're goin' to do, Smith—get a room over at the hotel?"

"Well," I said, "I reckon so . . . hadn't give it much thought but . . ."

"I hope he'll come back out to the homestead until he can travel." We all three, Sheriff Betters, Dr. Russell, and me, turned our heads toward an inside door beside the bed and looked at Autumn Lewis standing in it. Well, all I really did was to look in that direction. Not having any light behind her to give her an outline, I couldn't really see her, but I knew she was there.

"You think that would be a good thing to do, ma'am?" Sheriff Betters asked.

"Yes, Sheriff," she said, "I do think it would be a good thing to do."

"Begging your pardon, ma'am," Betters said, "but I didn't mean good as in right or wrong, but as in smart. I mean, you don't know much about this man, and I'm not sure it would be a smart idea to have him hangin' around. I know you want to take in every cripple you see, but there comes a time—"

"Sheriff," the lady said, sounding kind of riled, "Mr. Smith came here on an errand of mercy to tell me about Burl, and wound up coming within an inch of getting killed for his trouble. I think offering him a place to stay while he recuperates is the *least* I can do."

"I'll be stayin' at the hotel," I said. I couldn't see any future at all in going back to the homestead again, although I guess a blind cowboy would have pretty well rounded out her congregation of cripples and misfits. But I didn't want to be nursemaided by anyone, and I didn't want to be cooped up on some falling-down homestead where the biggest excitement to be had was to watch chickens eat bugs.

"Whatever you say, Smith," Betters growled. "Just don't leave this country until I say. You clear on that?"

"I've always been one to leave whenever the urge hit me, Sheriff—I ain't used to asking anyone's permission."

"I'm expecting something from the territorial capital any day now, and when it arrives I'd like to know right where you are." He paused a little bit to let that soak in on me, and then he said, "You just remember what I said, Smith." He stood in the doorway a few more seconds and then turned and walked out.

"I'll be leavin' tomorrow, Doc," I said. "Why don't you figger out the damages and we'll settle up."

Dr. Russell grunted, opened and closed his medicine cabinet, and said as he walked out, "I've got a call to make."

"I'll have Casey and Otis bring your horses to town tomorrow and leave them at the livery," Mrs. Lewis said.

I nodded. "Pole . . . did he . . ."

"No," she said, "he didn't."

"Thank you for the offer to let me stay out at your place for a few days, ma'am, but it'll be best all the way around if I just get a room here in town."

"You don't owe me any explanation, Mr. Smith," she said.

"I'm sure a man like yourself would rather be near saloons and dance halls when the sun goes down than on a homestead."

Before I knew what had happened, she'd gathered her skirts up and rushed across the room and out the front door just as Dr. Russell stepped inside. He walked across the room to his medicine cabinet.

"Forgot Mrs. Brown's sugar pills," he said. "What did you do to Mrs. Lewis? Looked like she was crying. Now look here, Smith, that lady's got big enough problems without you adding to them."

"Ain't tryin' to, Doc. I ain't trying to do anything but get to where I can see and get plumb shuck of this whole country, without causing her or anybody else any trouble. Seems like she's got a chip on her shoulder to me."

"More like a load than a chip."

"I've been wondering, Doc, about her and Burl. How'd that ever happen?"

"Well now," Dr. Russell said, and from the way he lowered his head I knew he was looking at me over the rims of his spectacles, "I figured since you and Burl were such good friends he told you all about her."

"To tell the truth, Doc," I confessed, "me and Burl weren't all that good of friends. I heard him talk about a lot of women all right, but he never once mentioned anything about a wife until he was dyin'. I was sure surprised when I found out, too, I'll tell you that. Burl never struck me as the homesteadin', wife-havin' kind."

"Hummph," the old doctor said, snorting and bumping his gums. "If you had enough sense to not be good friends with Burl Lewis, then that says something for you. In my own humble opinion, a tumble bug is a noble creature compared to what Burl was."

"You'll get no argument from me there, Doc," I allowed. "What I can't figure is how a man like him ever wound up breaking bread and settin' up housekeeping with a woman like that Autumn."

The doc sighed. "That's always gotten by me, too. Of course, they didn't break bread together for more 'n three or four months before he pulled out, or before she ran him off would be more like it."

"When did they settle on the homestead?" I asked.

"Oh, *they* didn't settle that homestead," Dr. Russell said, sitting down on the edge of the bed and taking his glasses off to clean them. "People call it the Lewis place now, but all Burl Lewis had to do with it was to loaf on it for the short while after they were married and before he left. You see, the place was originally filed on by Ben Marshal about three years ago. He settled here with his family—a wife and a little boy. They all came down with the fever in the winter of '93, and Mrs. Marshal's sister came out here from the East to take care of 'em until they got back on their feet. Well, Mr. and Mrs. Marshal were both dead by spring, but the boy recovered."

"And that boy was Casey and Mrs. Marshal's sister was a lady named Autumn, I bet."

"You bet right," Russell said. "I think she made some kind of vow to the Marshals as they were dying, that if there was any way she could, she'd stay on the place with the boy long enough to prove it up and get title to it. To say they've had a rough time of it would be an understatement."

"Okay," I said, "I savvy all of that, but if you've mentioned Burl's role in all of this I missed it."

The doc laughed and rubbed his chin. "Burl's role? Well, so far as I know his only role was to cause trouble for Autumn—and he handled that job with ease. He just drifted in here one time and hung around the saloons and dance halls. He had a way with the women, I guess there's no denying that, being big and good-looking like he was and knowing just how to use it. Why, some of those saloons girls would squeal like a horsing mare when he'd come around.

"One day after we'd had a big rain and the ruts were about yea deep in the streets and big puddles of water were standing everywhere, Autumn came into town to get some things at the mercantile. Burl 'just happened' to be there too—I say it like that because I noticed that when Autumn got to town in the wagon, Burl was sitting over in front of the saloon. As soon as she went inside the mercantile, he strolled right on over there. He 'just happened' along like a hawk 'just happens' to fall out of the sky and land on a ground squirrel.

"I saw Burl tip his hat to her as she stepped out carrying some things she'd bought. He smiled like a bashful cowboy and then helped her get the things into the wagon. He carried out two other packages and then they stood there a few minutes talking and smiling. That started their court-ship, and I'll swear, it couldn't have been more than three weeks later that they were married."

"Do you think Burl ever intended to settle down and stay out there on the homestead and put in crops and keep the place up?" I asked.

"Good Lord, no," the doctor said.

"Then I can't figure him marrying her to start with. It wasn't like he couldn't get a woman any other way."

"Oh, he could've 'got' other women okay, just like he'd been doing since he'd drifted into town, but none of them were like Autumn Meyerson—that was her maiden name."

"You mean none of the other women . . ."

"I mean none of the other women that handsome Burl Lewis could have had for a night and then went on his merry way were tall, pretty, thirty-year-old virgin nuns!"

"What!" I said, straightening up. "You mean . . ."

"I mean just what I said—Autumn came out of a nunnery somewhere back East. She was wearing a nun's habit the first day she stepped off the stage here, and she was still wearing it a few months later when Burl 'just happened' to bump into her at the mercantile the time I was telling you about. As a matter of fact, the first time I ever saw her in regular clothes was the day she came into town to marry him. I think that was one reason Burl thought he just *had* to have her—I mean her being a nun and so pretty and pure and all. I think he saw her as a special kind of challenge, a beautiful vestal virgin dedicated to serving God and seemingly forbidden him, beyond his filthy reach and his ability to desecrate, but he proved nothing was beyond that. He proved . . ."

Here the good doctor's voice began trailing away and he stopped speaking. Or, at least, if he didn't stop, his words were too soft-spoken for me to hear, even though I was leaning forward and tilting an ear towards him. In a few seconds though, and very softly, he said, "An animal . . . a beast . . . the devil's own child . . . that's what he had to 've been."

I waited for him to go on, but he didn't. I waited nearly a minute and then I said, "What, Dr. Russell? What did he do?"

The doctor then suddenly got off the bed and put his glasses on. As he was walking toward the door, he said, I think more to himself than to me, "You'd think I was old enough to know when to keep my mouth shut about things that aren't any of my business."

"Wait, Doc!" I said. "What did he do?"

"It's no concern of yours, Mr. Smith," he said, stopping for a second in the doorway before going outside. "You just get well and go on about your business."

I fell back on my pillow, listening to a wagon rumble by outside and to some kids hollering and playing. I laid there a long time like that, trying to make some sense out of a world that seemed to have lost what little sense it ever had.

CHAPTER 20

THE next day, along towards the middle of the afternoon, I stepped out into the street. The sun was bearing down hot and the sand in the streets was blowing. My left eye was covered by a black patch that Dr. Russell had given me, but through my right eye I could see good enough to see across the street. That wasn't very far, but in Liberty it was far enough. The town itself wasn't much more than one street wide and there wasn't much that a man with two good eyes would *want* to see—a cluster of adobe and rock buildings set out in the middle of a treeless sand-and-sage flat on the west bank of a blow-sand creek.

I started across the street to the hotel. I was light-headed and weak from being in bed all that time, and I wasn't used to having only half of one eye to see out of either, but it still felt good to get out in the sun again and to hear the jingle of my spurs with each step I took. Before I got across the street, I noticed the livery a couple of doors down from the hotel and stopped there first to see if Pat and my little packhorse were there.

"How much'll it cost to keep 'em here?" I asked when a little man with tobacco juice running out both sides of his mouth told me he had my horses.

"Half-a-buck a day fer the two of 'em," he told me.

"Pretty high, if you ask me," I said. "Just make sure they get a good bait of oats mornin' and night. I want 'em fit and ready to go when I come get 'em. And put some bacon grease on that sore on the sorrel's back, too."

When I was coming out of the livery I saw the sheriff's office across the street—on the same side I'd started from and two doors down from where I'd been laying up for the past four days—I also saw a man sitting on the step in front of the sheriff's office. My sight wasn't near good enough to read a face from that distance yet, but just on the chance that it was Sheriff Joe Betters with his undue interest in a certain half-blind cowboy, that same certain half-blind cowboy dropped on his hocks and spun around in the street smoother than half the cow horses he'd ever been on. Then he went around behind the livery and the mercantile and in the side door of the Brand Hotel.

"How much for a room 'n bath?" I asked the clerk, a baldheaded man in a baggy white linen shirt standing behind the counter.

"You want hot water?" he said eyeing me kind of queerly.

"You think cold water will start to knock off this crust?" I asked.

"Be a dollar and a half then," he said. "Aren't you the man who killed them two desperados out at the Lewis place?"

"Yeah," I said, "guess so. Which way?"

"Room number eight, right up them stairs. You'll get your bath in the room right behind me whenever you want it."

"I want it now," I said.

"I've already got some water heating up," he said.

"Good," I said. "I need some new clothes. Would you—"

"I'll go over to the mercantile and get 'em for you, Mr. Smith!"

I turned around and a boy about fourteen was standing there holding out his hand.

"I'll get you some new clothes, Mr. Smith," he said again. "I helped dig both graves for those two men you killed, and I'd be proud to get your clothes."

I tilted my head back so I could get a better look at the boy with the one eye I had that was working at all.

"You see my size—six foot and slim built? I need new socks and all new underriggin', and I need a pair of Levi's and a dark-colored flannel shirt, about like what I got on now only without the dirt and body grease—I'll apply them myself," I said handing him five dollars. "Get me some Bull Durham, too, and if there's anything left you can have it for yourself, son."

I stepped inside the back room where the baths were taken. The little room was hot and steamy and filled with the smell of soap and cigar smoke. A man about fifty years old with a big paunch and a little stub of a cigar was drying himself off. I looked at him and nodded my head a little and he nodded back and said, "Smith."

It seemed like nearly everybody in town knew my name. I nearly laughed. Here I'd come all the way from Wyoming, riding at night and bushing up in the daytime, eating cold, and sleeping like a coyote, moving so the cedars and the creeks and the canyons wouldn't even know I'd passed. I'd been doing all of that, and now here I was in Liberty, New Mexico, and everybody from the sheriff on down knew me. But so far they knew me as Will Smith and not Honk Ballard. That suited me fine and seemed to suit everybody else in town just fine too, everybody except for Sheriff Joe Betters. I'd have to sidle away from him until I left town, which I planned to do as soon as I could, like a wild cow heading for the tooles.

The other man left with his paunch and his cigar and I started scraping my clothes off, thinking the only fate fit for them was a fast and unceremonious cremation.

The hotel clerk came in with two buckets of steaming hot water and poured 'em into one of the tubs. "Cold water's right over there," he said, tilting his head toward a pump and an empty bucket in the corner of the room.

I tempered that scalding water in the tub with just enough cold water from the pump, so it took me about five minutes to get my delicate framework all the way in it. Then I just laid back and started to soak with only my head above the water, like a big old turtle. There was a big calendar on the wall and I started studying it, trying to figure out what day it was. When you'd been living like I had for the past few months, the days just sort of get lost in the scramble, sometimes the months do the same. I knew it was the month of September though, mostly because that's the month the calendar was turned to, and as close as I could figure, it was around the fifteenth.

That meant it had been over a hundred days since I'd had a hot bath—since the night before I left Tascosa, Texas with that XIT trail herd! The last bath of any kind I'd had would have been in a cold spring in Wyoming about three weeks ago, when me and Burl were sleepering calves for old Charlie Castle. But I didn't want to think about Wyoming or Charlie Castle or sleepering calves. I didn't want to think about Burl Lewis, either, or *anything* that had happened since I first met him. But there's a terrible truth about killing men—you think about it whether you want to or not.

I laid there soaking in the tub, and the thing I'd see every time I closed my eyes would be a big diamondback rattlesnake with his mouth wide open and his long fangs glistening like two daggers and dripping blood. If I didn't see that, then I saw Johnson Powers's head where Burl's bullet had plowed into his face and ripped out the back of his skull. Or I saw Ben DuPree's face twitch and jerk as my bullets tore into his guts.

I hollered at the clerk and told him to bring me a razor and a mirror and more hot water. When I looked in the mirror, I almost dropped it into the water. It was my hand handing the mirror, but the face looking back at me was the face of a stranger, drawn and bearded, and with a black patch over one eye. Then I grinned. That *wasn't* the face of Honk Ballard I was seeing, but the face of Will Smith! Since I never could stand a beard, I went ahead and knocked it off, but I left the mustache like it was, left it growing clear down past the corners of my mouth.

When the boy brought my new clothes, I got out of the water, dressed, and went out into the hotel lobby, feeling better. I stepped out into the street again and said to a man passing by, "Say, where can a man find some dead cow to gnaw on around here?"

He looked at me and blinked his eyes a couple of times but didn't say anything. He looked soft and was wearing fancy clothes and a bowler hat. I figured he must have been a drummer of some kind and didn't exactly savvy what I was asking, so I rephrased the question in more citizenlike terms, "Where's the town cafe at?"

"Oh, well, it's just two doors down thataway, Mr. Smith," he said nervously. "Rose's Cafe—with the big red sign. I guess you just didn't see it."

"You mean 'cause I'm damn near blind?" I said.

The drummer's soft, white face turned even whiter underneath his bowler hat. "Oh no, Mr. Smith," he said, taking a small step backward, "that's not what I meant at all. I just meant . . ."

"Thanks," I said and grinned as the drummer struck into a little town-gaited trot down the middle of the street, looking back over his shoulder now and then.

The four or five other people in the cafe all turned and looked at me as I stepped inside and hung my hat on the hat rack beside the open door. I stood there a few seconds, letting my eye get as adjusted as it could from the change of light from outside to in. Then I picked a table and sat down so I could see the door and the street, and so my back would be against the wall.

A Mexican lady came out from the kitchen and said, "Yes, sir, Meester Smith."

"What's for supper?" I asked.

"Beefsteak, bread, beans, potatoes, gravy, and cobbler," she said.

"Sounds good to me," I said, "but just knock the twitch outa my beef and warm it up a little." I always thought the rawer a piece of meat was the more strength it had in it—I guess because I'd never seen a wild animal sitting around a fire while supper cooked—and what I needed was strength.

The supper was good, although I couldn't get around all of it before I was full, and that wasn't usual for me. But it felt good to eat food cooked under a roof and eaten while sitting at a table instead of on the ground.

As I ate, I noticed the other people kept glancing at me. In fact, everywhere I went people either nodded to me and spoke, or else they just looked at me and sidled away like a spooked bronc, but no one acted like I wasn't there. As I finished off my third cup of black coffee and stood up, it hit me that it was a shame there wasn't some kind of city office I could run for, so all of that recognition wouldn't go to waste.

Back out into the street about sundown, all washed and scrubbed and wearing new clothes and carrying a full stomach like I was, I should have felt good. I did, but I didn't, if that makes any sense. I still felt empty, even though I'd just got through packing in all the food I could hold.

No bigger than Liberty was, there were still four saloons there. I started to go in one of them—before my trouble started up in Wyoming, I didn't think a man could pass through a town without visiting *all* the saloons in it—but I decided I wasn't up to the noise and that many people. Besides, I couldn't go in and drink like Honk Ballard the good-time cowboy, I'd have to do it like Will Smith the one-eyed tough hombre. Tough hombres—or even those who really aren't but have that reputation—and drinking establishments have been known to produce trouble. Trouble and I had grown real familiar the past few weeks but it had been a forced kind of acquaintance—not one of choice,—and the sooner I could slip off from him, the better it would suit me.

I went past the open door of a saloon and into the Brand Hotel. I walked up to the counter, thinking I knew, at last, what it was that was missing, what I needed to make me feel like a man ought to.

"Say, mister clerk," I said to the man behind the counter, the same baldheaded man who'd taken my money earlier and had brought the hot water for my bath, "I wonder if you could get me a bottle of whiskey."

"You favor any particular brand?" he asked without looking up from his ledger.

"Naw," I said, "just so long as it comes in a bottle about this big"—I held my hand about three feet off the floor—"and is mellow enough to raise a blister on a snubbin' post." Now I leaned toward the clerk a little and said with a little one-eyed grin, "And just to save you the bother, if you wanted to send it up by the way of the Silk 'n Lace Shippin' Company, I'd be glad to pay the freight."

The clerk looked up without grinning and said kind of sourlike, "Does that mean you want a whore with the bottle?"

"Yeah," I said, thinking that hotel clerks sure had a lot to learn about picturesque speech.

CHAPTER 21

I WAS lying on the bed in the room that was, by then, nearly dark, smoking a cigarette, when the door opened and I saw a woman's form silhouetted against the lantern light in the hall. "I have some whiskey here for Will Smith," she said.

"Come on in," I said, raising up and striking a match on the sole of my boot, and then leaning over to light the lantern that was on the table beside the bed.

The woman stepped inside the room and closed the door behind her. "Please," she said, "do you have to light the lantern?"

I held the match a second or two and tried to see what the woman looked like. I figured, by rights, being the big spender I was, I was entitled to at least that, but in that dim and dancing matchlight, and with only one eye—and it partly crippled—about all I could see before the match sputtered and went out was the big scoop of white skin between her neck and the low-cut saloon dress she was wearing.

There was no moon that night, or at least if there was going to be one, if hadn't risen yet. Whatever, it wasn't in the sky to throw any of it's blue light into the room. There was a little yellow lantern light from the hall coming in around the door, but that was all the light we had.

The bottle of whiskey landed on the bed beside me with a sloshing sound, and then I heard the slick fabric of the woman's dress rustle and I knew she was undressing. Now I had *the* two things I thought would make me feel like a man ought to—a bottle of cheap whiskey and a woman, by then probably naked, both within arms' reach. But I sat there on the edge of the bed a long time without reaching for either.

Then I picked the bottle of whiskey up off the bed and stood up with it in my hand, but instead of grabbing the woman like a bear grabs a slab of meat, and like I'm sure she expected me to, I walked slowly over to the window, my spurs jingling softly in the darkness, the sounds of revelry from the saloons coming in the open window. I didn't say anything but looked down into the street where lantern light could be seen through scattered windows—fuzzy lantern light in my eyes. A town dog barked and a coyote howled in the sage past the last dark building on the edge of town.

I uncorked the bottle and took a drink, a big one, and I chased that one with one that was even bigger. Then I got my breath and did the same thing over again—took two drinks as big and as quick as I could stand.

But something was wrong. Where was the fun and the excitement? If I was having a good time, I sure couldn't tell it yet. Two more long drinks of whiskey made my head swim and my chest burn, but I couldn't hardly call that fun.

"What's wrong here?" I said.

"What's wrong with *you* is the question, cowboy," the woman said. "I thought you wanted a woman."

"No . . ." I said. "I mean, I *do* want a woman. Whiskey and a woman. Have the woman and get drunk on the whiskey, and then the next morning not be able to remember much about the woman and be sick from the whiskey, isn't that the way to have fun?"

"Well, that seems to work with most men around here, but I'm not going to chase you all over the room, cowboy. If you want me, then you're gonna have to come back over here to the bed—that's where I transact my business from."

Maybe it was the whiskey already having an effect on me, maybe I'd drunk so much of the stuff over the past few years that it didn't take but a couple of stout drinks anymore to make me see and hear things that weren't there. But whatever it was, when I looked back down in the street, there stood Burl and Ben DuPree looking up at me and grinning!

This was the same street, of course, that a minute earlier would have been dark to a man with *good* eyes, but, there I was, with about half of one eye, seeing them just as clear as day.

"Ain't she somethin', Honk!" I heard Burl yell.

I squeezed my eye shut for a second, and when I looked back down in the street, it was empty and dark.

I turned back toward the woman. "Crawl?" I said, my voice shaky. "Did you say I'd have to crawl to the bed?"

"No—I didn't say crawl. I said—"

"And why are we in the dark? What are we, a couple of snakes breedin' under a rock?"

"Mister, are you crazy!"

I walked across the dark room and struck a match.

"No!" the woman said.

I lit the lantern and picked it up and turned toward the bed. The woman had pulled a blanket up in front of her, covering face and all.

I reached out and jerked it away.

"My God!" I said, stepping back in horror, wondering if what I was seeing could possibly be real.

At that moment, in that light and with those big, quick drinks of whiskey rushing to my brain, I'd have sworn that the woman on the bed was the same little ugly redhead that I found Burl naked and passed out with in Lusk, Wyoming—the only difference was that now she had red whelps and black bruises on her face, belly, and thighs where somebody had beaten her.

I wasn't in any frame of mind to stop and ponder how improbable it was that it was the same woman that Burl had been with in Lusk. I just grabbed my hat and the bottle of whiskey, threw five dollars on the bed, and was out the door, down the stairs, and into the street before my spur-jingle knew I had gone anywhere.

"You crazy son of—" the woman started screaming, but I'd

already put too much country between us by then to hear her recite my ancestry.

The same little man was at the livery stable when I got there in a long trot that had been there earlier—and he still had tobacco juice running out both corners of his mouth.

"I'll be gettin' my horses and gear," I said, handing him the money I owed him.

"Not till I tell the sheriff," he said, like that ended the matter for the night.

I grabbed ahold of his shirt front and jerked him close to me. "Then while you're at it, you can also tell the good sheriff how I rammed that wad of tobacco down your throat and plumb out the other end!"

"Okay, okay," he said, prying my fingers off his shirt, "the sheriff sure ain't goin' to like it none when I tell him in the morning, but you go ahead, mister, and get your horses and then get outa here—the sooner the better, too."

I made one other stop before departing Liberty that night. That was at Gerald's Mercantile Store, where Mr. Gerald lived in the back rooms with his wife.

"Mr. Gerald," I said after he answered my knock, "I sure hate to bother you at night like this, but I need to get some things out of your store."

He wrinkled his eyebrows and looked hard at me and said, "Well, I don't know . . ."

"Cash money," I assured him. "My money ought to be as good as anyone's—I've just got different hours. You see Dr. Russell told me not to get out except till after dark, on account of my eyes."

"Well, all right," he said. "I'll meet you at the front door."

When we got inside I dug around in my pockets and put all the money I had on the counter and asked him to count it. That money was what was left out of the XIT money Monte Canaster had paid me on the banks of Niobrara River the morning the XIT had gone on north without us.

"Eight dollars," he announced.

"Then load me up eight dollars worth of vitals in a sack—coffee, beans, canned milk, flour, tomaters, and stuff like that."

"Going somewhere, Mr. Smith?" he asked.

"Too blind to travel, Mr. Gerald," I said. "I just gotta get outa town and set me up a camp somewhere where a man won't feel so closed in . . . and someplace the devil can't ambush him."

When I left Liberty and rode into the night, I had just as well've had a patch over both eyes, because one was about as useless as the other in the dark. I couldn't see the stars up in the sky. I couldn't even see old Pat's ears, much less the ground, and although I'd had my share of dark-night rides before, this time was different. This time I felt handicapped and at a disadvantage from other night creatures, because it was an even *darker* night that surrounded me than surrounded any of them, be they man or beast. I don't know that I'd say it was fear I felt, but it was at least an uneasiness that bordered on fear, so as soon as I was far enough out that I couldn't hear the town dogs barking anymore, I pulled up and hobbled the horses. I got my bedroll off the back of the little bay and rolled it out in the sage. There I spent the night, Colt and Winchester on either side of me, listening to the horses graze and the coyotes yip and howl.

I wasn't scared, not anymore at least, about what I'd seen in town. I never had much sense, but I had enough to know that dead men don't hang around in streets looking up at windows, and that there was bound to be more than one redheaded woman of ill repute between Canada and Mexico. While I believed that, I still wasn't eager to go back to town and find out for sure. I figured that a man who was half blind didn't need the added burden of having to decide whether what he *was* seeing was real or whiskey-concocted.

"I'm swearin' off the stuff," I affirmed out loud. "I ain't touching another drop."

The horses stopped chewing and one of them, I figured it was old Pat, blew his nose. "I don't give a damn how many times you heard it before," I said. "This time I mean it!" I said that with the assurance that the bottle of whiskey I'd carried out of the hotel room was laying about two feet away on my saddle blanket. Being the experienced drink-quitter that I was by then, I knew that it put a lot less strain on an already overtaxed system if you have a bottle close by to check your progress. I mean, if you don't have anything to drink, it's kind of hard to tell whether you've really quit or not.

That night was darker than the pits of hell I remembered the Reverend Blackburn yelling about in church when I was a kid back in Kansas. And it was the longest and loneliest night I'd ever known, or ever would know—save one. I didn't sleep—not one time all night did my head droop or my shoulders relax.

Yes, it was a long, lonely, dark, and empty night. Like I said, the bottle of whiskey was close by, but I never reached for it. It had already failed me once in town, but from there I could run to the dark and hide. So, as much as I wanted a drink—as much as I wanted to be drunk—and as often as I started to reach for the bottle, I didn't. If it failed me again, and I was visited by ghosts and whoever, or whatever it or she was that had come to my room, where else could I run to? I guess, even though I was out in the middle of a big scope of sagebrush and hills, I felt more cornered that night than I ever had in my life.

CHAPTER 22

JUST like the night spent out in the sage after my running out of Liberty was the darkest and longest I'd ever known, the dawn that followed that night was about the most welcome I'd ever known. I put together a little pile of dead sagebrush sticks, built a small fire, and boiled a pot of coffee. Breakfast was a can of beans warmed over the fire. I'd done all of this and had saddled Pat and repacked the bay's load before the sun had ever broken free of the far eastern horizon.

I was disappointed in how little I could see. In fact, it seemed my vision was actually less than it had been the day before. The difference, of course, lay in what I had asked of my eyes the day before, and what I was asking of them then. The day before, I'd been in town where looking across the street and being able to tell the difference between the hotel and the livery had been enough. Now I was wanting—and needing—to look half a mile down a draw, or two miles to a mesa, or a dozen miles to the horizon. But everything much past a quarter-mile seemed to run together, like a watercolor painting that's gotten wet and has smeared. A quarter-mile limit of usable eyesight can keep a man from riding off something and getting killed, but it's sure not enough to let him pick out land features so he'll know where he is, or enough to let him see far enough ahead to figure on going around this or that wash, between those two mesas, and then topping out on that table above that creek, or so on.

So when I left the spot in the sage where I'd spent the night, I angled toward the northeast, traveling slow and mostly by instinct, and once I reached a tall mesa who's north

135

side dropped straight off two hundred feet into the Canadian River, I again made camp among some cedars and slept off and on until about the middle of the afternoon, when I broke camp and rode off the mesa and to the south.

It took even longer than I thought it might to find the homestead. I rode to the top of three different long ridges, all of which I'd have sworn was the one I was looking for, but they all had only grass and sagebrush at their base when I rode down. The sun had already started to go down again and I had begun to dread another night like the last one, when I topped another ridge and smelled smoke and heard a dog bark.

But I didn't ride on down right then. I wasn't sure if it was the right thing to do, so I held back, got off, twisted a cigarette, and smoked it down as the sun disappeared.

"Autumn said to come on down."

"I wheeled around, my gun jumping into my hand and my thumb earing the hammer back.

"Casey?" I said, cocking my head, trying to see in the dim light.

"Yeah . . . What's that black thing over your eye? Autumn said . . ."

"Good God, boy, what are you doin' sneakin' up on a man like that!" I lowered the hammer on the Colt and dropped it back into its holster.

"Weren't sneaking up on no one," he said, "just come up over there where it ain't so steep."

Then he bailed off the steep slope in front of me, digging his heels into the sand, quickly disappearing into the dusk. I gathered up old Pat's reins, mounted up, and went on down myself, still not sure it was what I should do or—wanted to do. I'm not sure which it was.

When I got down to the house Autumn was standing in the doorway holding something, I couldn't tell what, maybe a skillet.

"We're eating supper, Mr. Smith. Would you care to join us?"

"No, ma'am. Had me a big bait before I broke camp." I don't know why I said that, because I hadn't eaten since noon.

"Your eyes must have really gotten better."

I hesitated and then said, "Not so's you can really tell it."

"Oh, I thought with you out riding like this . . ."

"Pat's still got good eyes," I said.

I never was a man to ask favors of anyone, never needed any until then that I can recall, and I didn't exactly know the way to do it, especially from a lady like the one standing in the adobe doorway in front of me. She was the kind cowboys dreamed about at night and talked about around the wagon, but not the kind you ever expected to be leaning on your saddle horn in front of, asking if you could sleep in her barn.

"The invitation still goes, Mr. Smith, that I extended to you, about staying here until you can see better."

"I can stay in town, ma'am," I said, pushing my hat back with a thumb. "It's just that I think my sight might come back quicker out here where there's something to look at beside four walls and a ceiling. I can get along just fine campin' somewhere—or just rolling my bedroll out on top of the ridge yonder."

"Or you could roll it out in the barn," she said.

"Why, yes, ma'am," I said like that was one thought that had never occurred to me, "I guess I could do that for a day or two—if it wouldn't be any bother."

"And you're welcome to share what we have at our table."

"Mrs. Lewis, I'll do that under one condition," I said. "I'll work while I'm here, and you'll put the food I bought before I left Liberty in your cupboard and we'll all share that, too."

"Fine," she said, closing the deal. "Just help yourself to the accommodations in the barn. I'm sure Otis will enjoy your company."

Otis didn't enjoy my company that night—not that I thought he would anyway—because while everyone else was in the house, I turned my horses loose in the pen, rolled out my bed in the dark barn, and slept like a dead man.

By force of cowboy habit I was up early enough the next morning to smoke two cigarettes before the sun even began to push back the stars above the eastern horizon. As soon as I could see the windmill from the barn door, I walked over to it to get a drink and to wash my face. The wheel was turning slow and steady in the early morning breeze, but there was no more than a bare trickle of water coming out of the pipe. At times, that trickle tapered down to a drip. The trough into which the windmill pumped had only a couple of inches of water covering its bottom, where it should have had a foot and a half.

I wasn't much of a windmill man, but the truth is I'd worked on more of the things than I liked to admit. More and more outfits were putting them up in the cattle country where I did most of my roaming, and some of them even figured the cowboys ought to grease them and keep them pumping. I always figured I had too much money invested in leather to be doing common labor like that, and had quit more than one outfit for that very reason. Still, I knew enough about the greasy things to know what one sounded like when its pump leathers were wore out, and after listening closely to this one for a few seconds, I diagnosed that to be what was ailing it.

I remembered running across a couple of pulley blocks in the barn when I was looking for horseshoeing equipment during my first visit to the place. I found them in a corner, and as I was carrying them toward the door I met Otis coming out of the feed room, scratching his belly with his one arm.

"You think them pulley blocks will help keep you off the ground this time?" I knew he was talking about me getting bucked off in front of the barn and then later lying out there sick and passed out from a helping of that *Desierto de Pena*.

"Do you know if there's any pump leathers around here anywhere?" I asked, ignoring his remark.

"Yeah," he said, now scratching his head.

"Yeah what?" I said when he turned and started walking away.

He stopped and turned around again and said, "Yeah, I know if there's any pump leathers around here or not. That's what you asked, ain't it?"

"Let me see if I can put it some way so even your petrified brain can understand what I mean. If there's any pump leathers on this place and you don't hand 'em to me in five minutes, I'll cut some out of your hide and chink in the holes it leaves with screw worms."

His craggy old face split into a snaggletoothed grin and he walked back into the feed room, came back out in half a minute and handed me the pump leathers.

I climbed up to the top of the windmill tower and tied one of the pully blocks there. While I was up there, I greased the working parts of the motor with some axle grease I'd found in the barn, pretty well greasing myself in the process, too, of course. Like most cowboys, I was one who could get cow manure from tail-tassel to tongue-tip and not think much about it, but let me acquire a spot or two of grease and I started feeling plumb unsanitary. The rationale behind that being that cow manure was just good old clean grass that had passed through a cow and gotten limbered up, while there was no telling where the grease had come from.

After I got back on the ground, I tied the other pulley to one of the legs next to the ground. While I was doing that, I noticed that Otis and Casey were both sitting on the ground watching me. Then Mrs. Lewis called for Casey to come in so they could do his lessons, and Otis had the watching all to himself.

"Hope I'm doin' this to suit you," I said. The way he grinned, I figured I was.

I got the wrenches out of the barn and then put my saddle on the little bay, figuring I wouldn't embarrass Pat, him being a cow horse and all, by making him do windmill work.

I found a long, nester kind of rope in the barn and, after uncoupling the sucker rods above the ground, tied one end of it on the rod sticking out of the ground, ran the other end through the top pulley and then the bottom one, and then dallied it around my saddle horn.

I got on the bay, made him lean into the rope and walk forward, and the sucker rods started coming up out of the ground. It's hard, dirty work, pulling the rods out of a well, especially when you're doing it by yourself and you have to ride the horse forward until a place where two sucker rods are coupled together shows up above the ground; get off and uncouple the rods; get on and ride the horse toward the windmill until the sucker rod on the other end of the rope is on the ground; get off and take the rope off that sucker rod and put it on the next one sticking out of the ground. You do that as many times as there are sucker rods in the well, and if you do it like most cowboys, you get dirtier and madder with each one.

This was close enough work that I didn't have any trouble seeing what I was doing. Although by the time I rode the little bay out to the end of the rope, the sucker rods would be pretty fuzzy. The main trouble I had was that things just don't look the same when you're looking at them through one eye instead of two.

I'd worked about an hour when Otis stood up and dusted himself off. "You'll be havin' to do the rest of it by yourself," he said, "I gotta build a washin' fire for Miss Autumn."

About that time she stepped to the door of the adobe and said breakfast was ready.

"We don't say grace except for the evening meal, Mr. Smith, so you may go ahead and eat," she said, looking fresh and pretty in a clean calico dress and white apron and her auburn hair bunned up neatly at the back of her head.

We had fried eggs, hot biscuits, molasses, and coffee, eaten in silence except for the baby who kept crying and fussing and Mrs. Lewis who kept talking quietly to her.

"Thank you, ma'am," I said, putting my hat on and going out the door and back to work on the windmill.

I worked all through the hot morning. Some of the sucker rod couplings were covered with a mineral buildup from the water, and it took a lot of hammering and struggling and sweating and cussing to get them apart.

Casey and Otis sat on the ground and watched me until Mrs. Lewis called them to help her with a chore.

For dinner we had some of the food that I'd brought from Liberty—salt pork, beans, and potatoes. We ate in silence again—except for the baby again, who, this time, mostly gooed and bubbled. Mrs. Lewis's clothes weren't so clean now, and a few strands of hair were getting loose from the bun at the back of her head. As soon as I finished eating, I pushed back from the table, said, "Thank you, ma'am," and stepped out the door.

By the time I had the last sucker rod back in the well, the sun was no more than four fingers from the western horizon, and I was as wrung out as an old dishrag. I was covered with sweat and a tan, sort of greasy, rust. Every time I scratched my nose or touched my face anywhere with my hands, it left a dirty spot or streak. The new, blue flannel shirt and Levi's the boy in Liberty brought me from the mercantile were dirtier than if I'd been wearing them following a trail herd for a month, and even worse, where trail dust will shake off, the stuff from sucker rods won't.

I let off the brake on the windmill and put it in gear while Casey and Otis gathered around to watch. The wind blew and the windmill wheel whirled overhead, but no water came out of the pipe and the thing didn't sound any different than it had before I'd started to work on it about the time the sun was coming up. I saw Otis wink at Casey, and knew the old man couldn't have been any more pleased if I'd fallen off the top of the windmill.

But I knew that it takes pump leathers a little while to soak and swell up big enough to touch the sides of the working barrel and force the water up instead of letting it rush back. So I sat on the ground myself a few feet from Otis and Casey and rolled a cigarette and waited.

"I can pee a bigger stream than that," Otis said, looking at the trickle of water falling into the trough.

I rolled another smoke and waited some more, but no more water came.

"Supper," Autumn said from the doorway of the adobe.

I washed my face and hands as best I could in the trickle of water the windmill was making and walked to the house following Otis and Casey, convinced now, as they were, that my day's work had been for naught.

Mrs. Lewis's hair was now coming down in several places, there was black from the stove on her chin and forehead, her dress was dirty from cooking and washing and her face looked thin. She was holding the baby in one arm while she tended to getting supper on the table with the other. That left no hand to wipe off the sweat running down from her forehead and through the soot on her cheek.

"Our most gracious heavenly Father," she prayed softly before we ate supper, "the Maker and Giver of all things, we thank Thee for the day that is passing and for the blessings bestowed upon us in it. We pray that our labors have been pleasing in Thy sight. Forgive us our sins and shortcomings and watch over us through the coming night. Let us rest as well as we have labored, so we may be ready to labor again if Thou blesses us with another sunrise. We thank Thee especially tonight, Father, for the bounty Mr. Smith has brought us and for him fixing the windmill. We pray that his eyesight well be restored so he may soon leave. And we pray, Father, for the souls of the ones who lost their lives here. Just as Thy

Son showed mercy to a thief on the cross, so we pray for mercy for the souls of those two men. Amen."

I glanced over at Otis who was looking at me and grinning.

"I'm afraid I didn't get the windmill fixed, ma'am," I said.

"Then maybe tomorrow, Mr. Smith," she said.

We ate without talking anymore then, with me never taking my eyes off my plate unless it was to reach for some more food. About the time I was sopping up the last of the juice in my plate with a biscuit, Mrs. Lewis said, "If you want, I'll wash your clothes tomorrow."

"No water to wash 'em in," Otis said.

"If there is no windmill water," she said, "I can go to the river and wash."

"But I . . ." I started.

Mrs. Lewis stood up, went to a dark corner of the candle-lit adobe and came back carrying a shirt and pair of pants. "I didn't mean for you to go around naked tomorrow, Mr. Smith. These clothes belonged to my sister's husband. I think they should fit you."

I took the clothes, pushed back from the table, and stood up. "Thank you, ma'am," I said.

"We usually sing songs or read after supper, if you'd care to join us."

"No, ma'am," I said, "believe I'll go to the barn and see about my horses and then turn in."

On my tired walk from the house to the barn I happened to hear something that bent my course by way of the windmill. It was water—a pipe plumb half-full of it running into the trough. The windmill was pumping more than I ever thought it would, and would have the trough full and running over by morning. I couldn't help but grin.

I pulled off my dirty clothes, collapsed on my bedroll, and fell asleep in a few minutes, listening to a cricket chirping in the barn and the windmill working slow and steady in the background.

CHAPTER 23

THE next two days passed much like my first one back at the homestead had—that is, with hard work, big meals—but with the only meat being a little salt pork in the beans—and the passing of very few words between me and anybody else. There was much that needed to be done around the place, even an old leather-pounder like myself could see that. The tail end of one project would usually always lead to the beginning of another. Like putting in the new pump leathers in the windmill so it would pump more water meant having to fix the holes in the trough so it would hold that extra water. Or tying up the poles that made the corrals beside the barn meant having to dig postholes and reset the posts so they would hold up those poles.

I suppose I acted sullen, and I suppose I was. I was still feeling sorry for myself, I guess. Although I tried not to, I couldn't help but think about what all had happened to me since the day me and Burl came back to break camp on old Charlie Castle's range and found Powers and DuPree there drinking our coffee. It seemed like that particular little nightmare had occurred a long time ago, maybe a couple of years anyway, so much had happened since then. Of course, I knew it hadn't been very long ago that it happened, but when I got to figuring it up and realized that it had been only *nineteen days* it seemed . . . Well, it seemed as impossible to me as a cowpony learning to play pinochle!

How could it be that in a stretch of nineteen days—I guess, twenty if you count the actual day of the shooting up there in Wyoming—but that in twenty days I'd shot a United States deputy marshall twice—either bullet hitting him in a place vital enough to have surely killed him before sundown—had buried a man I once thought a friend in a shallow grave in Colorado, while watching what I was afraid was a posse out of the corner of my eye, had dropped into New Mexico hoping to find ten thousand dollars, but instead had killed two more men, lost an eye, and was then doing handyman work on a homestead! All of this to a man in twenty days, when for the first thirty-five years of his life he'd never been involved in anything more serious than a cowtown brawl, and whose idea of a wild time was riding a running horse across holey ground!

I tried not to think about it by staying busy. I worked harder than I had in years, maybe in my whole life. I worked and didn't talk. Otis said to me one time as we met at the door of the barn, "You were a lot more fun when you were gettin' farted off or drunk and sick."

For supper that third day we had one of the chickens. "She hasn't been laying," Mrs. Lewis volunteered. "Besides, a man working as hard as you've been needs more meat in his diet that a little salt pork in the beans."

"Mr. Smith?" Casey said, beginning just about the longest conversation at the table I'd been in. "Why do you always wear that gun?"

"Just a habit, I guess, Casey," I said.

"Are you a gunfighter?"

"Casey!" Autumn said. "Eat."

"Are you?" Casey asked again.

"Naw," I said, "don't even know what one is. I'm just a cowpuncher."

"Then how'd you know how to kill those two men like you did?" he asked.

I glanced to the other end of the table and saw Mrs. Lewis look hard at the boy and then look at me. I looked down at my plate and said. "I didn't use a gun, you know that. Besides, boy, killing—and dying—come natural. They can happen without your even trying, it's livin' that's hard."

After supper there was still a little daylight left so I went back to work, this time nailing loose boards back up on the barn. I was thinking about Pat, too, wondering if Casey had forgot about his evening chores, one of which was to go out and bring in their horse—and now mine, too.

There not being any feed on the place, I didn't have any choice but to hobble my horses out a ways from the house, so they could graze. I didn't like the thought of not having either of them right there near me so I could get to them if I had a sudden urge—or need—to leave quick, so I'd just let Casey take one at a time out to graze with their old brown, smooth-mouthed Chester and leave the other one in the pen beside the barn. I worried about old Pat most because, for all of his orneriness, I knew he had a lot more bottom and heart than the little bay, and he would be the one that would carry me out of trouble if any horse could.

For that reason, I didn't want night to come with Pat not in the corrals, so as soon as I saw Casey and Otis coming out of the house I said, "Casey, you better shinny up the windmill so you can spot the horses and get 'em in before dark."

"Oh, I was aimin' to tell you," Otis said, grinning like a dog passing a peach seed, "I seen that sorrel of yours runnin' off with a pack of mules." The day before, he had seen a panther kill him, and the day before that a "chicken-jumpin' sorrel-horse buzzard" had sucked out all of his insides and left nothing but the hide and hoofs.

"Better get up the windmill and get 'em spotted," I said to Casey, "and then I'll go with you to get 'em."

Casey stopped two-thirds of the way up the windmill tower, looked around a little bit, and then hollered, "There they are, over there," pointing toward the southeast.

"See anything else?" I asked, meaning, specifically, but not saying it in so many words, Do you see any high sheriffs heading our way?

"N-o-o," he said, turning his head around like an owl. Then, "Yeah, over yonder!"

"What is it?" I asked.

"Is it a little fat Mexican peddlin' *Desierto de Pena?*" asked Otis.

"It's some cows," Casey said.

Me and Otis both said, "Oh."

"But it looks like there's a milk cow with 'em," Casey said.

While Casey was climbing down, Mrs. Lewis stepped out under the sagging porch and said, "Do you think it could be our cow?"

"Can't say ma'am," I said. "After we get the horses in we can go look, though."

After me and Casey went out and brought the horses in and let them water, I threw my saddle on old Pat. Casey led Chester up beside the corral fence and jumped onto his bare back with Otis following in hot pursuit, looking like a pair of monkeys I saw one time riding a horse in a circus in Abilene.

By then Mrs. Lewis had walked over to stand beside Chester's left shoulder. She'd left her sun bonnet in the house and her soft hair was falling down about her shoulders, the slanting rays of the setting sun making it shine as much as her blue eyes sparkled.

"The baby is asleep," she said cheerfully, "so I think I'll walk out with you."

"A person afoot will probably booger the cows, ma'am," I said.

"Oh," she said, and I could see the happiness leaving from her face like those old cows would leave the flat if she wandered out there afoot.

"I'm afraid old Pat here or my bay are neither one the squirt-ridin' kind or you could ride one of them." Then I looked over at Chester and the pair of monkeys he was carrying and said, "Looks like the sway in old Chester's back is plenty big for three, though."

"What do you say, boys?" Mrs. Lewis said, looking up at Casey and Otis. "If I promise to never tell anybody you let a woman ride with you."

Otis couldn't have been any more agreeable, of course. He might have been old *and* snaggletoothed *and* one-armed, but he was still alive, and *any* man in that condition would have been more than agreeable to have a woman like Autumn Lewis ride with him. Casey could only see the humiliation in it, I'm sure. But he didn't say much and in a few minutes was all smiles again looking ahead like he was trying to see the far end of a strung-out head of Texas Longhorns going up the trail.

Chester wasn't craving the trail like Casey was, though, and hadn't moved a hoof since he was led up beside the fence. So Mrs. Lewis got on board like Casey and Otis had, being careful that her dress didn't come much past the tops of her worn shoes. She was laughing like a girl, and even a sullen, one-eye cowboy could see how beautiful she was.

The cows were southwest of the place about a half mile, just where the long ridge on that side sloped down to a small flat surrounded by low, sage-covered hills.

There were eight head of cows, some with calves. The bunch was a little ringy at the sight of us, but instead of breaking and running they just stopped eating and threw their heads up.

"Well, there's a Jersey in there all right," I said. "'Bout four or five years old. She's dry now, but she's springin' pretty heavy. Can't see a brand on her from here, but she's got an underbit earmark in the left ear and swaller-fork in the right. Her right horn turns in sharp near the tip like it's been broke some time in the past, and as short as her tits are, I'd say this'll be her first calf. Any of that sound familiar?"

"I don't even know what half of what you said means," Autumn said, still smiling. "But ours *was* a Jersey, the man I bought her from said this *would* be her first calf, and she *did* break a horn the day he brought her to us. If she had any kind of brand on her, I never knew it—but then I don't know a lot about cows—not yet, anyway. She was pretty wild before. Do you think we can pen her?"

"I think with *this* I can," I said, holding up my catch rope, "but I don't think we'll ever be able to *drive* her in the pens."

I stepped off and tightened my cinches, then got back in the saddle and dropped the horn loop over the saddle horn and pulled it tight. Then I started shaking out a loop.

"Ever use one of them things before?" Otis asked.

I cocked my head a little and looked at the old man like a bull on the prod. "Otis," I said in a low voice. Then I just looked at him for a couple of seconds with nobody saying anything, and nobody but him smiling. Then a smile that I couldn't hold back started creeping out of me, and I said, "I got this eye patch to prove it."

Then we all smiled—me, Casey, Otis, and Autumn. I guess that was the first time we all smiled at the same time. We didn't say anything, but our smiles grew bigger, all of us, I guess with the exception of little Casey, knowing what I meant and somehow seeing the humor in it.

"I'll circle around 'em and head 'em in the direction of the house until they start scatterin'. Then I'll build to your little wayward gal and give her a little hemp education."

The bunch pretty well stayed together until they were within a quarter-mile of the house, before they started fanning out. I gave Pat his head and touched him with both spurs. All I had to do was show him which one we were after and he would follow her like a coyote after a rabbit.

A cowboy ropes a lot of stock if he stays with the profession for a while, and there's no way he can remember them all. A few he remembers all his life, though. Some loops he's thrown he'd like to forget, but they were so bad he can't. And some were so good he reminds himself of them every chance he gets. But out of all the stock I ever roped, and out of all the loops, both good and bad, that I ever threw, I remember that Jersey cow and the loop that caught her the best.

Just about the time Pat had me close enough behind her that it was time to get my loop up in the air, I started wondering just what would happen *this* time. Would I get bucked off or get in some kind of a storm? That seemed to be the general run of things whenever the Homestead Congregation was on hand. I knew their eyes were all on me, and all of a sudden I felt the pressure to do this thing right.

I didn't know it until then, but I wanted to make a good impression on them. I wanted to prove to them that I could do *something* right, not only just right, but *good*, too.

I guess that's the reason I remember roping the Jersey that day so well and the loop I used to do it. It was the first loop I'd thrown since I'd become one-eyed, and that only added to the pressure, because I was still having trouble judging distance accurately.

I knew that the horns on a Jersey couldn't be depended on to hold—they might and they might not, but I didn't want to chance it. I spurred Pat on up to the cow, and she was running faster than I ever thought a Jersey could. She bent a little to the right, but I waited. It's hard for a right-handed man to throw a good neck loop going to the right.

Then she went back slightly toward the left, and I knew that was the loop I wanted. I reared up in my stirrups and mailed it to her. When I turned it loose, I knew it was a good loop—a man can usually tell the instant he turns one loose whether it will fit or not. It went around her neck like it had eyes. The slack in the loop formed a perfect figure eight that slapped her left side when I pulled it back. When I pitched the slack up in the air, old Pat knew we weren't going to trip her, so he dropped his sorrell butt and slid on his hocks for about eight feet. The cow hit the end of the rope running hard, was jerked up in the air, made a slow half-turn, and landed flat on her side facing me and Pat.

It all happened just the way I hoped it would, maybe even better. I glanced toward the Homestead Congregation all perched neatly in the sway of Chester's back. Casey had laid the reins across the old brown's neck and was clapping his hand. Mrs. Lewis was smiling. Maybe I couldn't from that distance, especially with my weak vision, but I thought I could even see the dimples in her cheeks, she was smiling so big.

CHAPTER 24

JUST before I'd roped the Jersey, I saw that she was springing even heavier than I said she was. As a matter of fact, I thought I could see a yellowish white hoof underneath her tail now and then. That meant that her time had come. Her water must have already broken and it was odd that she hadn't gone off by herself to calve, but she hadn't.

After I got the cow to the corrals at the house, I didn't slip my rope off her, but instead let her cross over it, and when she did, I spurred Pat out to the end of it hard enough to jerk her down again. Then I jumped off and ran back to her and tied her down with a piggin' string while Pat kept the slack out of the rope. When I stood up, I turned and said to the Congregation, all watching me from outside the corral fence, "She's tryin' to calve."

"Oh, how wonderful!" Mrs. Lewis said. "Isn't that wonderful, Casey?"

"I guess so," little Casey said, "but what does it mean?"

"It means she's going to have a baby!" Mrs. Lewis answered.

Casey's eyes got big. "She is? How's she gonna do that?"

I answered that question myself. "She's not—not without some help anyway." I walked to the back of the cow, rolled up my sleeve, and ran my hand inside her. "What I was afraid of," I said. "The calf's head is turned back."

"Oh *my*," Mrs. Lewis said. "Is there anything you can do?"

"I'll see, but the calf may already be dead. If he is, the rot may have already set in on the cow, and she'll die too." I rolled my other sleeve up and said, "We'll just have to see. I can't make any promises."

"This is God's world, Mr. Smith, and He is in control.

Somehow, I can't see Him bringing the cow back to us carrying a dead calf."

I started to say that I couldn't see the point in Him letting a cow carry a dead calf around in side of her no matter where she was; but I didn't say anything, I just went to work.

Remember the confession I made earlier about maybe being a little worthless when I hit a town? I guess I proved that in Liberty all over again just a few days earlier when I fell to the temptations of liquor and flesh, or tried to, even though I made a mighty poor hand at it. But I also said I wasn't useless *out* of town, on a cow outfit. Well, I wouldn't exactly call one hundred-sixty acres, one smooth-mouthed horse, and a Jersey cow a cow outfit, but even on a big outfit, when you have to pull calves, you pull them one at a time.

The Congregation came inside the corral and gathered around me and the cow, with Casey hanging back like he was afraid something might jump out of her and get him, but Mrs. Lewis got down on her knees beside me wanting to help.

I tried with one hand, and then the other, and then with both at the same time to reach inside the cow and pull the calf's head around, but things were too tight and slick inside there to get it done. The sun slid out of sight, but at the same time a huge orange moon started rising on the opposite end of the world and throwing off enough soft light to work by.

"Is the calf . . . ?"

I shook my head. "I think he's dead . . . I guess your God must've took the night off or maybe he took Mrs. God over to Endee to a dance . . . No, wait a minute! By golly, I was wrong, the little booger's still alive after all. He's sucking' on my finger right now."

"I guess God didn't go to Endee after all, Mr. Smith," she said, smiling a pretty I-told-you-so smile in the moonlight.

"Well, I can't hold that against Him," I said. "You ever been to Endee?"

She bent over in soft laughter. It was easy to laugh that night, and a really good time to be alive.

I finally managed to run my fingers in the calf's nostrils, and by so doing was then able to pull its head around.

"Now," I said, "if you'll take that piggin' string on the ground behind you, maybe both of us can get it looped around his front hoofs."

"Like this?" she said.

"You need to slide over closer to me," I said, "so we'll both have the same angle on the calf's legs. Now, you try to get it over the hoof on your side, and I'll try to get it over mine . . . Good. Now, you pull the piggin' string real slow and I'll try to keep it from comin' off . . . Okay . . . There it is. We're in business now . . . Let's both pull on the piggin' string, and we need to pull down toward the cow's feet a little instead of just pulling straight back . . . There comes his head . . ."

Then, suddenly, once we pulled the calf out past the shoulders, it came out in a gush. "A heifer calf," I announced.

"Oh, she's a pretty red thing too," Autumn said, "with a white face and white feet."

"Yeah," I said. I picked the calf up by her hind legs and shook as much slime out of her throat and lungs as I could. And then, seeing that the piggin' string around the cow's feet was coming loose, I said, "We'd better all clear out of here. When she gets up, she's gonna be a little out of snuff. Her and the calf will be better off if we stay plumb away from 'em till mornin'."

"I'll go in and boil some water for coffee then," Autumn said, "as sort of a celebration. Mr. Smith, you *will* join us won't you, since without your help we wouldn't have anything to celebrate."

I hesitated a second and then said, "Yes, ma'am, I will. I'll be in as soon as I unsaddle Pat and wash up."

That was the first time I "shared the candle" in the house. We sat in the dim and flickering light, talking and laughing about the cow and her new calf. I'd been on outfits where several thousand times as many calves were born without causing near so much joy. Twice during that first candle-sharing, the lady I couldn't keep my eyes off of caught me admiring her. I could tell it embarrassed her, but if it offended her in any way, she never showed it.

Anyway, I couldn't have helped it even if it had bothered her. I'd never seen anybody like her, so like an angel who had just laid her wings aside and dropped out of heaven on one hand, and yet, on the other, so capable of getting on her knees in a dusty corral and helping to pull a bloody, slimey calf out of a cow—and not only capable of doing it, but smiling the whole time too. And my admiring, this time, wasn't just for her face and figure, but for the whole person that was her. For, as I drank my second cup of coffee and watched her rocking the baby, I saw that it was that special warmth and love inside her that made the outside so beautiful. Then I grinned and thought to myself, as I said good night and stepped out onto the porch, Good grief, Honk, where in the thunder are you gettin' your thoughts lately? You better get on out to the barn and get a strong whiff of saddle leather and horse sweat, and maybe that will clear your head up!

Like I said, it was easy to laugh that night, even at myself. But the smell of saddle leather and horse sweat and even a little good-natured ribbing of Will Smith by Honk Ballard wasn't enough to keep him from laying awake way into the night, thinking about things that had nothing to do with killing or dying—or running.

The next few days passed quickly and quietly. I rode Pat to the mesa north of the house and chopped down a cedar tree that I drug back to the house and trimmed and placed under the porch, taking out most of its sag. I cleaned out the barn and rebuilt the milking stall, building a milking stanchion out of more cedars cut on the mesa top and drug to the homestead. I fashioned a halter for the cow since she had to be staked out to graze, and, a few days after her calf was born, I started breaking her to milk, which I could see would be no easy chore for she was about the world's best at cow-kicking a milk bucket and cowboy. All this time I never unbuckled the gunbelt from around my waist, but the number of times a day I stopped and looked carefully to the hills all around the homestead for riders coming grew less. I looked forward to each day of work in a way I never had before, and for a reason I wasn't quite sure of.

One night during supper, Autumn said out of the clear blue sky, "I've picked out a name for the baby."

"I thought that *was* her name," Otis said. "Baby Walking Horse."

"No," she said, "her name is Willa. This is the Sunday the priest comes to Liberty. I would like to get her christened and for everybody to be there. Will you go with us, Mr. *Will* Smith—since she's being named after you?"

I choked on my food and almost got down on the floor. "After me? *Why?*"

"Why? I guess because you've been a special person in our lives and—"

I got up from the table and went to the barn. I knew Mrs. Lewis would be out in a few minutes, and I decided that I had to tell her the truth. Just how *much* of the truth I'd tell her I hadn't decided yet—but how could I let her name the baby after me? How could I go on making her believe I was somebody special and something I was not? For if there was a Will Smith anywhere in the world who was a special enough person for a woman like her to name a baby after, it sure wasn't the feller standing in the boots at the ends of *my* legs.

I went out to the corrals and looked over at the milk cow and the little calf sucking her. I was there when she came out of the house. "I couldn't remember whether or not I'd shut the gate," I said, like that was the reason I'd left the supper table in so big of a hurry.

"I have something to tell you," I said. There was enough twilight left to see her blue eyes, but I didn't want to look into them, because they had a way of looking too deep inside a man, of seeing more than they ought to.

"No," she said, "first I have to tell *you* something. Do you remember the day you roped this cow and we pulled her calf? That cow was in terrible trouble and you saved her by delivering that calf. In a way, you came along and saved both of us. You saved her from not being able to have her calf and me from those two terrible men.

"A woman as old as I am ought to have known better than to think I was in love with Burl—or even more, to think that he loved me—then those two terrible men never would have been here."

"But . . ." I was going to say that I came here for the exact same reason those two terrible men had, but she wasn't finished.

"But you did even more for me than just save my life, Will Smith. You've restored my faith in life, and you've shown me there are decent, gentle men . . . And whether or not you believe it, Will, *I* believe you were sent here."

I looked down into blue eyes swimming in tender tears looking up at me, and I could no more have *not* leaned over and kissed the two soft lips so pink in the moonlight and slowly rising to meet mine, than I could have jumped over the moon.

The kiss didn't last but a couple of seconds, just long enough for me to feel the warmth and doe-skin softness of her lips, to smell her sweet breath, and know the excitement of her body gently against mine. That was all I felt during that short kiss, nothing more—just the things that have caused kingdoms to be built and lost and men to kill and die since the beginning of time.

The lady broke off the kiss as gently as she had begun it, and then turned and walked swiftly back into the house. Maybe a different man, a stronger man, could have stopped her before she got to the house and told her she had been right not to have had faith in life and in men, that she had been lied to from the very first by the man she had just kissed for restoring that same faith to her. I don't doubt but what that is what I should have done right then, but when a man's lips are burning from a fresh woman-warm kiss and the sweet smell of her is lingering in the night air about him, telling that woman what a fool she is and breaking her heart—not to mention her faith—somehow doesn't seem as honorable as it might if he were just looking at the cold facts in daylight.

CHAPTER 25

THAT night—the night of a lady's gentle kiss and a cowboy's failure to do the obvious most-honorable thing toward her—I lay on my bedroll for a long time, staring up into the blackness inside the barn. After a few hours of sleepless thinking, I lit a candle, rolled my bed, caught and saddled old Pat, and then started packing the little bay to travel.

In my shuffling around I woke Otis up and he stood in his doorway and watched me, not with any great deal of interest, but like it was the only thing he had to do at the time.

"Pullin' out, huh?" he said as I was tucking away the bottle of whiskey I had left over from my last frolicking, fun-filled night in Liberty into a safe fold of my bedroll.

"Yeah," I said without looking up.

"*Runnin'* out," he said.

"No . . . just pullin' out," I said, stepping into my chaps. "It's past time I was driftin'."

"You see all right now?"

"Good enough."

"You're not sayin' good-bye to Miss Autumn and Casey?"

"You can tell 'em for me," I said, checking Pat's latigo and pulling it a little tighter. "Anyway, I figure they'll be able to tell I'm gone."

"Hell of way to treat a lady, ain't it?"

I slipped into my mackinaw, gathered up Pat's bridle reins, and the bay's lead rope, looked over at Otis, and said, "A man does what he has to do, Otis . . . It ain't all the time what he *wants* to do."

"It must be a hard trail you're travelin', huh?" he said.

I stood up close to Pat and with one hand on his neck and the other on the saddle horn of my old Padgitt Brothers saddle, I put my left foot deep into an oxbow stirrup and said, "A hard trail? Yeah . . . it's called life." Then I stepped up on Pat, settled down into leather, and started our little traveling troupe towards the darkness waiting for us outside. As that darkness surrounded us, I said, "A *hell* of a hard trail, Otis . . . to nowhere—'cept maybe a lonely grave."

I rode to the top of the ridge west of the homestead and pulled up and looked back. My vision was better. It had improved steadily over the past few days without my really noticing it until then. With that one eye I could see about all the stars the night sky offered, but I couldn't see the homestead below me, not even an outline of the buildings. Maybe there's nothing down there at all, I thought, but sand and safebrush. Maybe there's no Autumn Lewis, just like there's no Will Smith.

It wasn't long before the dark night sky in the east began to grow a little pale, and the sun, somewhere still far below that side of the world, started snuffing out a few stars—not long, but long enough, if a man had kept a horse pulled up between his knees, to have trotted two or three miles. But instead of keeping Pat pulled up between my knees, I stepped off and squatted down on my haunches on top of the ridge and stayed that way like an old coyote without moving, while the east got more and more color in it. I couldn't put a conscious reason for staying so long on the ridge when my mind was so made up to leave, but the fact is I stayed there as the night slowly but steadily turned to dawn.

Then, where just a few minutes earlier there had been nothing but blackness, the homestead below me began to take shape. I heard the Jersey cow bawl to be let in with her calf. I could see a patch of soft, white frost, the first of the season, on the bare ground in front of the barn. From the small stovepipe sticking up from the flat roof of the adobe, a thin gray ribbon of smoke drifted lazily upward before tailing off toward the north and disappearing. One of the horses behind me stopped grazing and blew his nose, maybe impatient to be on the trail again.

"A hell of a hard trail to nowhere," I said under my breath, repeating the words I'd said to Otis and thinking about what lay ahead for me, the same thing that lay behind me—hard rides, hard women, and hard liquor to forget both.

I saw Otis walking from the barn to the house for breakfast, and a few seconds later Autumn came out of the house and went into the barn. In a few more seconds she came back out, walking slower and holding her arms against the chill.

Then she saw me and the horses up on the ridge where the sun had just reached, and came to the near corner of the house and stood there beside the little cottonwood, just like she had been doing when I saw her for the first time three weeks earlier. She had her apron on, and the morning breeze was just enough to move the long hem of her gingham dress. Seeing her down there looking like a strong but lonesome stand of timber, and remembering her warm lips on mine from the night before, a lump came up in my throat that I couldn't swallow, and some moisture from the cool fall air settled into my eye that I had to blink twice to get out.

I stood up and got back in the saddle, but I didn't head south. I pointed Pat downhill again, working on the lump in my throat and the collected moisture in my eye as the horses worked their way to the bottom of the steep slope on their hocks.

From there, you know the story for the next year and two months as well as I, Autumn. There was nothing untrue about Will Smith for the next fourteen months, and there was nothing untrue about us. God, we lived and loved, didn't we, Autumn! With the suddenness and brightness of a sky rocket going up on a black summer's night. If I told you now that many times over those fourteen months I wanted to tell you the truth about who I was and why I really came to the homestead, I'd be lying. Deep inside me I knew I *should* tell you, but there was never a time I *wanted* to or started to.

If I had've told you about me shooting Ben DuPree and leaving him to die in Wyoming, and of coming here to find Burl's stolen money and taking it to Mexico with me, I think you would have still loved me, but it would have been different between us, Autumn. Would your eyes still have lit up and sparked as much when they looked into mine, still seen me with as much admiration? I was afraid not. I was your hero, although not a very admirable one to begin with, but sent from God, or so you believed, to save you, and I was willing, as Will Smith, to play that role as well and as long as I could.

It seemed like we never were content from that moment on to sit back and watch life go by, but wanted to be a part of it, every minute, every second—you as much as me.

Beginning that very morning, we headed straight into life, sidling off from nothing, savoring everything. It is as real to me in this cold, lonely dugout with my last candle burning down as it was that sunny fall morning . . .

CHAPTER 26

HOW well I remember the chill in the air, the smell of horse hair and saddle leather, the strong feel of Pat between my legs as I stopped him a few feet in front of you, then as soon as I stepped to the ground, the feel of you, warm and soft in my arms, the clean smell of your dress and hair. You cried softly with your head on my chest—the only time I remember any tears shed between us, for, after that, we never had time for melancholy or tears.

I put a hand under your chin and raised your face. No words were needed and none were said. Your lips were soft, warm, and moist against mine, full of the soft promises of womanhood that are passed without words, full of the wild beckonings of a deep, beautiful, unexplored canyon.

Our lips came apart slowly. "You have a bad habit of leaving without saying good-bye," you said, wiping your tears with your apron.

"Old habits die hard," I said, "but . . ."

"Seems to me that for a man as far behind in his driftin' as you said you were when you *pulled* out before daylight this morning, you sure got back awful fast." We looked up and there stood Otis, his white-stubbled face stretched into a grin wide enough to have lost a wagon in, his hand on little Casey's red, tousled head of hair.

"Trouble was old Pat," I said. "He's been around you nesters so long, he's barn-spoiled. When we got up there on the ridge, he sulled up and wouldn't take the trail. D'rectly he took the bit in his mouth and down off that ridge we came. Wouldn't much else I could do but come along with him."

163

"Want me to get in behind him and try to drive him off?" Otis said. "Or could it just be that the problem ain't one of being barn-spoiled but widder-eyed sweet, and I ain't talkin' about horseflesh here neither."

"Otis," I said, trying to rib him as deep as he was me, "it's a dirty shame there's not some way to bottle some of your hot air and ship it to the Klondike, where somebody might appreciate it at least a little bit!"

Then I looked around the homestead and said, "Right after breakfast I'll hitch my bay here and old Chester to the wagon and go up on the mesa north of here to chop firewood. Winter's comin' on, and I better get busy."

"Oh, good! I'll pack a lunch and go with you," you said, your eyes dancing.

"Oh, boy, a picnic!" Casey and Otis exclaimed together.

"But not for you two," you said, "you'll have to stay here and watch Willa. Will and I will cut wood by ourselves today."

Do you remember how much wood I chopped that day, Autumn? According to Otis, about enough to build a fire big enough to singe the pinfeathers off one chicken! It was a little more than that, but not much to show for a whole day's work! But it wasn't a day for chopping wood and working hard. It was a day for talking and laughing . . .

"Why did you come back this morning?" you asked, when we were barely out of the hearing of Otis and Casey.

"Because I couldn't leave," I answered truthfully.

"Are you going to stay?"

"Stayin's something I haven't practiced much for over twenty years."

"*I* want you to stay, and I think I can make *you* want to stay too."

"Wanting doesn't always rule, Autumn . . . Why do you want me to stay?"

"Because I love you."

"You know it just like *that?*" I said, snapping my fingers.

"I know it because it feels right for us to be together. Because I'm happy when we're together. I know it because . . ."

"Because God meant for it to be?"

"You don't believe in God do you, Will?"

"Probably not. Not like you do, anyway. That's all pretty hard for an old cowboy to understand. There's some bad things happen in this old world—three people have died right there on the homestead since I rode in—and I killed two of 'em!"

"Does that bother you a lot?"

"To tell the truth, Autumn, while I remember it, it all seems to have happened in a dream and wasn't real. It seems like I was watching somebody else do it all. You think God brought me here to kill those two, don't you?"

"No, I don't believe He brought you here to kill anybody, but I believe He watches over us in a broad sort of way. Those men didn't have to die—they chose to do what they did. And I even think God loved them too."

"Then God must be a pretty easy feller to get along with, is all I've got to say.

"You talk about the bad things that happen, but there's good things too."

"Yeah, there's good things, but even some of them are hard to understand."

"Like love?"

"Yeah, I guess so."

"It's God's greatest gift to us."

"But what about you and Burl?"

"What about us?"

"You thought you loved him, didn't you? You probably thought that God sent him, didn't you? I've talked to Dr. Russell some about you and Burl and . . . Well, it didn't sound like a marriage made in heaven."

"Sometimes evil can be dressed up to look terribly good,

Will, and just coming out of a convent, I'd been so protected I didn't realize that. When my sister and her husband died and left me alone with Casey and the homestead, I was scared. It seemed impossible that we could make it. And then big, strong, good-looking Burl Lewis came along and charmed me right off my feet! I was a fool, and I admit it. I was looking for nearly *anybody*—although I didn't realize it at the time—and then along came Burl . . . Just believing in God doesn't keep us from making mistakes, Will—and Burl was a big one."

"Dr. Russell has a theory that Burl saw you as a 'thirty-year-old vestal virgin' of some kind, and that's what he was after," I said, having trouble believing I'd said it after it was out of my mouth.

"I think Dr. Russell was right. At least I think he was right in theory . . . but he was wrong in fact—just like Burl was."

I thought about that for a second or two and then said, "You mean . . ."

"I mean, why does everybody automatically think every nun is a virgin? I wasn't born a nun, you know, wasn't one all of my life—not until I was eighteen years old."

I said again, "You mean—

"I mean, if *that's* why Burl married me, he was about fifteen years too late. A boy back in Pennsylvania named Freddy Fodheckler beat him to it."

"What!" I said.

"Well . . . the girls all called him *Fancy* Freddy Fodheckler," you said with a teasing grin.

I laughed so hard I had to stop the wagon and get out and lay on my back in the grass. When I could finally talk, I leaned up on an elbow and said, "Do you mean that some skinny kid named *Fancy Freddy Fodheckler* beat charming, handsome Burl Lewis to you . . ."

I can see it like it was happening right now, see you sitting on the wagon seat with your legs crossed, an elbow on your knee and your chin in your hand, your eyebrows raised.

"That's ri-ght," you said. Then we both laughed until we cried.

When we finally quit laughing enough so we could start on toward the mesa, you said, "Will, I don't want to talk about Burl after this, but I think you have a right to know about us. When he found out I wasn't a virgin, he became furious. He called me more filthy names than I knew there were. Some of the milder ones were whore, slut, and cheat. Then he hit me with his fists. Some honeymoon, wouldn't you say?"

"After we'd been married about three months, I was in town one day and Dr. Russell asked if I'd come by his office alone. When I got there he was embarrassed and nervous, but he said there was something he had to tell me or he wouldn't be able to live with himself. He was one of the first people, other than my sister and her husband and Casey, that I met after I got out here. He was out at the homestead a lot because of the fever we had then, and we came to be pretty close.

"He said he hated to have to tell me, but there were a couple of 'girls'—prostitutes—in town who had disease, and he knew for a fact that Burl was not only 'cavorting'—that was the word *he* used, but I could have used another—but he told me Burl wasn't only cavorting with the ones who had disease, but with nearly all the others as well.

"It wasn't any great shock to me that Burl was cavorting in town—I learned real quick not to be shocked by *anything* he did. But the disease and all . . . It was the last straw, and when Burl came home about three days later, he found all of his things piled up outside. He was already mad because just a couple of weeks before that was when I let Otis move into the barn.

"Burl knocked the door down and came in the house, beat me again, and forced himself on me. Then he left. Once a week for the next three weeks, he would come out about half drunk and do the same thing—beat me with his fists and force himself on me. Dr. Russell found out about it and went to Sheriff Betters, but Betters told him what went on between a man and his wife was none of the law's business.

"The last time Burl came out he even brought along a friend . . . No, the friend didn't have me too, but he was sitting at the table while Burl did! After that he never came back, though. Then you came a few months later and said, thank God—and may He forgive me for saying it!—that Burl was dead."

"I was lucky—I never got the disease . . . And now here you and I are. So you see, something good has come out of something bad."

After we got to the top of the mesa and chopped a little wood, we stopped for a snack underneath a cottonwood tree.

"What are you looking at?" you asked.

"I was just wondering . . . If I had *two* eyes would you look twice as good, or half as good."

You picked up a stick and threw it at me, but missed and hit the horses, boogering them and making them run off with the wagon. They stopped two hundred yards away, snorting as loud as we were laughing.

Another time I slipped getting out of the wagon and fell down.

You said, "They say the balance is the first thing to go when you start getting old."

"Well," I said pulling myself up and laughing, "being an old widder woman like you are, I don't think I'd say much."

"Old widder woman, huh?" you said, getting out of the wagon and sitting down beside me in the grass. "And what 'old widder woman' has a certain cowboy been eyeing rather indecently lately?"

"Wouldn't have the foggiest idea," I said.

"Am I to take it then that you don't have any improper notions towards me?" you said, flirting and rubbing my chest.

"Mrs. Lewis," I said, "to tell you the truth, if you took all the improper notions out of me right now, there wouldn't be much left."

I grabbed for your arm, but you were too quick. "Let's go cut some more wood," you said.

"While your virtue is still intact?"

"No," you said, handing me the ax, "while yours is."

Yes, we laughed and talked a lot in the time we were on the mesa that fall day. It was a time for laughing and talking. But most of all, it was a time for this . . .

We spread our lunch on a blanket on the west side of the mesa, at the edge of a thick growth of cedars and scattered pinons, where a small spring fed a clear pool of water next to a rock bluff covered with the fall-colored leaves of mountain mahogany. The afternoon was crisp and sunny, fall heavy on the air.

We ate our lunch, not talking, but listening to the day crickets and the murmuring of the spring. You took down your hair and lay down with it spread on the blanket.

After we ate we lay beside each other for another half hour without saying anything. It wasn't an uneasy silence, though, but natural peaceful, just like the talking and laughing had been.

"There's another flock of geese," you said after a while, looking up at the sky. "How do they know where they're going?"

"How do we?" I said. "They're the lucky ones, all they have to do is follow their instinct."

"And we have to be able to look ahead and plan, don't we?"

"I guess that's what we try to do," I said, looking up at the sky with my hands under my head, "but it's the things we don't—and can't—plan that turn out to be the most important things in our lives."

"Like us being here?"

"Well, we sure didn't plan it, did we?" I said. "It seems like the really big things happen like that."

"Will . . . Do you love me? You never had said."

"I said love was hard to understand, Autumn, and I haven't thought much about it for years and years, no more than I've thought about not driftin' and settling down. There was a time I didn't believe in love, at least not for me."

"And now?"

"There's been a lot happened to me in a short time, Autumn. There's been killin' and dyin' and bein scared . . . but just as much has happened to you, too, and you beleive in it. You believe God gives us love. Isn't that what you said?"

"I believe he gives us the *ability* to love, Will, but it's our choice whether we do or not . . . If you can't say you love me . . ."

"Nobody can help but love you, Autumn. It's not possible to *not* love you."

"Burl didn't."

"Burl was an idiot, a fool, and men like Burl don't count."

"What about you then? You count, and you still haven't said whether *you* love me or not."

"Autumn . . . how could *I* not love you? I feel things for you I didn't know I had inside. I just can't explain them. But love is scary, Autumn."

"Life is scary, Will. But we can't be afraid to live—or love."

"I just don't trust life, Autumn, not for a minute. I've seen it turn on people too quick to trust it."

"Then that's why it's so important to grab happiness when it's within our reach, Will. If we're going to wait until we're certain our happiness will last forever, then we'll *guarantee* ourselves nothing but sadness. I'd rather risk happiness than guarantee sadness, wouldn't you?"

Neither of us spoke again for ten minutes. Then you put your hand on mine and said, "Will . . . I want you to make love to me . . . now . . . right here."

I turned my head and looked at you.

"You're shocked?"

"I don't know . . . it's not the thing pretty women are in a habit of saying to me."

"And it's something I never thought I would say. But I've lived a lot since I came out here. I've learned that a marriage license and a priest's words can't make something right that's wrong to start with—and the lack of them can't turn something right into something bad or shameful. If you stay, I think we should be married, but for right now, all I ask is that you love me. Who knows what tomorrow might bring, Will. All we'll ever have is right now . . . And right now I want you to hold me."

We came together on the blanket and kissed, soft and tender at first, and there was no turning back, no wanting to. There was no shame in our nakedness, no guilt in our passion. With you, Autumn, making love was as natural as the change of seasons, as pure as the pool of spring water we lay beside.

CHAPTER 27

TWO days later, on the twenty-sixth of September, 1895, we were married in a little adobe church in Liberty. On the same day the priest christened little Willa, just twenty-six days after I shot Marshal Ben DuPree in Wyoming. No writer of dime novels could have ever dreamed up such a story.

The winter of 1895 came early, stayed long, and showed no mercy of those unprepared for it.

The day after the wedding, we started building another room onto the house for Casey and Otis to sleep in, and were still working on it when I woke up on the nineteenth of October and saw two inches of fresh snow on the ground.

"It'll be too wet to work with the adobe today," I said, pulling on my Levi's, "but the game ought to be moving up on the mesa, so I'll saddle old Pat and ride up there to hunt. It won't be easy, but we'll get by."

On the twenty-ninth of October, as I was slipping into my clothers in the dark, you woke up and said, "Where are you going, Will?"

"A storm hit durin' the night," I said. "Hear that wind? The ground's covered with powdery snow, too, and it's still coming down. We just barely got the roof on the new room finished in time, but working on that got me behind in gatherin' firewood. We could be in trouble if this storm sets in and lasts a few days, so I'm goin' to hitch the horses to the wagon and go up on the mesa and cut some now, before it gets any worse."

That storm lasted until the next night and covered us up with eight inches of drifted snow. When I came off the mesa, the wind was whipping it around so hard I couldn't see where the road was and passed by on the east side of the house without knowing it. By the time I finally realized what had happened and turned around and got back home, it was two hours past dark. I was able to get enough wood to last us through that storm, but before we saw the ground again it was all gone, and it was back up on the mesa with wet boots and an ax for old Will.

One night before supper in the middle of November, Casey said, "What's Will drawing?"

"Flies is all he can draw," Otis said.

"He's making posters to take to Liberty," you informed them. Then you said, "Will . . . I've been thinking. I'll bet I could work in Mr. Gerald's store for a while."

"And what about the kids?" I said. "No, I've told you I'll get us by, and I will. Now how do these look?" I held up two posters that said:

> I WILL BREAK AND SHOE HORSES
> 50¢ a saddling—No horses too rank!
> $2.00 per head for cold shoeing.
> Leave a message here for Will Smith.

The must have looked good enough, because I had a customer before I'd tacked up the second one!

I'd put one in Gerald's Mercantile and was on my way to the post office with the other one when Mr. Bingham called out behind me, "Wait up a minute, Smith!"

When he caught up with me, he said, "Say, I just saw that poster you put up over at Gerald's store. Your price is cheaper than gettin' it done at Perkin's Livery, and I was wonderin' if you wanted to shoe a couple of horses for me?"

"I sure do," I said.

"Trouble is," he said, " is money . . . I was wonderin' if you'd shoe 'em on credit. I'm good for it, but I just don't have the cash right now."

"Sorry, Mr. Bingham," I told him, "but if I was fixed to

where I could give credit, I'd be home by the fire instead of huntin' for work at this time of the year."

"Yeah," he said, "I know what you mean . . . Say! I just thought of something—how are you fixed for hog?"

"Got a one-armed one out at the place," I said. "Why?"

He looked at me like I was missing a couple of slats and then said, "Well, I've still got one left from this summer's litter, and I was thinkin' that maybe I could trade him to you for shoein' those two horses of mine—they're gentle old things and won't give you no trouble at all."

"A hog, huh?" I said. Then I nodded and said, "Sounds fair enough to me."

I followed him right on out to his place a couple of miles south of town. He was right about the horses not giving any trouble at all, because they didn't—not after I'd lost patches of skin and tufts of hair and they were both tied down flat on the ground like big old beef steers! I found out later that the reason he didn't get them shod at Perkins Livery wasn't because of the price, but because Mr. Perkins told then he wouldn't shoe them at *any* price!

But I did, and when I was going back home with that hog tied down in the wagon, and he was squealing like he was hung under a gate, I pulled my collar up against the wind and said out loud, "And just think, I could be settin' up batchin' quarters at some big outfit's line camp about now, with a good supply of liquor and no one to worry about all winter but myself."

Then as I turned back east with a cold, setting sun to my back, I smiled, thinking about a warm adobe house at the foot of a long ridge and the smiling woman in it who was fixing my supper and wondering when I'd be home.

During the next two weeks I shod three more horses and put three saddlings each on two more—not much, but enough to keep the wolf at bay for a little while.

Then just after the first of December, late in the day when I was stacking wood against the house, I heard Pat nicker and looked up to see two riders leading two horses each coming around the bend in the road at the end of the ridge.

I acted like I hadn't seen them and eased over to the door and reached inside and slipped my old Colt out of the holster hanging on a nail beside the door. I was quiet and careful not to let anybody inside the house see me get it. Then I stuck it inside the waistband of my Levi's, pulled my coat around it, and went back to stacking wood.

When the riders were almost to the barn, I stopped and watched them, like that was the first time I'd noticed them coming. They stopped a few feet away and a stocky, middle-aged man with graying hair and a slow, deep voice said, "Will Smith?"

"That's right," I said, slipping my right hand inside my coat on the pretext of warming it, but ready to get it curled around the handle of the Colt.

"I'm J. L. Shaffer," the man said. "I own a outfit southeast of here, and this is Clyde Henry, one of my hands."

I nodded to them both and held my breath. I'd worked with Clyde Henry on the Diamond O outfit in Arizona fifteen years before. He had changed a lot and I don't know if I would have known him without hearing his name. I knew that I'd changed a lot in those same fifteen years, especially with the recent addition of the eye patch and the mustache, and I didn't *think* he would recognize me. But still I couldn't be sure, so I made it a point to keep my head down as much as I could without raising suspicion.

"I understand you're a pretty good hand at startin' broncs," Shaffer said.

"I don't claim to be the world's best at it," I said, "but I've started my share that have turned out to be good horses."

"I've got four four-year-olds here." the rancher said. "Do you want to ride em?"

"For four-bits a saddlin' and you furnish the feed for 'em," I said, "I'll ride 'em off hell's rimrock."

Shaffer smiled a little and then said, "Four bits a saddling is too high if I've got to send feed over for 'em. Tell you what I'll do, I'll give you two dollars a head for a week's ridin' on 'em. These four ain't all I got either. After a week, I'll send a man over to pick these up and drop you off four more."

"How many head total you got, Mister Shaffer?"

"Twenty-one. If you're interested in the deal, you can break 'em all—or you can break all of 'em you're able to before they break you, whichever comes first. A few of 'em might have a little pitch in 'em."

I studied his offer a little bit and then said, "I'll ride 'em all for two dollars per head per week, you furnish the feed for them, *plus* I get to feed our three horses and milk cow out of your feed."

He looked down at his saddle horn, twisted his mouth around, and then rode up and handed me the lead ropes of the broncs he was leading. "Deal," he said. "I'll send a wagon over with a fresh set of broncs and more feed."

Clyde Henry rode up and handed me the horses he was leading, and then the two of them nodded and rode off. Henry never recognized me, but I never could completely shake the fear that someday some cowboy I'd worked with somewhere would see me, and maybe you'd be with me, and he'd just come up, stick out his hand to me and say, "Honk Ballard, where in the hell did you get that eye patch!" The fear of that lessened as the months rolled by, but I was never plumb shed of it.

The Shaffer broncs were all big, rangy types of horses with little pig eyes and ears that hooked and almost touched at the tips. As a whole they were the rankest set of broncs I'd ever seen raised on one outfit. The very first one I climbed aboard (the same day Shaffer and Henry left the first four) made a couple of circles around the pen as quiet as old Chester would have, and then came apart underneath me like a stick of dynamite. He didn't buck me off, but he caused me to pull a groin muscle that didn't heal till spring.

The third saddling on that first set of broncs, I got bucked off by a thin blue roan with a shaggy mane and a long tail. He wasn't just satisfied to buck me off either. He stuck my head through the fence and nearly tore off my left ear.

On the second set of broncs, I had one slip on the frozen ground while he was pitching and fall flat on his side with my right knee providing a little padding between his ribs and the ground. The knee stayed swelled up all winter and never did completely heal.

I don't know how many times I got bucked off during the five weeks that I rode Shaffer's broncs, but it must have been fifteen at least. Even old Otis got to feeling sorry for me after about seven or eight times and stopped teasing me so hard. You tried to get me to tell Mr. Shaffer not to bring any more after the first set. But I was not only getting two dollars a week per horse, we were also getting feed for our stock when we had *none*. So, you see, Autumn, I *couldn't* quit. A man with a family to feed will stick and see a lot of things through that a single, drifting man might be inclined to ride away from.

Besides riding those broncs and shoeing what horses I could, I had to go up on the mesa every time I had a chance to hunt game and cut wood. When you let a hard winter get the jump on you like it had me, the best you can hope for is to stay even with it, and that only comes from working daylight till dark, wet and cold or not, sore and aching or not. From the middle of November until some time in February, I don't know if I ever saw you or inside of the house except by candlelight.

But I didn't mind. When I'd be coming down the road in the wagon, or finishing up with the chores, or riding in on Pat with a deer slung across his withers in front of the saddle, and I'd see the yellow light coming from the windows of the house and breaking through the dark, and smell the woodsmoke of home, I'd know it was worth it all.

And those long, dark winter nights? God, how I loved 'em! When I'd come in out of the dark and the cold into the light and the warmth of the little adobe. See your smiling face. Pull off my wet boots and put on a pair of clean dry socks that you'd hand me. Tell you about my day or listen while you told me about yours. Smell the fresh coffee and the aroma of supper cooking. All of us sitting at the table and eating together while we laughed and talked. Glancing across the table and catching the twinkle in your eye—the special twinkle reserved only for a bowlegged, stove-up cowboy who at one time thought twinkles only came from stars and fairy tales.

But it was after all of that, after Casey and Otis and Willa were asleep, that I loved most of all. When I'd lay in bed and watch you brush out your long hair, watch you get up and blow out the candle, hear the gentle rustle as your gown fell to the floor around your feet and you came to me, always a lady . . . But, God . . . God! How much a woman. How much a woman!

CHAPTER 28

COLD and wet, 1895 was committed to memory and to history, and, just as cold and wet, 1896 was born.

Somehow, we survived. You not only survived but flourished and seemed to grow more beautiful and contented as winter wore on. I think I flourished, too—wintered pretty good, a cowboy would say. But not on the outside—my flanks got higher and higher, and I moved around like I'd been foundered. But something *inside* me sure wintered pretty good. I guess that was a pride for having a tough job to do and doing it, and a sort of unexpected happiness that comes from doing things for others instead of only for yourself— as I had done my whole life until then.

One morning just after sunup, when I should have been out milking the cow and doing the other chores but instead was still in bed next to you, I said, "Well, Mrs. Smith, look there, there's a robin on our windowsill. I think we've made it."

Lying on your stomach, smiling without raising your head, you said, "I never doubted for a minute but what we'd make it. Did you?"

"Naw," I said, pulling myself out of bed and then giving to that sore Shaffer-bronc knee. "In fact, if I'd a known takin' care of a wife and family was going to be this easy, I'd have had three or four by now."

Half an hour later when I was carrying a steaming bucket of milk back to the house across three inches of crusted snow and smelling the coffee you had boiling, I looked up to see Sheriff Joe Betters, no more than two hundred yards away.

I waited for him on the porch holding the milk bucket. I

was sure enough wondering what he had on his mind, and I felt a quick jolt of panic hit me, but then you opened the door and came out to stand beside me, and somehow I knew that whatever Betters's business *was* it was with Will Smith. I wouldn't let myself think anything else.

"Mornin', Sheriff," I said. "You're out early on a cold morning."

He pulled up in front of us, tipped his hat at you, and then said, "When I got business to tend to, I like to get out and get it done. I never did get a chance to congratulate you folks on your wedding last fall. Before I knew that you'd even . . . Well, you know, before I even knew anything about it, you were done married.

"You sure are a lucky man, Smith. I mean you come in here to tell Mrs. Lewis, er, Mrs. Smith now, ain't it? But you come here to tell her she's a widow lady, save her from them two bad hombres, and then before anyone knows it, you're married to her. Just like in a fairy tale where they always live happily ever after."

"I didn't exactly volunteer for any of them jobs but the last one, Sheriff . . . But you didn't ride all the way out here in the cold just to congratulate us, did you?"

"No," he said, unbuttoning his coat with a smile I couldn't read and reaching inside it. "I came to give you this hundred dollars."

We looked at each other with blank faces and it was you who said, "Why would you give us a hundred dollars, Sheriff?"

"Oh, it ain't me," he said, opening the envelope and showing us the cash. "It's from the Territory of New Mexico— reward money on the one of those two men you killed that was called Pole. Real name was Norman Henry. Pole was his nickname, and it was short for Pole Ax. He was called that because of a habit he had when he was mad of 'pole axing' whoever he was mad at. I finally run down a poster on him and found out there was a reward. And here it is, you'll just need to sign . . ."

We looked at each other again, thinking the same thing, I guess. "Sheriff," I said, "you can just keep that money—we don't need it."

He looked at me and then at you like he couldn't believe it.

"But I can't keep it," he said. "Don't you have any sense, Smith?"

"Been accused of that before," I said. "But you keep that money or send it back . . . Or even better yet, Sheriff, why don't you find some poor people and give it to them."

"Okay," he said, putting the envelope back inside his coat. "But you're a fool if you ask me . . . Before I leave, Smith, there's something I want to tell you. There's plenty of folks around who think you're some kind of hero—but I'm not one of 'em."

"Then that makes two of us, Sheriff," I said.

He looked at me a few seconds and then jerked on his reins, wheeled his horse around, and left.

"But you're some kind of hero to me," you said, coming beside me and putting an arm around my waist and smiling.

"Stop that, Autumn," I said, pulling away. "I'm no more a hero than I can jump on a broom handle and fly to the moon—and you know it."

"You're a hero to me, not because you killed those two men, but because you have a set of values."

"Stop it, Autumn," I said. "Just stop it! Don't make a big deal out of me not taking that money. Don't make me into something I'm not."

"How many men wouldn't have taken that hundred dollars?"

"Autumn, do you want to know the truth about why I didn't take the money? It wasn't because I'm sort of noble saint or anything. I'm selfish in that I don't want anybody else providing for you—even though that hundred dollars would buy things we need. But the main reason I didn't take it was because I didn't think *you* would want me to! So your noble hero turns out to be nothing other than some bowlegged, stove-up cowboy trying to impress a calico skirt."

You smiled, big and pretty. "You have the sweetest way of putting things."

"I give up," I said, lifting my hands in the air. "Let's go eat."

A couple of weeks passed, spring came, and one day J. L. Shaffer dropped by again.

"Will," he said, not having time to get out of the saddle long enough for a cup of coffee, "I'd like to hire you to go out with my brandin' wagon this spring. A man that sees twenty-one head of my broncs through in five weeks is the kind of man I want. I'll pay you thirty-five dollars a month—plus, when we get through, I'll give you a yearling heifer. It'll take us about sixty days, but I realize that a man with a place and a family to take care of has to come home now and then. Just as long as he don't over do it, that's fine with me. What do you say?"

"Well, I don't know. There's a lot of work to get done around here, but we could sure use the money—and the heifer. There's an awful lot of work to do around here, though."

"Mr. Shaffer," you said, "could I talk to my husband alone for a minute."

When we were inside the house, you laid the law down, but not the kind of law I'd heard other men talking about that they'd had laid down to them: "Now, Will Smith, you've cowboyed too long and have it too much in your blood to just completely stop because of me. If I let you do that, I'm afraid you'd start hating me in time. All I've ever asked is that you love me, I've never asked for you to try to be something you're not. We'll get by fine, just don't forget where we are."

"Mr. Shaffer," I said, back outside, "I'll help you brand,

but first I'm going to build an adobe spring house by the windmill to keep milk and things cool this summer, and I'm also going to build a wooden water chute out to the garden, so Autumn won't have to work so hard to keep it watered."

"The wagon's pulling' out the first day of May," Shaffer said.

"Thirty days from now, huh? With any luck I'll be ready by then, Mr. Shaffer. See you at the wagon."

I enjoyed the work with the wagon and being around a bunch of cowboys again. You were right in saying it was in my blood, and it would be hard to completely stop. The days in the saddle and on the ground flanking calves all fled by. But those nights in my hard bedroll—alone—crawled by! It was then, when I was laying out under the sky, watching the stars blink on and off and hearing our night horses stomp and blow their noses, that I couldn't help but think about home and you and wonder if everything was okay.

I didn't know what Mr. Shaffer's "now and then" meant as far as going home was concerned, but I'd ride home at least once a week no matter what. Sometimes, I would get home about sundown, and have to leave again by midnight in order to get back to the wagon in time for breakfast the next morning, but it was always worth it.

Cowboys have a sort of vulgar expression for men who can't seem to stay away from their wives for very long. They don't mean, really mean, anything indecent, just a way of razzing a man, and I got plenty of that when I'd say I was going home for the night. It didn't bother me any though, I'd just smile when they were through and say, "You reckon it's terminal?"

Sometimes, I would just stop up there on top of the ridge before I'd come on down. I could hardly believe what a lucky man I was. I was living the best life any cowboy could. I was not only able to punch cows, but I had a home and a wife to come home to. I had the best of both worlds, and for once in my life, I was smart enough to realize it.

The last week of the branding, I was able to take Casey with me and let him ride my little bay and a gentle horse of Shaffer's the wagon boss loaned us. You fixed him a little bedroll and he slept on the ground beside me. When we came back to the homestead, through with the branding and leading that heifer yearling, I don't know who was the proudest, me or him. But I *do* know who was the proudest he wasn't going to have to sleep in a cold bedroll by himself for a while!

We had good rains that summer that forced us to put a new roof on the house, but also let us raise a good garden and pick a lot of wild fruit along the river. We grew a lot of grass that summer too, enough so we could cut a lot of it and stack it in the barn for winter stock feed.

It seemed that I'd barely come in from Shaffer's branding wagon when he was back at the place trying to get me to go out with his fall wagon.

"No, Mr. Shaffer," I said, "I'd like to help you, but I've got too much work to do. Last winter we barely got by, because we weren't ready. This winter we *will* be ready, though."

A steady month of twelve-hour days followed with all of us working. By the last of October, there was enough wood to last all winter stacked beside the house and in the barn. I had killed, cleaned, and cured three hogs and three deer. You had enough plum and grape preserves to last all winter, and there was plenty of feed for the livestock. We had thirty dollars clear after stocking up with groceries, and our cow herd was now numbered three head.

We'd been married over a year, and I now had little time or inclination to think of Honk Ballard and his drifting, reckless ways. The geese were still passing by high overhead in big flocks going south in front of the coming winter, but they held no spell over me now. To say I was contented would be like saying green grass follows a soaking rain. Honk Ballard could never have even imagined living such a life—Will Smith could imagine no other.

Did I think it could last forever? Right after the shooting in Wyoming, and all the way down across Colorado, my thoughts of the future were of only the next few hours, at times only of the next few minutes. By the time I rode Pat down from the top of the ridge above the homestead, the first time a week after the shooting, the future for me then was the next day. After things happened between us like they did, and the days and weeks rolled by, I gradually began to think of next week, and then next month. After that first winter, a part of me started to think in even longer terms. So, I guess, yes, at least a foolish part of me, had begun to think it could last forever. But deeper down, another part of me refused to trust life even a little bit and stayed convinced that what had happened so suddenly and wonderfully, could and would just as suddenly come to an end.

The first real warning for me came about a month ago, Autumn. I wonder if you remember it. November was mild up until just after the first week, and it was a warm afternoon that day. We were walking to the house together from the barn where I had just finished milking and doing the chores. I was carrying the milk pail in one hand and my other arm was around your shoulders. We were talking about how, now that we were ready for winter, we probably wouldn't even have one.

From far, far away, from the mesas to the north, a howl drifted across the homestead. A single howl, drawn-out and lonesome as the hard trail I'd followed from Wyoming had been. It was no coyote's wail this time, but the howl of a wolf on the hunt, the first I'd heard from the homestead since I'd been there. A shiver raced through me, end to end.

"Why, Will," you said, "what's wrong!"

"What *could* be wrong?" I said. "Let's just go on in the house where it's warm."

"But it's not cold out here at all," you said.

I tried to smile, but the chill reached my bones again. "Sometimes," I said, "it's colder than you think."

CHAPTER 29

IT was the first of December. Dark outside. A light snow falling, the first of the winter. We were sitting at the table eating a supper of venison steaks, laughing at how Willa had gravy all in her hair.

"There was a man up on the ridge today," Casey said.

"A man?" I said. "Could you see who it was?"

"No. He was just there a little bit, and then he rode away."

"Probably somebody just passin' through," I said.

The next night it was Otis. "Seen a man on the ridge 'bout sundown."

"Doing what?" I asked.

"Just sittin' there on his horse."

"For how long?"

"Don't know how long he'd been there before I seen him, but no more 'n five minutes after I did. Probably somebody missin' some cattle and lookin' for 'em."

"Probably," I said.

I got up before daylight the next morning and slipped out of the house without waking you up. When I went out the door, I took the gunbelt off the nail it had been hanging on for over three months. I saddled Pat and rode up on the ridge.

What I found as soon as there was enough daylight was about the last thing I wanted to find. But I didn't do anything but nod my head slowly and then shake it just as slowly. There were two places, about ten feet apart, that had four or five snuffed-out cigarettes scattered on the ground. I didn't even *think* anything, just nodded my head slowly, and then shook it slowly. Then I followed a set of horse tracks that

187

went off the ridge toward the west. A half mile west of the ridge, the tracks disappeared underneath a bunch of cow tracks, so I turned Pat around and rode home.

When I got out of bed the next morning, the cold stars were twinkling above about three inches of snow that had fallen overnight without drifting. As soon as I did the chores and ate breakfast, I said, "I'm goin' into town today to see a man about ridin' some broncs for him."

"Did you do something with your gun and gunbelt?" you asked. "I notice it's not hanging by the door anymore."

"Yeah," I said, slipping into my coat. "I got it down so I would remember to take it to town today and get it fixed. It feels like the cylinder has too much slack in it, and I was afraid if I had to shoot a snake or skunk or something, the thing might blow up."

"When will you be back?"

"Could be late," I said.

I circled around the south end of the ridge and was planning on riding to the top and seeing if somebody had been up there during the night. But before I even started up, I picked up two sets of tracks in the snow. One set was going up and had been made before it had quit snowing. The other set, coming down and angling toward the northwest, had been made after the snow had stopped sometime during the night.

I followed the tracks across the snow-covered sand and sagebrush, up one hill and down the next, for about five miles to the foot of a high mesa. There the tracks went up a steep deer trail that angled up the side of the mesa and finally came out on top.

I followed the tracks across the mesa and off a steep trail on the other side. Two miles after they came off the mesa they veered back south, then back to the east.

By sundown the tracks had brought me right back to the same trail going up the side of the same mesa I'd been on earlier in the day. Somebody was playing with me, and I know a man who plays another man's game is a fool. I turned Pat around and went home, trying all the time I was riding back to figure who this phantom rider could be. I eliminated the law—they didn't toy with a man like somebody was doing with me. Some of Burl's friends—his business associates because Burl never had a real friend in his life—who might be after the same thing Pole and Scalp had been after? Then a sickening thought hit me—maybe one of them had lured me away from the homestead so another could . . . I touched a spur to Pat's ribs and long-trotted and loped the dozen or so miles back home, but found, much to my relief, everything normal when I got there.

"Did you see that man today, Will?" you asked over supper.

"Man?" I snapped my head up. "What man?"

"The man you rode to town to see about riding some broncs."

"Uh . . . No, he never showed. I waited a long time, but he never showed."

There was a bright moon over the snow that night, and a man could see to the top of the ridge. I eased out of bed every half hour all night long and looked, but saw no one.

The next day was warm and sunny. All the snow melted, and there was no sign of anybody anywhere near the homestead. The same thing the next day. I began to relax a little bit. Maybe it had been a false alarm.

Two more busy, peaceful, warm days passed, and I returned to normal—even sleeping *most* of the nights through.

One week to the day after Casey had seen a man on the ridge above the house, I found a piece of paper with a childlike drawing on it in the barn on my saddle. The drawing was of a large United States deputy marshal's badge with a stick-figure man hanging from a gallows in the center of it.

I thought I was going to be as sick when I saw that drawing as I had been on that *Desierto de Pena* right after I first came.

Somebody knew. Somebody knew and was playing with me.

I didn't sleep at all that night.

"What's the matter, Will?" you asked sometime after midnight.

"Just got a little stomach ache," I said. "Nothing to worry about. You go back to sleep . . . Autumn, you do know how much I love you, don't you? I've never told you much, but . . . Autumn?" You were already asleep.

Although I thought I kept a nearly constant watch both up on the ridge and around the barn all night long, the next morning there was another picture laying in my saddle seat. This one had a cross with the words *Burl Lewis 1863–1895* printed across it. The cross was in front of what was supposed to be a grave, and a stick-figure man was rising up out of the grave.

This picture made less sense than the first one had. It was common knowledge that the reason I'd come there in the first place was to tell you that Burl was dead and that I'd helped bury him. So what was the picture supposed to mean? And why the stick man rising out of the grave?

Just before I wadded the picture up, I saw something that I'd overlooked before. I was so interested in the grave and the cross that I didn't notice the word printed in small letters below the grave—*Colorado*.

My God! How could *anybody* know that I'd buried Burl in Colorado instead of Wyoming? I was the only person in the *world* who knew that! It was eerie, ghostly, and although I never once believed in ghosts and still didn't, I felt a sharp chill race down my spine.

CHAPTER 30

IN the afternoon of the same day I'd found the second picture in the barn, a man came riding down the road and stopped in front of the house. I'd been watching him from the barn and when he stopped, I stepped out with my rifle in hand.

"Need something, mister?" I said.

He turned his horse around and rode him closer to me. "You Smith?"

"That's right," I said. "Who's askin'?"

"You break horses?"

"Times I do. Who's askin'?"

"You interested in ridin' some for us?"

"Has 'us' got any names?"

"Yeah . . . You interested?"

"In the names," I said.

"Powers and DuPree."

"What!?"

"You wanted names, didn't you? Then there's some names for you—Powers and DuPree."

There was a live round in the firing chamber of my rifle. I pulled the hammer back behind that live round and walked closer to the man on the horse. "What'n the hell are you talkin' about?" I said.

The man grinned. "Maybe you'll want to follow me down the road a ways and talk particulars on our deal."

I had to go. I had to find out who this was and what he wanted. Pat was already saddled. I led him out of the barn and got on.

"Will?" You were standing in the doorway of the house. "Where are you going?"

"Just going to talk to a man about ridin' some horses," I said.

"This late in the day?"

The stranger tipped his hat and said, "He'll be back before long, Mrs. Smith. You go ahead and start supper."

When we rounded the curve in the road that swings around the end of ridge, there was another rider waiting for us. As soon as we stopped in front of him, he drew his gun on me and told me to hand my rifle and the Colt over to him.

When I hesitated he said, "If we'd wanted to kill you, we could've done it a week ago. Now if you want to bring this thing to a head and find out what's goin' on, just do as you're told."

I handed over my guns, and we all three sat in the road without saying anything as the day got shorter and colder.

When only half a sun was left in the west, a rider appeared far down the road, seeming to come out of the sun itself. He rode his horse in a slow walk, getting closer and bigger, but no clearer.

I couldn't tell who it was until he was ten feet away. And even then it was his voice I recognized first. "What're you hidin' behind that eye patch and mustache for, Honk?" He rode a couple of steps closer and then said, "You could have at least left me the money Canaster paid me in Wyoming. After you buried me and I went to hell, I didn't have the price of admission, so the devil sent me back."

"Burl!?" I said in disbelief, ducking my head to get a better look at him.

"In the moldered flesh," he said.

It would hardly do justice to the way I felt to say I was stunned. Of all the possibilities I'd considered about who it was that knew I wasn't Will Smith, this had never been one of them. "How . . ."

Burl laughed, loud and long and wicked. "Goddamn you, Honk, do you know how I've been lookin' forward to hearin' you ask that, and to seein' the look on your face that's on it right now?" Then he laughed again, just as loud and just as long and just as wicked as before.

Then he said, "Honk, I don't care a damn thing about palaverin' with the likes of you, but I want to tell you this story. It just shows that there is some justice in this old world after all.

"I don't remember you burying me *alive*. The last thing I remember is us leaving Wyoming with our shirttails stickin' straight out behind us and you complainin' about me slowin' you down. The next thing I know, I'm wakin' up in some doctor's office in a little burg in Colorado. They said some cowboys had been ridin' down this creek when they heard some funny noise coming from a tamarack thicket. What they found was a man in a shallow, sandy grave with some brush pulled over him, makin' what they thought was his death rattle. They didn't think I'd ever live till they got me to town, but, by God, I did. The doctor never thought I'd live either, but, by God, I fooled him too. They said I was on the brink of death and unconscious for ten days.

"Then one day I surprised them all and come to. But my hands were tied to the bed I was on and the law was standin' over me. They wanted to know how I got shot, who buried me and left me like that, and was I by chance comin' from Wyoming.

"You've got to always be thinkin' in this business, Honk— always. I could tell that the law was tryin' to tie me in with that little affair we had with those lawmen in Wyoming. But I could also tell by the way they were talking that they didn't know who I was or anything else about me, so I figured you must have took everything I had with you except for the clothes I had on—and you even cleaned out the pockets.

"Not knowing exactly how much they knew, I was afraid to say I didn't know anything about any shootin' anywhere, because once the law catches you storyin' to them once, they tend to not believe *anything* you say. So I come clean with 'em, Honk. I told 'em I was Bob Shaw and I'd come upon some cowboy's camp in Wyoming as I was passin' through and he'd invited me to stay a couple of days with him while my horse rested up. One day these two lawmen came by and had some of our coffee, and all of a sudden this goddamn cowboy just opens up on 'em like a crazy man and shoots 'em both. I said I didn't have the *foggiest* idea about why he did it. I said that I got hit by a stray bullet, and the cowboy wouldn't take me to a doctor, but instead made me go with him until I couldn't ride anymore, and then I guess he buried me and stole everything I had.

"I was gambling that if old Charlie Castle was ever talked to, he'd say he'd never seen me before in his life. I figured he'd like to keep the arrangement we had with him secret as long as he could.

"I couldn't think of any fake name to give 'em for you, Honk, so I just told 'em it was old Honk Ballard that did the terrible thing in Wyoming.

"Then they said, as soon as I was able, they would take me back to Cheyenne and let a jury decide if I was tellin' the truth, as the whole story sounded a little farfetched for their tastes.

"When they got me back to Wyoming, guess what? I found out that Ben DuPree was alive! He identified me as one of the cowboys there when the shooting took place and said he would testify to that at the trial. You see what I mean about always thinkin', Honk? If I would have said I didn't know *anything* about the shooting, and then DuPree identified me, they would have figured I was guilty as hell.

"At the trial last November in Cheyenne, DuPree said he couldn't say who had started the shooting, or who had killed Johnson Powers, because when all of that happened he was turned around takin' a pee. All he could testify to for sure was that when he *did* turn around, me and Powers were both on the ground and the other cowboy—you, Honk—shot him twice in the stomach and then left him for dead.

"I thought the jury was awful rough on me, because they still sentenced me to five years in prison for being an accomplice to murder. I never could see how they figured that with all the evidence in my favor, and me still lookin' so sickly from being an innocent bystander and takin' that stray bullet through the lung like I had.

"But how I looked was nothin' compared to how Ben DuPree looked, Honk—and how he *still* looks. Them two leaks you put in his gut just won't heal right, and he stays in a lot of pain. He came to see me a lot during the year I spent in prison. It wasn't that he was so fond of me, but that he had such a hate for you. I kept tellin' him that if he could just get me out, I bet I could find you for him. I said we were a lot closer friends than I'd let on at the trial. I finally convinced him, and he pulled some strings with somebody close to the governor and got me out a couple of weeks ago.

"Thought you might enjoy seein' your name in print, so I brought this along to show you." I unfolded the paper he handed me and it was a wanted poster that said:

WANTED: DEAD OR ALIVE
FOR THE MURDER OF SHERIFF JOHNSON POWERS OF
LARAMIE COUNTY, WYOMING
AND THE SHOOTING OF UNITED STATES DEPUTY
MARSHAL BEN DUPREE
HONK BALLARD
$500 REWARD

There was a drawing of a face that might have looked like mine—without the mustache and the eye patch—just like it might have looked like a thousand others. Then it went on to tell how dangerous I was, and how, if I was spotted, extreme caution should be used in dealing with me.

I looked at Burl over the wanted poster and said, "You son-of-a-bitch."

Burl laughed again. "I can't wait to see my wife's face when she sees me again . . . and I can't wait to spend a few nights with her and get caught up on our . . . uh, conjugal matters. A man sure misses them conjugal things with his pretty wife when he's in prison, Honk. Of course, you wouldn't know a goddamn thing about that, 'cause all the while I was in that stinkin' hellhole, you and her were conjugatin' up a storm."

"Burl," I said, looking him straight in the eye, "you ride out of here right now, or I swear to God, I'll kill you."

"No, you won't, Honk, and that's your downfall. If you'd went ahead and killed DuPree like I tried to get you to, you wouldn't have half the troubles you've got now. And if you'd have killed *me* like I told you, you wouldn't have *any* troubles. Honk, I'm afraid you just don't have the nerve it takes to survive in this business. Oh, sure, I heard about your killing Pole and Scalp—and by the way, I want to thank you for not letting them have the money—but the way I hear you did that is a long ways from lookin' a man in the eye and shootin' him.

"Man, Honk, I just can't believe that you left me to rot in an unmarked grave and came right in here and took my money and my woman!"

"There never was any money there, Burl," I said, "and you know it. Or maybe you've lied so much you don't even know what the truth is anymore. And as for Autumn . . . One woman is the same as another to you, Burl. Why would you want to hurt her anymore? Why don't you just ride on out. There's nothing here for you. You've caused me enough trouble by getting me blamed for what you did in Wyoming. Can't you be satisfied with that and leave us alone. Burl . . . I'm *asking* you."

Burl laughed again, louder than ever, longer than ever, and more wicked than ever.

Then he stopped laughing and said, "I'll tell you what I'll

do, Honk. Nobody around here has seen me. The boys have been to town to learn what's been goin' on, but I've stayed out of sight. I guess people around here still believe that lie you told about a horse fallin' on me and killin' me while I was makin' a hell of an effort to head some cattle up in Wyoming. Now, you give me that ten thousand dollars, and we'll just let people keep on believin' that lie. I'll leave and you'll never see or hear from me again. You can go on bein' the local hero, and we'll *all* live happily ever after."

"But, Burl," I said, "I never have found a dime of that money."

"If you *don't* give me my money, Honk," he said, like he hadn't heard me at all, "here's what I'll do—I'll telegraph Wyoming and tell DuPree where you are and drop in and see how surprised Sheriff Joe Betters is to see me back from the dead. . . . Then me and Autumn can get caught up on those conjugal matters we've got so far behind on like a man and wife should. We'll stop conjugatin' long enough to go watch you hang though, you can bet on that."

"Burl," I yelled, "there is no goddamn money there!"

"But there is, Honk. The oat bin in the barn has a false bottom in it, and that's where I hid it. When the boys here were in the barn putting those pretty pictures on your saddle, they looked. They said it wasn't there now, so that means you must have found it and done something with it. You give it to me and I'll be gone forever. You don't, and I'll do just what I said I would.

"Three days from now at three o'clock in the afternoon, Outlaw Honk, you bring that money, or at least what's left of it—and I expect that to be *at least* eight thousand. Bring it to the top of the mesa there behind the homestead or I go straight to Liberty and do what I said I would—talk to Betters and get a message to DuPree. As soon as they haul you away, I'll move in with Autumn, and there's not a law in the world says I can't. She still belongs to *me* in the eyes of the law, and she has certain obligations to me by *right* that the law won't stop me from taking *if,* by some rare chance, they're not freely given."

By then Burl had his horse turned around and he looked over his shoulder and said, "Stay here with him, boys, until I'm out of sight, and then give him his guns back and let him go. In three days, Honk."

CHAPTER 31

FIVE days ago, Autumn—at least I think it was five days ago, but where I am now time is hard to judge—those frantic and worry-filled three days began. The longest, the shortest, the worst seventy-two hours of my life. Like a trapped coyote staked to the ground on a short chain, I went to the end of my chain this way and that way and then back this way again, back and forth, back and forth. Thinking, thinking, thinking. There had to be some way out, there *had* to be! But what?

To make it even worse, I didn't know how much of what Burl told me was the truth, and how much of it he was making up. All I really knew for sure was that he was not dead, and that I was wanted not only for the shooting of Ben DePree, but also for the murder of Johnson Powers. The one I was an unwilling participant in, the other completely innocent of, but that didn't matter now. But what about the money? Where was it now? Had somebody else found it and taken it? Had somebody at the homestead found it and hidden it in a different place without saying anything about it? I couldn't see that at all. You wouldn't have. And Casey wouldn't have any more known what it was than little Willa would have. That narrowed it down to Otis and Mary Walking Horse before she died. But would a man as old as Otis, and one who had been forced to accept charity, sit on ten thousand dollars? No, I didn't think so, especially not as much as he thought of you, Autumn. He would have shared it, if he had found it.

Mary Walking Horse? I didn't know her at all, so I couldn't say. Life had been hard on her, too, so it was possible that if she happened to've stumbled upon it, she might have moved it and didn't say anything, planning on leaving with it after the baby was born. But how would she have ever found it if Burl had hidden it where he said he did? I *looked* for it, and looked hard for it, too, and I never once thought about it being in a false bottom of the oat bin, so how would anybody ever "stumble" upon it.

And the oat bin *did* have the kind of bottom where the money could have been hidden. I looked as soon as I got home the night I met Burl on the road. And someone, I guess Burl's boys, had pried the boards loose and looked. For all I knew, maybe they had actually found the money there and Burl was just playing with me like a cat with a mouse.

But I looked. I looked *everywhere* I could think of. What other hope did I have, did we have, for I was looking for you Autumn, even more than for myself. I was looking for us, I guess, because I couldn't make myself think of one without the other. That possibility I wouldn't accept yet. But I found no money.

With that hope gone—although I never stopped looking—I latched onto another. This hope was small and, looking at it with a cold eye, was more of the blind faith I'd seen in you than any realistic hope. But now I began to think, If the money had been here, I would have found it by now. Therefore, the money is *not* here—and Burl knows it. That means he's playing with me. But when he's through playing, what will he do? Wire DuPree and go see Sheriff Betters? I could believe that *only* if I could believe what he'd said about legally getting out of prison and being in such good graces with the law *and* Ben DuPree.

The more I thought about that, the more unlikely it seemed. If he'd been in prison, would they let him out after only one year? Not likely. If he'd been in prison, then he must have escaped. That sounded more like it. That would account for him staying hidden now. The more I thought about it, if everything *was* like he said it was, why wouldn't he go straight to Sheriff Betters, tell him the same story he said he told the jury in Wyoming, show him the poster, collect the five-hundred-dollar reward on me, and then watch and grin as Betters arrested me? No, I decided, two days into the allotted three, he had lied *again*. This time about his own standing with the law and Ben DuPree. What that meant to me—to us—exactly, I didn't know, but I felt a little better just knowing that Burl didn't hold all the cards.

During this time, did I ever want to tell you the truth? It would be better said to admit that during this time, just the same as for all the happy months before, I wished I wasn't having to hide a lie, but I never *wanted* to tell you the truth. And especially now. It would look like (and would have been true) that I didn't tell the truth of my own free will, but because circumstances had forced me to. I wanted things to go on forever like the last fourteen months had been, and if you knew the truth, they couldn't. You might say you would never doubt me, but you would.

The time for the truth had been long before Burl ever came back to life, even before we "knew each other" on a blanket beside a pool of spring water on that first day we talked and laughed and loved—not now, not fourteen months later.

I never told you before, Autumn, but several times during the time we shared the same bed—I would say a dozen times at least—you would start crying and thrash around in your sleep, saying something like, "No, Burl, please. Don't. No! No! No!" Whenever you would do that, I would just hold you in my arms, and before long you would be sleeping quietly again. The last time you did it? The night of the afternoon when I met Burl on the road. In your sleep you thrashed and cried and pleaded with him to stop. I held you close to me, and in two minutes you were still and quiet. But after that, how could I have told you if I had wanted to, that I'd made a slight mistake and that instead of your nightmare being forever dead and buried in Wyoming, he was actually alive and camping nearby.

Time rolled on. It was noon of the third day. December the sixth, 1896, thirty–six years and forty–nine days after Honk Ballard was born, one year and ninety days after Will Smith was.

The day started out warm and sunny. Otis and the kids were their usual ornery selves. You were your brightest and prettiest self. I tried to act like it was just another normal day on a busy homestead waiting for winter. I did my usual work, but couldn't keep my eyes off the sun, wondering how close to noon it was.

"Will," you said at dinner, "is something the matter?"

"Uh . . . No," I said. "I was just noticing that it's gettin' cloudy outside, and that if there's a snow coming, I'd like to have another deer hanging in the spring house."

"But, Will," you said, "there's two deer hanging out there now, besides all the meat we have cured."

"Can't ever have too much laid up this time of year," I said, not looking at you. "Think I'll go up on the mesa after we eat."

I saddled Pat, slipped the Winchester in its scabbard, buckled my gunbelt around my waist, and pulled my coat over it.

When I rode Pat out of the barn, you were standing on the porch watching me. "Will, it's sure starting to get cold."

"Oughta make the game move," I said, turning my collar up, and heading Pat toward the east to go around the windmill and then up the old wagon road to the mesa.

"Will?" you said.

I pulled up and turned Pat around.

"Good-bye," you said.

I'm not sure how long it was before I answered. I put on my gloves without even knowing it until later. Suddenly, I was afraid to go to the mesa. It *was* much colder. I wanted to stay there with you in the warm house. Pat's breath was now frosty, and the wind was moving the hem of your dress.

"Goody-bye, Autumn," I said at long last, reining quickly around while I still could.

"I'll have supper ready for you," you said.

I didn't look back.

Up on the mesa, Burl's boys found me before I found them, just like I knew they would. They came out of the cedars, took my guns, and we rode a half mile to another bunch of cedars where Burl was off his horse waiting for us.

"Get off, Honk," he said.

As soon as my foot hit the ground, he said, "You got the money?"

I said, "You *know* I haven't got it Burl, because it's not there."

Burl's face turned red, and not from the cold. "I always said you didn't have a lick of sense, Honk, but I never knew how dumb you really are till now."

I nodded my head. "That's right, Burl. Now you just as well go on and get the hell out of here. I've been figurin', and I don't think you want to see the law anymore than I do, or any more than Honk Ballard does, anyway.

"And I've already told Autumn the truth," I lied. "So I don't figure there's a hell of a lot more you can do to me."

"You figured wrong, Honk," Burl said, gathering up his bridle reins. "Betters is out of town, but is supposed to be back by dark. I'll be in his office when he does. He'll be out to the homestead with a posse an hour or so after that, and I'll be with him to watch while they take you away. By tonight I'll be sleeping with my wife again—and the *only* way you can stop me is for you to get to Liberty with my money before Betters gets back there from his business."

I looked down at the ground, thinking, wondering if Burl

was that good at running a bluff, or if I had misfigured after all. I didn't even hear him move, but when I glanced up he was standing close to me, and the three-foot piece of cedar branch in his hand was coming at my head.

CHAPTER 32

I DON'T know for sure how long I was knocked out, but when I came to, Burl and his friends were gone and Pat was grazing about a hundred feet away. There was blood all over the side of my face, and my right cheekbone was swollen so big, I could see it out of the side of my eye. It had gotten even colder while I had been out, and now a few flakes of snow were drifting down out of the sky. I found my guns not far away in the grass, and after picking them up, I caught Pat and started for home.

My mind was as unsettled then as a milling herd of wild cattle, and I couldn't put together a string of thoughts long enough to make much sense, much less long enough to make a plan out of. I guess I was still partly addled by the blow to the head Burl had given me. On top of that, I still didn't know what Burl was going to do, because I didn't know how much of what he had told me was the truth. I didn't think he would go to the law. Oh, I knew he might wire DuPree— that is, *if* DuPree was actually still alive—but I sure didn't think he would actually talk to Sheriff Betters. And I was still pretty well convinced, in spite of all the sincere-sounding things Burl had said to the contrary, that the money was not at the homestead and he knew it.

But what bothered me more than anything was that whatever *did* happen was up to Burl, not to me. Burl had figured all along that no matter what he did, I would just sit back and take it, and that is exactly what I had done.

It was a lonely ride back home that afternoon underneath the heavy clouds and in the light snow and the cold. I felt I had failed in every way that I could have. Failed you. Failed myself. Failed us.

By the time I got within a half mile of the homestead, I had decided that I had to tell you the whole truth. What else could I do? Happiness does not come without its price. I was willing to accept that—*unless* that price was the breaking of your heart, which it now appeared was the exact price life had put on the past fourteen months of happiness. As I rode Pat into the barn, I slowly shook my head, thinking to myself, Autumn would have been a lot better off if I had've just keep rattlin' my hocks down that lonesome trail to nowhere.

When I pulled the saddle off Pat, I noticed a small cinch sore just behind his left elbow. It didn't amount to much more than a little hair rubbed off, and ordinarily after I'd been away from the house all afternoon, I'd have been so anxious to see you that I wouldn't have doctored it right then. But now was different. Now I dreaded going in the house, and out of all the times to be worried about a place the size of my fingernail with the hair rubbed off, I picked right then!

You know that cabinet in the barn that I guess your brother-in-law made out of old shipping crates, the one just to the left of barn door. I led Pat over to it and started looking for the can of bacon grease I had in there somewhere. I reached behind some stuff on the bottom shelf, felt a pack rat's nest, and pulled it out. I threw it down, but, just as I did, something caught my eye. I leaned over and picked it up again and looked at it. There were pieces of old gunny sacks, bits of dried leather, hay, horse-hoof trimmings, dried pieces of horse and cow manure, and some funny-looking small pieces of paper.

I looked at the pieces of paper closer.

My God, it was pieces of paper money! Pieces of hundred-dollar bills it looked like!

"Will," I looked up and there stood Casey in the doorway.

"Autumn said supper was almost ready, but she needed some milk to make gravy . . . What happened to your face?"

"Uh . . . Old pat slipped coming' off the mesa and fell with me, but it's nothin'," I said. "I'll go ahead and milk before I come in. You run along in and tell Autumn for me."

As soon as Casey went inside the house and closed the door, I pulled everything out of the cabinet and let it lay wherever it hit the ground. But no money. No more rat's nests lined with money, either.

I looked everywhere in the barn I could think of, mostly places I had already looked a dozen times. No money.

But it *had* to be there somewhere. Surely if a pack rat could find it, I could too!

I went back to the cabinet and looked at the bottom shelf again and saw a hole in the corner of it where a rat had gnawed through the wood. The hole was dark inside. That mean the backing of the shelves was not against the wall of the barn, like the sides of the cabinet were.

I reached out, grabbed the cabinet with both hands, and pulled it over. There was a space of a couple of inches behind the backing that couldn't be seen from the sides all right . . . but no money. Nothing but more rat's nest litter.

I raked away the litter with my boot . . . and that's when I saw it.

It wasn't much—just a little piece of canvas barely uncovered by a digging rat, but I knew what it was the second I saw it.

Down on my knees, I went to digging like a hungry coyote smelling a fresh mouse. In a matter of seconds I pulled out a canvas bag. I knew what it said before I shook the dust off and read it—MINERS STATE BANK OF HILLSBORO!

I looked inside. It was full of hundred-dollar bills. I didn't know how much was there, and I didn't take time to count it, but it was more money than I'd ever seen at one time in my life, ten times more money than I'd ever seen.

But I didn't care *how much it was*. It was just *what it was* that was important. And I didn't know or care who had buried it under the cabinet. Whether it had been Otis or Mary Walking Horse who hid it there didn't matter. Or maybe even Scalp had found it in the oat bin and buried it there while Pole was in the house with you and the rest of us were locked in the feed room. Whoever had put it there and for whatever reason mattered none at all to me, only that I now had it in my hands—now had our future in my hands! I never stopped to wonder how much of a future ten thousand dollars of stolen, bloodstained money could buy. I could just see me handing it to Burl, him leaving, and me rushing back to milk the cow so you could make the gravy!

Without wasting a second or a single motion, I threw my blanket and saddle on Pat again, cinched him up, and stepped on him, cradling the money bag in my arms like it was a baby.

I lined Pat out on the road to Liberty, gave him his head, and let him run. The snow was coming down harder now and stinging my face as we ran into it, but I just ducked my head and kept going. Pat ran the first three miles without a bit of coaxing from me. From then on I had to touch my spurs to him, only now and then for another couple of miles, but nearly every jump after that until we got to town. A six-mile run at brim-bending speed is a lot to ask of any horse, but old Pat never quit me or even threatened to. For all of his orneriness, when the chips were down, there wasn't another horse in the world that I'd rather had between my knees than that sorrel.

When I pulled Pat to a walk at the south edge of town, it was terribly cold and the snow had turned to sleet. The ground was white and slick. The wind had picked up considerably—but there was still close to another hour of daylight left.

I heaved a sigh of relief.

I had made it in plenty of time.

I'd find Burl, give the sorry son-of-a-buck his stolen money, and then . . .

The only sign of life in town, other than three or four horses tied up in front of a saloon, were three men standing in the middle of the white street with their backs turned to the weather. They were facing me, but not looking at me. Instead they were talking with their heads down.

For some reason I stopped and watched them for a few seconds and then rode on up the street slowly toward them. The big man in the middle was holding something that the other two were looking at. It was a piece of paper, the edges flapping in the wind as they looked at it.

I stopped again and ducked my head, looking into the wind and sleet at the men.

I rode Pat forward a few more steps until I was only thirty feet from them. Again I stopped and ducked my head. Then I recognized them. All of them.

I think I knew who they were before I was even close enough to see.

That was Burl in the middle holding the poster.

That was Sheriff Joe Betters on his left looking surprised.

And that was U.S. Marshal Ben DuPree on the right! I guess I should have been glad to see that, in fact, he *had* survived my two bullets, but I couldn't find it in my heart for rejoicing or thanksgiving.

I didn't have to see the paper they were looking at to know what it was—a wanted poster with Honk Ballard's name, his ill-drawn picture, and a brief summary of his murderous exploits.

Burl must have sent a wire to DuPree a week ago, as soon as he knew for sure where I was. The only reason he said he would wait until dark of that day was just on the chance that I might be tricked into giving him the money before the law came for me.

I slowly nodded my head as I saw how everything had

really been. But I didn't panic. As strange as it was, I felt a calm come over me like I had never known before.

In less than a heartbeat, without any conscious effort at all, without even really forming any thoughts in my head, just *somehow* I saw the cards in my hand that fate had dealt me, and I started discarding them one by one.

There were two running cards—running with you or without you:

How could I ask you to run with me, to flee in the middle of a cold winter night with the kids, taking only the clothes we wore? And how far would we get? And what kind of life would if be if we escaped *this* time, because there would be another and another and another.

Running without you? And leave you alone with no one to protect you from Burl?

The "turn myself in and have faith in the law" card was discarded immediately. I had faith in the law all right—faith that they would take me back to Wyoming and hang me for the murder of Johnson Powers. My testimony against charming Burl Lewis and U.S. Marshal Ben DuPree? They would start building the gallows in Wyoming as soon as they got word that I'd given myself up in New Mexico.

The last two were a pair of black cards. One for Burl. One for me. Death cards.

I hope that someday you can see it as clearly as I did in that wind-driven sleet storm in the middle of Liberty's wide street. *There just was no other way,* Autumn. I was dead. You surely see that, don't you? I was dead the moment my first bullet broke flesh on DuPree's stomach. It's funny, in a sad sort of way, that while I died when that happened in Wyoming well over a year ago, the best part of my life was still ahead of me in New Mexico with you.

The strange calm that I said had come over me continued. The game had been taken out of Burl's hands now, and, although he wouldn't know it for a few seconds yet, I was now dealing and calling the game. But I had to act fast, right then, while I had surprise on my side, while I could ride right up to Burl without Betters or DuPree having a chance to stop me.

I pulled my old gun out of its stiff holster, and, still holding onto cold Colt steel, slipped my hand into the money bag.

I ducked my head into the wind and sleet, so the three men ahead planning my destiny couldn't see who I was. Pat's head was held level, his sides heaved, and his hot breath met the cold air in small gray clouds of steam. I pulled the hammer to full cock inside the money bag and started walking Pat forward. I knew how to use the gun now. Burl had taught me. Burl taught me everything I knew about the business at hand now.

"I'll go along with the posse, Sheriff," Burl was saying with a laugh in his voice as I drew closer. "After all, that's my place and wife he's got out there. It'll restore my faith in justice to see him hauled away and locked up."

"I still can't believe it," Betters said. "I never did really trust that guy—but I never thought anything like this!"

"It's true," DuPree said, "so let's get a posse together and go get him before he runs again."

They stopped talking when I was about ten feet away. I guess they were wondering who I was and what I was doing.

I didn't hear a thing from them until their boots appeared under my hat brim no more than four feet away.

Then I looked up and held out the money bag at the same time. "Here's your money, Burl," I said, like I was handing him a beer.

I never looked at Betters or DuPree, but Burl's eyes were wide with surprise. He looked at me and then at the Miners State Bank money bag.

Then he stepped forward and reached for the bag. I tightened my grip on the curved handle of the Colt, and when Burl's fingers were two inches from the bag, I pulled

the trigger and played both death cards—Burl's *and* mine—
with a deafening roar and a cloud of gunsmoke.

Two hundred grains of powder-heated soft lead hit Burl in
the hollow of his throat.

The bag was blown off the gun by the explosion and
hundred-dollar bills scattered down the street like dried
leaves.

Betters and DuPree fell out of my side vision. Burl stag-
gered backward, his eyes big, his lips already rimmed with
dark red blood. The gun roared again and jumped in my
hand, but unlike the time I shot DuPree when all of this
started, it wasn't acting on its own now.

Burl sank to his knees looking up at me in disbelief. I held
the old Colt out at arm's length and shot him twice more in
the center of his chest as quickly as I could cock the hammer
and pull the trigger. I glanced up and saw brave Sheriff
Betters running for cover.

Burl slammed backward, much like Johnson Powers had
done, and lay in the snow with his arms outstretched, his
front covered with blood.

I saw movement to my right. It was DuPree's gun coming
up. My Colt turned toward him. "Drop it to the ground," I
said. "I ain't done here yet."

DuPree didn't drop his gun but he didn't bring it on up
either. We looked at each other over Colts like we had the
other time. "You'll never understand this, DuPree, so don't
even try. I'm not the kind of man you think I am. I got no
grudge against you, but I can sure as hell kill you right now
if you get in my way."

"I'll get you," he said, then dropped his gun.

I rode Pat over closer to where Burl was lying face up. I
looked down into his face. His eyes were set and glazed,
seeing nothing. Around him swirled hundred-dollar bills in
the street. I looked at Burl's blank face and said, "I bet you
got the price of admission this time."

Then I looked at DuPree for a few seconds. I could see the hate in him for me. Then I nodded to him, wheeled Pat around, and loped into the wind and sleet, hearing the town come to life behind me with shouts and orders.

CHAPTER 33

PLANS are excess baggage on the trail that dead men travel, and I had none upon leaving Liberty. I only knew I wouldn't let myself be captured. I wouldn't put either of us through the torture of a trial and a hanging. But running from the Reaper's blade comes natural and is what a man does as long as he can, so I put my faithful Pat into a hard run once again.

The sleet had turned back to a hard, blowing snow again, and I held out hope that a posse couldn't be organized before my tracks were covered. But it was. DuPree knew his business.

Any hunted animal tries to climb. So it was to the nearest mesa to the northeast that I fled.

Though I could tell Pat's heart was still game, his lungs and his legs weren't. The posse was on fresh horses and had closed to within a quarter-mile of us by the time I struck a narrow deer trail that angled steeply upward over the slick snow.

Darkness fell suddenly that day and had covered the land by the time Pat carried me to the top of the mesa. There would have been hope in that if we had been able to maintain the quarter-mile lead we had as we'd begun our climb. But that lead had been cut in half by the time we hit the first heavy growth of cedars on the level top of the mesa.

Several shots rang out in the darkness by men armed with powerful rifles and the firm belief that "right" was on their side.

Pat went down.

He kicked wildly on his side a few times and then regained his feet and was gone, leaving me lying in the snow.

I jumped up to run, but quickly went to the snow on my face again. I reached down and felt my right leg just above the knee. I felt the warm blood, the torn Levi leg, the jagged end of bone.

I heard the posse thundering down upon me and turned with cocked Colt to greet them. But they passed by thirty feet away, horse's hoofs plowing through the snow, men shouting like a pack of wolves closing in for the kill.

The the sound of angry, bloodthirsty men and running horses faded into the darkness and was soon suffocated. completely by the falling snow.

I lay there a few minutes waiting for the sounds of horses and men coming back to finish their work. But only the silence of a winter night and the moan of the wind through the cedars came to me.

I was unaware of pain right then, but I was weak and dizzy. I stopped the flow of blood by tying my neckerchief tightly as I could above the wound. Then I started crawling and dragging myself through the snow, thinking only of getting some protection from the wind.

I had no idea where I was or in what direction I was going. I don't know how long I struggled or how far I came, but at last I found myself behind a rock ledge where the cold was as chilling, but the wind didn't drive it into you like a sharpened knife.

The my foot slid through the snow and into a wide hole. Without any command from me, the rest of my shivering body followed.

Now not only had the wind stopped, but so had the snow. With numbed, stiff fingers I was finally able to get to the matches in my shirt pocket and stike one of them.

To my surprise, instead of finding a sleeping bear like I thought I might, I found a candle at my elbow and quickly held the sputtering match to it.

In the dancing candlelight I saw that I had crawled into some sort of small, crude dugout, maybe an old trapper's camp. There were several half-burned candles and some cans of food without any labels on them, sitting on top of an old wooden box. Inside the box, along with four steel traps, some mouse-nibbled jerky, dead centipedes, and a pen and ink, was the paper upon which has fallen the truth about Honk Ballard and Will Smith, outlaw and homesteader, drifter and family man. Different men, yet both wanderers, and learners about life much too late.

It is later now, Autumn, much later. Maybe a couple of days has passed since I crawled inside here, as least as well as I can measure night and day by the coming and going of the small amount of light that filters down through the thick blanket of snow that has covered the dugout.

No doubt you've been told by now about the terrible thing that happened in Liberty. I'm sure the word is out all over the country, as not even a blizzard can stop the spread of bad news. No doubt you are racked with unanswered questions that no one but me can supply the answers to. That is why I have written constantly ever since finding the pen and paper.

But where is the posse?

I am weak and cold, although I have been able to keep a small hand-fire going most of the time out of bits of cedar the pack rats have drug in here over the years. My leg wound is painful, although not as bad as you would think since it is swollen to twice its normal size and I have picked pieces of bone out of it since I've been here. It is beginning to smell though, and I think the rot has already set in on it below the neckerchief.

Autumn, don't let what's happened destroy your faith. Marry again, but maybe this time try a rich city man who can give you what you deserve—and who won't take forever to bring the milk in! Stay away from the men of the trail dust and saddle leather. There is something about most of us that ends suddenly and lonely.

I hear noise outside now, Autumn, and I think I know Who it is. I've wondered all my life where I would meet Him. I must close and put these pages in an empty lard can I found. When the posse does its final appointed work, I'll be holding the can, so they can't help but find it and give it to you. I wish things had been different, Autumn, but this runaway horse that I've been on, called Life, is hard-mouthed and hard to handle. Just about the time I thought I had him under control, he took the bits in his mouth and took off again. Now he is running blind toward a tall bluff with no bottom.

I would like to be able to crawl out of the dugout and go to the edge of the mesa and see one more big scope of country before I go to my long home in the earth, but I am too weak and the snow is too deep. I'd like to hear a herd of cattle bawling again, or Otis's raspy voice poking fun at me, or Willa and Casey playing. Most of all though, I'd just like to hear you laugh again.

I keep remembering what you said about this being God's world and Him being in control of everything in it. I'd like to be able to see that, Autumn. Maybe there is an eternity somewhere where we will meet again, but I can't see it from here. I don't know where it is or how to get there, so I'll not promise that we will meet there sometime, in the future . . . But, God, Autumn, can you imagine the sweet reunion—the joy of that first touching—if we do!

EPILOGUE

I found Honk Ballard's last letter in the fall of 1983 in a fallen-in dugout on a lonely mesa in New Mexico and wanted to know more. Maybe I would find it in the dugout from which I'd pulled the old lard can. As the sun dipped close to another mesa in the west and the air grew colder and colder, I worked a hole big enough for me to crawl through and get into the dugout.

Over the years dirt had slowly shifted in and raised the level of the floor, while the roof sagged. There had also been enough sunlight let in to allow scattered sprigs of grass to grow in the drift dirt.

I could barely see inside, could *not* see really. My boot struck something hard, so I struck a match. A piece of old leather. I pulled on it and pulled out a brittle gunbelt and holster. Another piece of old leather. A curled boot with rusty spur.

I fashioned a small torch for a better, longer look. I found an old Colt revolver, its hammer and cylinder rusted down solid. I found another curled boot and spur.

Against the far side of the dugout, I found a gleaming, white human skull with a hole in the forehead and empty eye sockets greeted me!

Chilled, I continued to dig until all the bones I could find had been laid outside the dugout on a blanket. Even a shattered leg bone was there—the leg bone shattered by a posseman's bullet the cold night of Honk Ballard's last ride that I had just read about in his letter. These were Honk Ballard's bones, and they had lain undisturbed in the hidden dugout with the letter that was never delivered, while the cold snows and the lonely winds of eighty-seven winters passed on the mesa.

What had happened? Who put the hole in Honk's skull and left him there? Did Autumn never know the truth?

As I put Honk Ballard's bones and the blanket containing them back inside the dugout, the sun had just set, the coyotes were howling, and a cold breeze had come up out of the north promising snow.

I got back on my horse and hit the trail that would carry me off the mesa just as darkness fell. Below me I could see the dim lights of the cow camp where I lived. I knew my wife would be fixing supper, looking out the window nervously toward the barn, wondering why I was so late coming in. I thought of dried bones and lonely mesas and hurried my horse a little faster.

I tried to find the answers to the unanswered questions left by the dried bones and the brittle letter over the next couple of weeks, but found only this report in a December 8, 1896 copy of the Las Vegas, New Mexico *Territorial Reporter:* BAD BLOOD BETWEEN GANG MEMBERS LEADS TO LIBERTY KILLING!

An apparent "gone wrong" partnership between members of an outlaw band led to a vicious and cold-blooded attack by Honk Ballard upon Burl Lewis in Tuesday's bitter-cold afternoon.

It is believed that both outlaws, Ballard and Lewis, were involved in the robbing of the Miners State Bank in Hillsboro of the Territory some two years ago, in which a bank employee was killed. The money was hidden on the Lewis homestead east of Liberty under the watchful eye of Autumn Lewis, Burl Lewis's wife, while the two outlaws fled north to "cool their hocks."

During that time, Ballard killed Sheriff Johnson Powers of Cheyenne in a Wyoming shootout and badly wounded U.S. Deputy Marshal Ben DuPree who is now helping Sheriff Joe

Betters with his investigation. Lewis was badly wounded in the same fracas, and Ballard left him to die along the trail.

Details from there are sketchy, but apparently Ballard came to Liberty under the alias of Will Smith, took up with Lewis's wife and sat on the stolen bank money, pretending to be a simple, law-abiding homesteader.

The viciousness of Ballard's nature was seen last September when he killed two other gang members who came to the homestead to collect their share of the ill-gotten booty.

It was thought at the time, however, that Ballard's (Will Smith's) actions were completely honorable if not heroic in the defense of Mrs. Lewis.

It has only come to light with the recent brutal killing of Burl Lewis what an animal-like creature the citizens of Liberty had in their midst, since Ballard came there posing as a friend of the Lewis family. It is not known for certain what role Autumn Lewis (or "Smith" as, in time, she came to be married to *both* men!) played in the whole insidious affair.

It is a mystery to lawmen why Ballard left the stolen money scattering down the streets of Liberty in a strong north wind after his unprovoked attack upon Lewis.

Lewis died on the spot, and, as of the writing of this report, Ballard had still not been apprehended, and it is feared he may somehow have pulled off yet another escape.

Our Territory will never attain statehood status until we show the rest of the nation that the actions of men like Honk Ballard and those of similar felonious and murderous intent will not be tolerated.

Those few, mostly erroneous, words were all that was ever officially and publicly recorded of the "outlaw" Honk Ballard.

Autumn left even less trace of herself behind. I'll have to admit to entertaining the romantic notion of finding her grave and burying Honk's bones alongside hers.

I searched in the library, the museum, and the county

courthouse in Tucumcari, the nearby town that sprang to life a few years after Honk's death, but I found no trace of either an Autumn Lewis or Autumn Smith, no Mrs. by either name was found. No gravestone bearing her name could I find in any cemetery.

The answers to all questions concerning Autumn, even to her final resting place, were locked tightly within the earth, and the earth is The Great Keeper of Secrets.

I went back to the mesa on horseback with my wife and showed her the dugout where Honk Ballard's blanket-wrapped and waiting bones were. I then dug a deep grave on the nearby rim overlooking a big scope of country and buried him—his bones—there. To the southwest a few miles, where Hereford cattle now graze, was where Liberty once stood. And to the southeast, east of a long ridge in a spot now forgotten, was where the homestead where he and Autumn found their happiness had been.

After I had put the last shovelful of dirt over Honk's bones, my wife put some flowers on the grave and said a soft prayer through tears for him and Autumn. Women are like that. The moisture that collected in my own eye while she prayed must have settled there from the cool mesa air.

Today mesa grass covers the place where I buried Honk Ballard's bones, and no one but my wife and I know where they are. No curiosity seeker or weekend souvenir hunter from the city disturbs his long sleep. Coyotes and bobcats pass by on soft, padded feet, mule deer browse nearby, hawks and eagles soar silently overhead, and now and then a cowboy passes by on a horse.

Ride on, Honk Ballard.
    Ride on if you can.
They say you died like an outlaw—
    I say you died like a man.
Pull a spirit horse up between your knees
    and head for the further slope.

There—somewhere—you'll find the trail to eternity,
 and, *God*, don't I hope—
That when you top the final ridge in glory
 you'll see a homestead waiting there . . .
And a tall pretty woman, with shining auburn hair.

Sam Brown
Quay County, New Mexico

If you have enjoyed this book and would like to receive details of other Walker Western titles, please write to:

Western Editor
Walker and Company
720 Fifth Avenue
New York, NY 10019